crazy
free

To Teresa —
Cheers to Being crazy free ♡
Tori Starling

crazy free

A Novel

by

TORI STARLING

JUNIPER RAY

Published by Juniper Ray Publishing
Atlanta, GA
Written requests for permission to use specific material or for bulk orders should be sent to the publisher.
juniper_ray@yahoo.com

ISBN: 978-1-7348762-2-2 pbk
ISBN: 978-1-7348762-1-5 ebk

Library of Congress Control Number: 2020910498

Editing and book design by Stacey Aaronson

Printed in the United States of America

This is a work of fiction, loosely based on real events. Names, characters, places, and incidents are either the product of the author's imagination or are used fictitiously. Any resemblance to actual persons, living or dead, is entirely coincidental.

Then you will know the truth,
and the truth will set you free.

JOHN 8:32 NIV

chapter one

KORA

December 18, 1959

"Mama . . ." My daughter's breath warms my ear, and her stubby fingers dig into the meat of my arm as she tries to nudge me awake. The sheets are tucked tight, my body safely sealed in, but I'm freezing. I crack my eyes open just enough to see the sun shining in through the window, a beacon of light encouraging me to start the day, to keep moving, to seize the moment.

Blah, blah, blah. Morning, I don't care if you request my presence today or what your desires are. I am not your slave, and I don't have to abide by your precious rules.

I glance over at my husband standing guard at the bedroom door—tall, lanky—arms laced against his chest, all business as usual. Daniel Mitchell is a master at barking out orders day in and day out; I bet his men rue working for him just like I do.

I pretend to fall back asleep. The scent of smoke curls around me like something is burning. But I know better. I smell tobacco because I haven't emptied my husband's ashtrays. The smell is so intense I can taste how good the smoke would be swirling around in my own mouth. Lord help me, what I wouldn't do for a drag right about now, along with the company of an intriguing book and a cup of coffee loved on with a little cream and sugar. But alone of course, not with an audience. The girls at Mother's, the man of the house at work.

"Mama . . . up." Fern presses again.

Damn, she's back. Her over-pronounced "p" puffs against my cheek.

I groan and bury my face in the pillow. The sound of the clock annoys me. *Tick-tock, tick-tock, tick-tock.* My husband's boots make dragging sounds across the floor. He is, conveniently as usual, leaving my girl to torment me.

My incessant list of to-dos for the day start to ramble through my head. Cook eggs, bacon, and grits for breakfast. Pick up the blocks strewn about in the living room. Polish the silverware. Swipe away the dust on the furniture. Plait the girls' hair, dress them like little ladies, gussy my own self up with powder and lipstick, tease out my curls and set them with Aqua Net. Go to the market, pluck the blackberries peeping through the fence in the backyard. Throw some eggs, butter, and flour with them for tonight's dessert—blackberry cobbler, one of Daniel's favorites. Fingers crossed, he will love it. Perhaps even toss me a few extra dollars this week, kiss me in front of the girls, or spin those sweet babies over his head, beard their bellies, make them laugh.

I slide my elbows under my stiff body and try to prop up, but I only get a few inches off the bed before I collapse back into my pillow. Milk leaks out of my breast and through the cotton of my translucent summer gown.

My daughter points to my breast, then whimpers. "Mama . . . hungry." This time she yanks at my arm as if she may throw a full-out temper tantrum if I don't pay her some attention. *Dear*

Lord. Tears begin to pool behind my closed eyes. I just want to rest; I feel like I've been hit over the head with a cast-iron skillet—the one that clumps up with grease every morning when I fry sausage. Sleep takes the pain away, and oh, how every part of my body hurts, aches for relief.

My eyelid twitches, the right one, just like it always does. *Please Lord, make her go away. Make her leave me alone. This is still my life, dammit. They want to take it from me, but I'm still the one in charge here.*

Leave me alone.

Alone, alone, alone.

I just want to be left alone.

"Go!" I finally manage to spout.

With the last ounce of strength I have, I lift my hand and point a trembling finger toward the door. "Your daddy can feed you—his hands aren't broken! And anyway, you're a big girl now, you don't need your mama's milk."

After a few seconds, I hear her slide out of the room and creep back to wherever she came from. Maybe to wake her babies up and start her own fastidious morning routine. Changing Suzy's diaper, the doll with the blonde hair who looks like she's been electrocuted ever since the girls got hold of the scissors last week. Then there's Molly, the runt I got on sale last year on Christmas Eve at Woolworths. She's still drinking that itty-bitty bottle that never runs out of milk. *How convenient.*

My girls don't know it now, but it's hard to be a mama. Very, very hard. Sometimes I think I might shatter into a million pieces and no one would be able to put me back together—if anyone would even care enough to try.

Mother comes in just as soon as I'm starting to have some

peace and quiet. "Kora, time to eat." Her words take me back to when I was a child. She'd be an acre, perhaps two away, in the red clay field, her hands wrapped around a cotton boll. Her voice faint, distant, tired. Always so very, very tired. Like me.

My eyes are heavy, but I force them open anyway.

"Good girl," she says with a pleasant smile and a coddling voice I'm not accustomed to. "There you go." She lifts my head and slides a second pillow underneath me.

"I've got some chicken soup for you. Got these carrots fresh out of the garden and wrung that chicken's neck yesterday at sun up."

Scowling at her, I pat my curls; the matted clumps of oil don't even feel like my hair anymore. The odor from my sticky underarms wafts into the air. I try to ignore the stench, ashamed Mother has to see me in this state.

My gown is starting to dry, and I rest my palm on my chest.

"Now, now. Don't you worry about that baby. The Lord will see to it that your family is taken care of." She grazes her fingertips over my forehead. "Come on now, eat for me." She puts the spoon to my lips, and the warmth of the salty broth fills my mouth.

She continues on, silently feeding me, bite after bite until the whole bowl is gone.

"There now. That was good, wasn't it?"

I want to nod yes, tell her thank you, but I can't. Instead, I lie back down and turn to face the window. Her bedroom slippers pad across the floor toward the door. It sounds as though she is leaving, but then she stops and comes back.

"Kora, you're the one who chose to marry him." Pitying me, she brushes my bangs to the side. I glare at her, doing my best to make her feel guilty for being so blunt, but it doesn't seem to work because she keeps blabbing. "Sometimes I think you would've been okay if it wasn't for that polio. It gave you too much time to read and write, want more for yourself. But the Lord didn't intend for a country girl like you to lead some glamorous life. You've got to learn to accept that and make do with what you got."

A tear slides down my cheek, and I swipe it away.

"Just like I said when you tried to leave him a few years ago . . . you made your bed and now you gotta lay in it. Things don't always go like we want them to. You gotta dig deep, Kora, find the strength to get yourself out of this. I didn't raise no quitter."

She walks over to the door, creaks it open. Her footsteps fade down the hall as panic sweeps through me. She's right, I should've tried harder, been stronger. Should've been the wife Daniel Mitchell deserves. Should've been like that confident, red-bellied robin I see every night while I'm cooking dinner, flying into the bush to take care of her babies, fending off enemies that pose a danger. But instead I'm like her little fledgling that fell out of the nest the other day, matted feathers coated in dirt, beak opening and closing in desperation, squalling for love, food, acceptance.

I had no idea I was so close to the edge. No idea that home sweet home was only made of brittle branches and flimsy leaves. And certainly no idea I was so high off the ground when I fell.

chapter two

EMILY

Present Day

T he horns blare at the Five Points intersection as a college student on a bike with a bookbag strapped to his back speeds across the street out of turn. A couple sits on a bench waiting for the bus, so into each other they don't even notice all the commotion. An eighties song comes on the radio, and I turn up the volume, attempting to tune the rest of the world out.

My phone, resting on the console, lights up with a text from Bernadette, my editor: *I know it's late, but can you swing by the office to discuss this month's articles?*

I roll my eyes. Usually, I'm at home this time of day, but this afternoon I went into the office to catch up on a few things and then left a little before five. Going back to *Southern Speaks* to chat with Bernadette, who was on a conference call when I left, is the last thing I want to do. Especially since I have dinner plans with Mom. She won another case today, and I'm treating her to a celebratory meal.

Once the red light turns green, I pull into the parking lot of Baxter's local health food store. After I grab an open space near the back, I glance at the clock and see that it's 5:10. As long as Bernadette is respectful of my time, I should still have plenty of time to make it to Mom's house by six.

I pop a piece of gum into my mouth and peck out a quick reply: *Sure. Be there in twenty minutes.*

I toss my phone into my bag and hustle in, heading straight to the buffet. I pick up two takeout boxes and circle the choices of food, trying to decide what I'm in the mood for. A Billy Joel song comes on—"I Love You Just the Way You Are"—and I smile as I hum along to the melody. Mom used to always play this CD on Sunday mornings, the only time of the week she would allow herself to relax, sip on a cup of coffee, and read the newspaper.

I stop at the chicken alfredo and spoon some into Mom's container, then load mine up with noodles and marinara sauce. I'm eyeing the desserts a few feet away when I hear Colin's voice over the beeps of the registers and droning conversations.

He's standing at the checkout line, flicking his sandy blonde hair with a cocky smile, putting a *Sports Illustrated* back on the shelf and ignoring the copy of *Southern Speaks* beside it. He greets the pretty cashier in front of him.

I freeze. My heart races in my chest as I wait—hope—for Colin to leave without seeing me. I'm not ready to confront him, at least not yet. I've just started sleeping through the night without waking up at two a.m. to think about him, and I no longer check my phone ten times an hour to see if he's called. I've even stopped overthinking if it was right to pressure him to get married after three years of dating.

The girl scans Colin's pizza and puts it in a paper bag.

"Thank you, sweetheart," he says, his voice reverberating through the store. "I'm working tomorrow night, so you better come see me." He leans in and whispers something that makes her blush.

She hands him his bag, and he starts to walk away, but a

little boy behind him screeches, begging his mom for candy. Colin pauses to look back, and our eyes meet.

I take a deep breath and wave.

He smiles and struts toward me. He's got a five o'clock shadow now, and it appears he's put on a couple pounds, but he's still just as handsome as ever.

I feel like I could pass out, but somehow I manage to return his smile and come up with something halfway witty to say. "I'm surprised to see you here. I thought this place was too granola for you."

He runs his fingers through his hair. "Yeah, it still is, but I was craving one of those cheese pizzas we used to always get."

I nod absently. "So, when did you get back?"

"A couple days ago. Sorry, I was gonna call, but then I got crazy busy in Charleston and the time flew by . . . and well, here I am."

"Are you home for good?"

"Yeah, I got the bar up and running. I thought about staying . . . they offered me a job, but I decided I like Baxter too much to leave."

I press my dry lips together, wishing I'd touched up my makeup or at least put on some lip balm before I came in.

"You look good," he says, trying to be nice. "What have you been up to?"

"Not much, just working." I stare down at my takeout boxes. "Mom and I are having dinner tonight."

He winks. "Emily, Emily . . . such the overachiever. I guess Pam's doing well?"

"Yeah, she's still working like a mad woman. I don't think she'll ever slow down."

I shift my eyes back and forth. A girl about my age is standing in the middle of the bread aisle, squinting as she types into her phone and shoppers maneuver around her. A little girl grins and licks her lips as her mom scoops mac and cheese into a container. A couple in the aisle across from us hunts for the perfect bottle of wine.

Colin puts his hands in his pockets. "You know, I'm sorry how everything worked out between us. I'm just not at the point in my life where I'm ready to settle down yet. Being by myself for the past few months has shown me that. Maybe we can still be friends? Meet up for a drink or coffee sometime?"

I look away briefly then back at him. "Yeah, sure." Then I glance at the exit. "Sorry, but I probably need to get out of here. You know how Mom is . . . if I'm not on time, she'll be all over my case."

He gives me an awkward hug goodbye. "All right, well, see ya."

I close my eyes and exhale as he turns and walks away, feeling the tension slowly leave my body. I've spent the past seventy-two days trying to convince myself that being alone is better than being with someone who doesn't love or respect me, and as I watch Colin saunter out the double doors, I finally know I made the right decision. Colin is who he is; I'll never be able to change him. It's simply time for us to go our separate ways.

I lay the pasta boxes on the counter and make the salads, a little slower than usual, taking time to really think about Mom's favorite veggies instead of just throwing them on. When I'm finished, I go to the line of the same cashier Colin was flirting with. She fans herself with her hand then pushes up her sleeves; a small tattoo of three flocked birds flies from her wrist toward her bicep.

As I wait, I pick up the latest issue of *Southern Speaks*. This month's cover is a glossy photo of a trail on the outskirts of the city, one I've always wanted to hike. I think back to the first article I ever published and how proud Mom was. It was for my college newspaper. A story about the three most influential business-women in Baxter. I wrote about how they got their start, learned to overcome their fear of failure, and the strategies that made them successful.

Mom framed the article and gave it to me as we feasted at a fancy restaurant downtown. "You must always remember this moment," she said. "The passion that went into this piece, the dreams you have for yourself. The exhilaration you felt when you held that newspaper in your hands and read your words in print for the first time."

As I flip through the pages, inching ahead in the line, I can't remember the last time I bought a hard copy of something I'd written.

"Find everything okay?" the cashier asks, startling me out of my thoughts.

I force a smile. "I did, thanks." I put the magazine back, pay for dinner, then head to the office to see what mind-numbing topics Bernadette has for me *this* month.

chapter three

✤

PAM

Present Day

It's dusk, and I'm home a few minutes earlier than usual. I adore my two-story brick house atop a manicured grassy hill. Living at the end of a cul-de-sac on a spacious acre lot, with plenty of trees and neighbors on both sides who keep to themselves, is my idea of bliss. My daughter thinks it's too much square footage for a single woman, but it's perfect for me, Ms. Pam Sharp, who makes so much money I can do whatever I please.

If Emily weren't coming over tonight, I'd be tempted to pour myself a glass of chardonnay, watch old episodes of *Law and Order*, and go to sleep early. I simply don't have the stamina for these lengthy, exhausting trials like I used to. My body isn't as cooperative. My toes cramp up in my heels, my lower back aches if I sit for too long, and two cups of coffee give me the shakes.

But I wouldn't have it any other way. Nothing brings me greater joy than taking a victim's shred of hope and transforming it into a victorious debate with their perpetrator. This means my clients regularly put me on a pedestal and view me as their hero. They want something done and I make it happen. After it's over, another person with a new injustice is waiting in line behind them. If only all relationships were this simple.

Today the jury found Professor Fisher Marberry guilty of sexually harassing a college student. All my cases tug at my heart, but this one did especially because my client, Samantha, reminds me so much of Emily when she was that age: smart, ambitious, mature. I've always tried to put myself in the shoes of the victims I defend. I think it's one of the reasons I've been so successful in my career. This mental exercise in empathy helps to feed compassion back into the code of law.

In this case, to say it's not fair when something like this happens to someone so undeserving is an understatement. As far as I'm concerned, there's never forgiveness when someone in an authoritative position abuses their power. But at least Samantha stood up for herself and took action. Because of her assertiveness, Fisher Marberry, one of the biggest scumbags to ever step foot on this planet, will be held accountable for his actions—and I'll make sure Samantha receives every single last dime she's due.

I sling my briefcase and purse over my shoulder and drag myself through the garage door. Switching on the lights, I deadbolt the door behind me and yawn as I walk down the hallway. I run my fingers along the chair rail to make sure the housekeeper remembered to dust it. Sometimes she forgets, but not today. I smile as I admire my spic-and-span house: vacuum lines in the carpet, polished furniture, shiny hardwood floors, the fresh aroma of glass cleaner mixed with a hint of bleach.

In my bedroom, I turn on some classical piano music and kick off my heels. After I hang my suit in the closet, I change into lounge pants and a faded, stretched-out sweatshirt. I catch a glimpse of myself in the mirror and wince. Despite getting Botox on a regular basis and promptly dyeing my bobbed hair black every five weeks, I see age setting in: wrinkly bags under my mousy brown eyes, a sallow complexion. My designer suits can only hide so much. I've definitely been working way too many hours and spending far too little time on myself.

I plop down and stretch out on my king-size bed, pushing away the vision of myself and embracing the stillness of my tranquil, gray room. My face may not reflect the youth it once did, but at least everything in my home is tidy and where it belongs. Mechanical pencils and two Tiffany gold-plated pens sit in a cup on my desk. My computer alternates landscape scenes of places I've never been. A painting of dogwood trees at sunset hangs above my desk—a picture that Sadie, my childhood nanny, gave me when I graduated law school in '85. Besides an old photograph in the kitchen of Emily and me, this piece of art is the only item of sentimental value in my home.

My phone rings and startles me out of my thoughts. When I see John's name, I know I better take it. He'll keep badgering me if I don't. He was in court today too, but he was on the other side of the building, so we never ran into each other.

I prop a lumbar pillow behind my neck and answer.

"I heard the good news," John says. "Congratulations, babe." His velvety voice has always reminded me of the guy on the radio who does the afternoon traffic report.

"Thanks, I'm glad it's finally over. Now I can have some peace for a day or two."

"Emily bringing you dinner tonight?"

"Yes, my girl enjoys taking care of me, I suppose." I study Sadie's painting and the swirls of red, orange, and white that blend perfectly together. "Though, lately . . . I can't help but wonder . . ."

"Wonder what?"

"If I've been a good mother."

For some reason, John laughs. As usual, it irritates me. "Of course you have. Why would you say that?"

"I don't know. I've just been thinking that I haven't exactly been the best role model. Sometimes I don't think I've really been there for Emily the way she needs me to be."

"You're there for her in your own way. Every relationship is different, there's no formula for success. Besides, ultimately our goal as parents is to raise children who are independent and contribute to society in a positive way." He pauses for a moment. "And you've done that. She's got a college degree, a good job. Right?"

"Yeah, but I just worry about her. I wish she could meet a nice guy, fall in love, have a family. I want more for her than what I've had."

"Well, she does have a lot of you running through her veins."

"Yeah, but I'm different. I'm fulfilled. My career gives me everything I need."

Once I say the words, I regret them. John asked me to marry him last year, but I told him I wasn't ready—even though out of all the men I've been romantically involved with over the years, he is by far the best fit for me. I've always had an analytical, intellectual side to my personality and he appreciates this because he's the same way.

"I think you need a little TLC. There's more to life than work, you know." I imagine the crevice between his dark eyes deepening.

And if I were a man with dreams of shooting nine holes of golf each day or relaxing on the beach with my grandchildren every summer, that would make superb sense.

I ignore his comment and shortly afterward, we say our goodbyes.

I'm feeling anxious all of a sudden, and to calm my racing heart, I attempt to focus on my breathing like my yoga instructor taught me. My thoughts halt for a minute or two, but then they tiptoe back one by one.

No matter how hard I try, I can't seem to stop scrutinizing my client's family. Samantha and her mom, Kathy, are a blonde-haired, blue-eyed duo who seem like a few sisterly years separate them rather than two decades. Her mother actually reminds me of Sadie when she was younger. I spied on the three of them from my car as they walked through the parking lot today. Husband and wife holding hands, looking at peace for the first time since I met them, and Samantha striding confidently a few steps ahead of them. The dynamic of their family seemed to flow so effortlessly, so naturally. I couldn't help but be envious over their relationship.

Most days my past feels like a story that happened to someone else. But every once in a while, I still feel like that same submissive little girl who wants nothing more than to be loved by her parents.

It's a travesty that Kora, the woman who was my mother, had to die.

And I don't know if I'll ever understand why Daniel Mitchell, my angry, self-centered father, spent a lifetime making me pay for it.

✿

chapter four

KORA

January 8, 1960

The general of Daniel Mitchell's army only lets me rest for a minute before she ambushes me again.

Mother is ready for battle. Long, dark hair with strands of gray wound in a bun, shirt tucked into an ankle-length skirt, lips pursed, and armed with a suitcase. She sets it on the floor and marches over to flick the space heater on. The room is dim; the sun has shifted, now hiding behind the clouds.

"Time to get up, Kora." She claps her hands. "We've got ourselves a little bit of a problem. Daniel's had enough of you, so he's carting you to Hamilton Meadow today. Thought you'd rather hear it from me than him."

I gaze outside at Ivy and Fern bundled up in their coats, playing with their dolls. Ivy is cradling one of them in her arms and skipping around, belting out "This Little Light of Mine," a song she learned in Sunday School last year. My newborn baby pops into my head and I envision her asleep in her crib with a sweet smile on her face.

"I'm not going," I say. "Y'all can't make me."

"You don't have a choice. He's got a court order." Her words fire through me like a bullet, but she doesn't stop to nurse my wound.

"You had a mental breakdown," she continues. "I've heard it happens to some people and it's nothin' to be ashamed of. But . . . it's time for you to stop feeling sorry for yourself. You've been laying here for three weeks now. Gracious, slept straight through Christmas and your twenty-seventh birthday. So it's time you get moving."

"Are you sure it's been that long? Hardly seems like it." I don't sound like myself. My voice is raspy, weak.

"Dr. Parsons came to speak to you after your breakdown. You remember that?"

I shake my head as tears begin to flow down my cheeks.

"I didn't want Daniel to do it," Mother continues. "I suggested he take you to your Aunt Cecile's house in South Carolina for a while, since it's only a couple hours away. Or just give you a little more time here so I could nurse you back to health. But you know how he is. Once that man gets something in his head, there's no talking him out of it."

I open my mouth to speak, but my brain is still pondering this conundrum I'm in . . . how I'm going to prevent my husband from getting his way, how I'm going to be a mother to my little ones. The thought of living without them splits my chest in two. They developed in my belly, sipped from my breast. They need me now more than ever.

Don't I have a say-so in my own life? Is my fate really being determined by a boy who thinks half his paycheck should be spent on whiskey and poker each week? A boy who can't even pick up his own underwear off the floor?

"What about my girls?" I grumble.

"I'll take care of them. Managed to raise you just fine, didn't I? Besides, you'll be out of there in no time."

"No . . . Mother . . . no. The baby . . ." I place my hand on my breast, but it's no longer full.

She leans down and squints. "Stop feeling sorry for yourself. You'll see, this is all going to work out for the best."

Even though I feel like death, I smirk at her optimism.

"Think of it this way, you're sure not gonna get better here, living under the same roof with that man." She pats my back. "Come on now, let me help you with your bath."

Mother escorts me into the bathroom where she's already filled the tub. I allow her to slide my gown over my head, not caring what she must think about my stretch marks and sagging skin. She eases me into the water and proceeds to lather every body part with Ivory soap. I breathe in the fresh scent as she shaves my legs and underarms, and washes my hair as if I'm a baby and she's spiffing me up for church on Sunday morning. After she's finished, she announces she's leaving me for a few minutes to make the bed and to just stay put. I luxuriate in the warm water until she returns, then I allow her to dry my flaccid body off and rub my head with a towel until my scalp burns.

Next come my bra and panties—one leg in, another leg in, one arm in, another arm in—*Frick, frack, Cracker Jacks.* Mother helps me with my checked dress and inches my stockings up the length of my pasty white legs. Then she fastens the hair dryer bonnet over my head. When the timer goes off, she brushes my hair out and shapes the natural curl with a comb. Next, she maneuvers each finger into my wrist-length gloves. She intends to send me off like a real lady, I suppose. To let everyone know she did her job as a mother, even if her own daughter wasn't capable of doing the same.

I slump before her, my broken soul now camouflaged, and

she hands me the mirror with a proud smile on her face. "There now. You clean up pretty good, if I do say so myself."

I shove the mirror away.

"You can make this easy or hard. It's up to you." She sighs and plops the suitcase onto the foot of the bed. "Now then, what should we pack?"

Sliding deeper into the chair, I mentally admire the stellar job Mother did making the bed. The fabric of the thin quilt is worn in places and the ends are frayed, but she has managed to make it lovely by smoothing out the wrinkles and making sure each side hits the bottom of the mattress just so. And the freshly bleached pillowcases sit crisp at the top, looking as if they're not going to miss my mucked-up mind one smidge.

Mother steps into the bathroom and comes back with her arms full: toothbrush, mirror, brush, purple-red Hazel Bishop lipstick, powder, and Maybelline mascara. She plunks these things into the side zipper of the suitcase and then picks up the Bible from my nightstand, along with the book *A Woman Called Fancy* and last year's issue of *Ladies Home Journal*.

She sidles over to the closet and snatches a dress for every occasion: my favorite light green one, another that she sewed for me on my birthday, a few others, and finally, my least favorite— the dingy lavender one I clean the house in. She places them in neat squares into my suitcase and lays my white sweater on top. From the top drawer of my dresser, she pulls out two pairs of stockings, seven pairs of panties, and the most modest night-gown I own.

Once she's finished, I scan the room to see if there's anything I can't bear to live without. This is all moving so fast, it's hard to process the rapid speed at which the grand finale of my life is approaching. I wish more than anything I could muster up the courage to throw in a plot twist right about now. Do better, be more, switch back to the person everyone knows and loves, do something useful with myself, *for* myself.

But it's not that easy. Lord knows I've tried. It's as if another person has taken up residence inside my body, and though we could certainly tolerate each other for a while, it's now time for her to go. The problem is she likes it here. She's real comfortable kicked back on the screened-in porch, sipping on a glass of sweet tea. There's no way she'll ever leave now.

There's a picture of Ivy and Fern lying on my nightstand that Daniel's sister took the last time they went to the city to visit her. I push myself up and snag it, tucking it into my bra. I never got around to taking a picture of the baby. Mother's already made her way across the room and is now waiting at the bedroom door, suitcase in hand.

When we walk into the living room, everyone is chattering as if they're merely passing the time, waiting for the Barnum and Bailey circus to begin. The newspaper rests in Daddy's lap, and he's laughing at something Daniel just said. The girls have come back inside and are now spread out on the rug, constructing the second story of their castle. Ivy's hand slips from the rectangular wall she's positioning and the blocks crash to the floor. My head throbs, and I bring my hand to my forehead as my bottom lip quivers.

The girls stare at me with expectant eyes and panic sets in again. Who's going to cook them breakfast, brush their hair, read bedtime stories, and push them on their swing? How in the world am I ever going to live without them? Surely there's a better way, something, anything I can do, some way to get out of this.

My heart thunders, the room starts to go black. I latch on to the chair. Everything is silent as the seconds pass, but then life comes back into focus. The refrigerator hums in the kitchen, Daddy clears his throat, my husband sighs. Mother sets my suitcase down and takes a seat in my glider, where she begins rocking anxiously.

"Here, Mama, take this with you." Ivy is beneath me, holding up her *Wonder Woman* comic book. "It'll help you feel better."

It's clear she's been told some story about my leaving and has accepted it. My first instinct is to hide my face with the book and soak up my tears with the pages, but I stop myself from falling apart. The last thing I want to do is scare or confuse my children any more than they already are. I've got to focus, do my best to get back to normal so I can return home as soon as possible.

"Thank you, baby." I wiggle my fingers out of my right glove. I've barely taken the comic from Ivy before she scurries over to Mother and jumps into her lap, snuggling her head against her chest.

I've read the Wonder Woman stories to the girls over and over again. We adore everything about this heroine: her narrow waist, the patriotic colors she wears, the way she can always get out of whatever bind she's thrust into. It's a shame she's not here right now.

I glare at Daniel Mitchell. If he is feeling any remorse, his expression doesn't show it. Suddenly, the thought of getting a couple hundred miles away from him doesn't sound so bad. Sounds blissful, actually. I consider for a moment what's in this for him, why he's so quick to get rid of me, why he is refusing to give me just a few more weeks to recover. *Does he want freedom? The privilege to drink as much as he wants, spend money we don't have? Traipse around town with his arm draped around another woman? Lasso up someone who could be a better mother to our children?*

"I wanna get there before lunch," he barks, looking at his watch. "I gotta be back by this afternoon. Got some lumber to load up for the job I'm starting tomorrow."

"I need to say goodbye to the baby."

Daniel ignores me and exchanges glances with my parents. Then, what little energy I have left drains out of my body. The girls bounce over to me and say they love me, wrapping their matchstick limbs around my legs, but I don't lean down to hug them back. I'm afraid to. Instead, I graze the tops of their heads and squeeze their shoulders, a gesture of love I pray they are able to pick up on.

My father is next in line to say goodbye. He appears to be on the verge of a breakdown himself as he takes both of my hands into his and peers down at me. "Remember, baby girl, it doesn't rain forever. Eventually, the sun will come back out for you, I promise."

He gives me three dollars from his wallet. "I've heard cash comes in handy where you're going."

I cram the bills deep into the pocket of my dress even though I don't want his damn charity. He's a man. He could do something about this, stand up to my husband. He's supposed to take care of me, especially since I'm a girl and his only child. He starts to put his arms around me, but I turn and walk toward Daniel—smile pasted on his face, boot tapping, holding the door open for me. He has my suitcase gripped in one hand and my tweed coat in the other.

The rational side of me that's barely hanging on wants to say to my girls: *Be good while I'm gone. Daddy's in charge now. I love you, and I'll be back just as soon as I can.*

But like always, I don't say anything. I don't want to be disrespectful or speak out of turn. I know my girls get it—no giggles, no sass, no singing, no crying.

Only the sweet sound of nothing.

Just like Daniel Mitchell likes it.

chapter five

✤

EMILY

I look out the window and watch the red, yellow, and orange leaves glisten as the afternoon sun shines through them. Bernadette is finishing up a call and I check my watch, mindful of the time.

"Okay," she finally says, setting down her phone and drumming her fingers on this month's copy of *Southern Speaks*. "Here are your assignments for October." She slides a typed list across the conference room table. "Make sure you have them back to me by the fifteenth."

I swivel toward her. "You know you can just email these to me, right?"

"Ha, ha. But then I wouldn't get to see your pretty face, and what fun would that be?"

I throw her a smirk.

Bernadette has been my boss for five years now. I often complain about being bored, but I still meet my deadlines and never take a vacation or call in sick, so she puts up with my occasional bouts of sarcasm.

"I'm due at my mom's house in half an hour," I explain.

"Don't worry, I'll have you out of here in time."

I glance quickly through the topics: *Botanical Garden annual fundraiser, businesses owned by university alumni, holiday concerts and plays in Baxter.* The rest of the sheet is filled with much of the same, but the last one grabs my attention: *Hamilton Meadow—mental institution in Sparrow—sells 200 building, 2,000-acre campus.*

I sit up straighter in my chair. "What's up with this one?" I flip the paper toward Bernadette and point.

"Ah . . . Hamilton Meadow. They've been downsizing for decades, and everything's finally shut down now. I just need you to go there and figure out the details. I'm curious if they're going to try and renovate any of the buildings or if they're just going to plow it all down." Her fingers fly over the keypad of her tablet, then she turns the screen around. "Here, take a look. Eerie, right?"

A tall, ornate brick building stares at me with vines growing all over it, windows busted out, and weeds surrounding it.

"You think they'll let me go inside? This place would be amazing to photograph."

"From what I've seen, there are 'No Trespassing' signs up everywhere. But you could probably get plenty of shots from the street. You've still got that good zoom lens, right?"

"Yeah, but I'm not sure where it is. I can't remember the last time I used it."

Bernadette leans back in her chair and crosses her slender arms. "You know, Emily, this would be a great opportunity for you to write a feature article. I bet there's a ton of human-interest stories hanging around that place. I read that at one point, the hospital had ten thousand patients."

"Hmm . . ." I look out the window again. Leaves dance in the air and fall onto the sidewalk as people crunch over them. A conversation I overheard between Mom and her sisters after my grandfather's funeral this summer suddenly comes to me. They were on the front porch, eating slices of apple pie, and I was inside reading on my Kindle. Mom said to my aunt, "Ivy, have any new memories surfaced for you about Mother?"

"No, I can't think of any. I just remember her crying a lot when I was a little girl. She was always pent up in her room . . . and I remember her eyes changing. She didn't look like our mama anymore. The next thing I knew, Daddy had her committed, and we never saw her again. Shortly after that, Sadie moved in to help take care of us."

Mom and I were stuck in the car with each other for two hours on the way home that day, but I didn't dare mention what I'd heard. She's always made it abundantly clear that she doesn't talk about her family, and I've learned not to challenge one of the best attorneys in the south.

I can't help but wonder, though, *What if this is the same hospital where my grandmother was committed?* I toy with the idea of prying a little more with Mom tonight. Since her trial is over, she won't be able to shoo me away with her typical excuse of being too busy.

Bernadette waves her hand in front of my face. "Earth to Emily—what's with you today? You keep dazing off. Did you not have your coffee this afternoon?"

"Sorry. Just thinking about a possible story idea."

"Well, good. Try to figure something out . . . something no one else is writing about. Since Erin's been working less, we really need you. You're one of our best writers . . . I know you can do it." Bernadette tucks her tablet and yellow legal pad into her bag; she never leaves home without either of them. "Besides, we've got to do something to get our sales numbers up. I swear, blogs and social media are going to be the death of this industry."

I stand up, poised to leave. "I know. I saw that advertising fell by another fifteen percent last month." I smooth out the thigh of my worn-out flare jeans, thinking about the times I turned in feature articles on a whim that ended up in her slush pile. "I'll see what I can dig up."

Bernadette slings her bag across her body and walks to the door. "I'd ask if you want to join me for happy hour tonight, but . . ."

I tip my head. "How about a raincheck?"

"Sure. And keep me posted about when you decide to go to Hamilton Meadow. I'd rather you go sooner than later." She raises her eyebrows. "I have to warn you, though—I've heard that place is haunted."

I pick up my papers and laugh. "Thanks for the warning, but I'm sure I'll be fine. Just give me a day or two and I'll get back to you."

I TAKE A left instead of a right out of the conference room so I can swing by Erin's cube. Erin and I both majored in journalism and have been friends since we shared a dorm room our freshman year at college. As seniors, we both interned at *Southern Speaks*, and as luck would have it, two jobs opened up when we graduated: one writing features, which we both interviewed for, and the other covering news and events.

Erin got my dream job as a feature writer, probably because her uncle is editor-in-chief of the magazine, and I somewhat graciously accepted the other position, which typically consists of writing about local events going on around town.

When I step into Erin's cube, she's not there. Now that she

has a baby, she's always checking out early, asking me to cover for her, take an article here and there. I take a moment to drink in her workspace, which is totally different from mine. Teal and beige striped wallpaper, a white lamp sitting on the shelf, a quote hanging on the wall that says, *Live less out of habit and more out of intent.* Framed photos are everywhere, including a new one of her and Michael—her handsome, dark-haired husband—sitting on the grass at the park. Erin is holding her baby Sophie, who has a crooked smile and an enormous fuchsia bow strapped to her head. A lake is behind them, and Erin's highlights are luminous in the sun.

I caress the dainty sapphire necklace Colin gave me on our first anniversary. We were at his family's lake house, swaying together in a swing down by the water. Back then, both of us were in school, bar hopping every Thursday night, sleeping in on the weekends, watching movies and taking walks together. Everything seemed perfect. But when he got his job at the bar, he gradually morphed into a totally different person. Once he quit school to bartend full time, I knew I'd never get him back.

Tears fill my eyes as I fumble around in my brown fringe bag to find my car keys. Then I head to Mom's house.

🦋

chapter six

PAM

E mily sets our food down on the kitchen table, and I peek
into the boxes she says are mine. "Well, I must say, my
daughter knows me better than anyone. And I'm doubly glad
you're on time because I'm absolutely famished."

"I thought you would be," Emily says. "How many wins does
this make for you now?"

I hand her a water bottle and grab my glass of chardonnay. "I
don't even keep up anymore. It may sound cliché, but you know
me . . . it's really about uncovering the truth and righting wrongs.
I'm glad Fisher Marberry got what he deserved, but I still hate it
had to happen in the first place."

"Your client must be pretty gutsy. This week I read that
ninety percent of sexual assault cases on college campuses don't
get reported."

"That's true. And because Samantha had courage, it will
inspire other girls to do the same."

Emily arranges our meals on plates as I sit down at the table.

"You've been so busy lately," Emily says. "John's probably
ready for you to take a break. What's he been up to?"

"Oh, same as me. Busy, busy, busy. We did see a good movie
last weekend, though. That new one with George Clooney." I

pick up my glass of wine and within seconds have to wrap my left hand over my right to steady it, hoping Emily doesn't notice. My hands have been shaking ever since Dad's funeral. I reason that it must be lack of sleep or my hormones acting up again.

"You really should rethink his proposal, you know. He's a catch."

I set my glass down as Emily sits across from me, then stab a few lettuce leaves with my fork. Emily sneers at my silence.

"All I'm saying is, he's a great guy. Just because it didn't work out with Dad doesn't mean things with John will end the same way." She takes a bite of pasta.

I refrain from responding and instead flip the conversation. "What about you? Been on any compelling dates lately?"

"No, I'm on a dating fast right now. I'm actually enjoying the freedom."

"You sure? You're not still hung up on Colin, are you? I told you from the beginning he was trouble—blonde, bartender, flirt—nothing good was ever going to come from that relationship."

Emily rolls her eyes, just like she always does. "Mom, I'm not still 'hung up' on Colin. I'm fine. I've just been slammed at work lately. I don't have time for a social life."

"Well, I'm glad you're keeping yourself busy. I just hate you putting in all those hours and not getting paid more. If you would've gone to law school like I told you to, you'd have a lot more money in your bank account right now."

That comment merits another eye roll, this one accompanied by a defensive sigh. "I almost failed my public speaking class in college, remember? I wouldn't have made it one day as an attorney."

"Oh, please. You could've overcome that fear. But don't get

so worked up. You know I'm just trying to get a rise out of you." I wink. "So, how are things going at work?"

"I'm supposed to be going out of town this week to the old mental hospital in Sparrow."

I freeze for a second. "Hamilton Meadow? What have you been doing for Bernadette to send you there?"

"I guess you know it's closed now, so they've put all the land and the buildings up for sale."

"Really? Wow, that place has been there forever. I'm glad to see that chapter in our nation's history is officially coming to a close. We're a long way from having mental illness figured out, but at least people aren't living like caged animals anymore."

Emily lays her fork down. "Is that where your mom was committed?"

Her question catches me off guard. "How did you know about that?"

She eyes me sheepishly. "I overheard you and Aunt Ivy talking about her after Papa's funeral."

My heart pounds as I take in a breath, hesitating before quietly answering. "Yes, that's the God-forsaken place my father shipped her off to."

"Why?"

"I'm not sure. All I've ever known is once I was born, she snapped. I guess she could've had postpartum depression, or my father could've driven her mad. He drank and gambled too much, and he always loved his friends more than his family. It's a miracle I turned out as normal as I did."

Emily pokes around at her pasta. "I don't suppose you have a picture of her?"

My heart softens as I contemplate sharing this part of my

life I've never talked to anyone about. I'm also swayed by the tinge of assertiveness from my only daughter, by her expression that tells me she needs something to believe in.

"I only have only one . . . I keep it in my nightstand." My chair screeches, almost as if in protest, on the hardwood floor as I push it back. "Hold on, I'll be right back."

The lamp is on in my bedroom, and the James Patterson novel I was reading right before Emily arrived is still lying on the comforter. I go straight to my nightstand and rummage through the top drawer until I find the picture underneath the unused journal Emily gave me last year for my birthday. I slide my reading glasses on. My parents are standing in front of the Fox Theatre with their arms around each other. My father's jawline is rugged, sexy, and he's showing off the lipstick kissed onto his cheek. The picture is not in color, but I can tell my mother's plump cheeks are rouged, her lips darkened, her skin fair. She's wearing a dress, and a fancy hat sits on her wavy brunette hair that disappears down her back.

Before I can think about it too much, I return to the kitchen and set the picture on the table in front of Emily.

"This is her. Kora . . . that was my mother's name. I don't know if you remember that from the family tree project you did when you were a kid. I'm actually named after her. Pamela was her middle name."

Emily shakes her head as her emerald eyes glimmer under the light of the chandelier. She tucks a few strands of honey brown hair behind her ear, then picks up the photograph and studies it closer. "Why haven't you ever shown me this before?"

I shrug. "I learned to stop thinking about my mother a long time ago. What happened to her is impossible to understand.

Plus, I knew you'd have questions, and since I don't have answers, I didn't see what good it would do."

Emily props her chin with her palm, not taking her eyes off the photograph.

"I've always thought you favored her," I say softly. "I'd assume she's about your age in this picture."

She smiles gently. "I guess that's Papa? Doesn't really look like him."

I sit back down. "Yeah, time has a way of changing people."

"Do you know how she died?"

"All I know is she passed away a year or two after she was committed. And you know Ivy and Fern . . . such melodramatic princesses. They always said she died of a broken heart, which as a kid, and even as an adult, I've never been able to make much sense out of. I mean, a broken heart about what? Being a mother? Marital problems? Being locked away in a mental asylum?" I knead my fingertips into my neck to massage the knots. "Anyway, I don't know what the real story is. And when you grow up with a man like my father, you don't ask questions."

Emily nods. "Where'd you get this picture from?"

"Sadie Johnson gave it to me—the nanny who lived with us when I was growing up. She said she found it when she was cleaning out my mother's things. I'm sure I've mentioned her to you at some point. You actually met her a couple of times when you were little."

"Oh. So why didn't you two stay in touch?"

I pick up my phone, grasping for a distraction by scrolling through my emails. "We were always close, but we had a bit of a falling out when your dad and me got a divorce."

"That's too bad. I didn't know."

"Well, it's not something I like to talk about. Our fallout is actually one of the reasons I've been seeing a therapist for the past few years. I thought about calling her when Dad passed—Ivy said she's a nurse practitioner at one of those medical centers in Sparrow now—but since she didn't come to the funeral, I figured she didn't want to dredge up the past."

Emily nods. "I'm surprised she'd still be working. Isn't she pretty old by now?"

"Yeah ... probably close to eighty. But she was always the type to keep herself busy. I can't imagine her *ever* getting old."

"Hmm." Emily pauses. "What would you think if I did some research while I'm in Sparrow?"

"On what?"

"On Kora. Maybe I could find out why she was committed ... or how she died. I'm guessing the hospital's admin offices are closed, but I know there's a community college there, so I'd think the library would have some resources."

I feel my face flush. "I don't know, Emily. What's the point?"

"I guess I just don't see what it would hurt. I know you're busy. I'd take care of everything myself."

I take a deep breath. "It's not that I don't want to help, but Marberry's being sentenced next week and I've got another case right after that. Then, of course, Ivy's been on me to help her get Dad's house sold." I pick up my plate and my glass, then walk to the sink and dump the last few sips of wine into it.

"Mom, I get it. I won't ask you for help, I promise."

"I know." I cover my plate with plastic wrap and put it in the refrigerator. "Look, I've got several urgent emails I have to get out tonight. I'm going to have to cut dinner short."

Emily's mouth drops open. "But I just got here."

"I know. But if anyone knows how demanding my career is, it's you."

"Yeah, but . . . you're kicking me out so soon?" Emily then tries to backpedal. "We don't have to talk about your mom anymore."

I walk toward the hall. "I know . . . I just really have a lot of work to do."

Emily's shoulders fall with a loud sigh. "Okay. I guess I'll go then."

"You don't have to rush off. You can stay a little while longer if you want. Just let yourself out, okay?"

Emily doesn't respond. She simply nods her head quizzically as if she's not sure what to make of all this.

"By the way, you can keep that picture. I've never had much use for it anyway."

Emily perks up a bit. "Really? Are you sure?"

"Yes, consider it a gift." I plaster a smile on my face, wave, then escape to my room.

I sit on my bed and drape my ivory faux fur blanket around me. I hear water running in the kitchen, then the grinding of coffee beans. *She must be making herself a cup for the road.* An odd feeling comes over me. I'm not sure why I gave Emily that picture. Typically, I don't need to be my daughter's hero, but for some reason, at that moment, it felt like the right thing to do. I hate it that she grew up without any grandparents. It was never my choice for things to end up like they did. So, if that picture gives her some peace, then I want her to have it. My shrink would be oh-so-proud of such a grand gesture.

A few minutes later, the front door closes and relief washes over me. I'm proud of myself for opening up to her, but I imagine she's perturbed that I refused to cozy up with her on the couch and tell her stories about my childhood. She's always been sensitive like that.

I stare at my computer across the room. *I wasn't deceitful, I do need to get caught up on emails.* But tonight, I don't think I can make myself do it. Right now, all I want to do is say goodbye to this day and sink into a deep sleep under my freshly washed 400-thread-count sheets.

chapter seven

KORA

"Kora, wake up. We're here." My husband throws his Chevy into park.

I lift my head from the car window, massage the crick in my neck, and gently open my eyes. A beautiful white-columned building stands majestically in front of me and stretches into the sky. The flags on the manicured lawn wave hello and I wave back.

I peer at him, confused. *Did you make a wrong turn? Change your mind? Decide to take me for a picnic on the lawn at the governor's mansion instead?*

But then I see the sign on my left—HAMILTON MEADOW HOSPITAL. A shrilling ambulance disappears around the side of the building as an old, beat-up Dodge pickup pulls under the awning. An older man in dark pants and a white button-up shirt bolts out the door and jogs down the steps to open the passenger door. Even though her hair is short, I think it's a woman inside. The man bends into the car and coaxes her, pulls her, just like Daniel Mitchell did with our dog that time she ran and hid under the bed, afraid of the storm. A gust of wind rustles the trees and the metal ADMISSIONS sign sways as the man manages to drag the woman inside, then the truck whizzes away.

I zoom in closer and see people bustling about in the distance, men carrying briefcases, women scurrying around in white dresses and matching caps, some by themselves, others escorting what I assume to be patients. Vast acres expand in every direction with enormous brick buildings joined together by roads and parking lots. The air in my lungs drains out of my body and I squeeze the door handle until my knuckles turn red.

Dear Lord, we're here.

"I'm sorry," my husband says.

I turn abruptly. These are not words Daniel Mitchell typically utters.

For a brief moment, remorse spreads across his face. "I don't know what else to do. I just can't live like this anymore."

Tears pool in my eyes. Instead of telling him not to worry, that I understand he's done the best he can, I start twiddling my thumbs and humming a lullaby, the one I sing to the girls . . . the one I attempted to sing to the baby. The lullaby that didn't work. The one that didn't soothe, comfort, make my gift from above feel adored.

Daniel Mitchell slams his fist against the steering wheel. "Goddammit, what's wrong with you? Just when I start to feel sorry for you."

My tears, seeming to cower in fear, drain back into my eye sockets. I quickly turn away again, longing to feel the heat of the sun, a refreshing breeze through my hair, my feet grounded on the pavement. Anything but what I'm feeling now.

My husband gets out and pulls my suitcase from the backseat, then pokes his head back in. "Come on, let's get this over with."

Before I even open the door, his back is to me, marching toward the building.

I fall in line behind him, just the right amount of space away, careful not to get too close.

I let my husband take the lead. Just like always.

"THE DOCTORS ARE too busy to meet with you," the lady behind the counter says. Daniel Mitchell says that's fine as she pushes the paperwork across the counter. I survey the room as he fills out all the necessary information. The people waiting frighten me, and I edge away where I can prop myself against the wall. I wrap my coat tighter around me as I try to imagine why each person is here. Finally, I see my husband sign the last form and slide it back to the lady. He scans the room briefly, then walks toward me. I shrink as he gives me a half-smile and pats me on the head. "Bye," he says.

And then, turning his back abruptly, he is gone.

A nurse—young, pretty, wearing lipstick—approaches me right away and ushers me back to a room. She jots my height, weight, and blood pressure into a brand-new folder. She draws blood from my arm then riffles through my suitcase and swiftly confiscates my things.

"What are you here for?" she asks.

I search the room for a trash can in case I have to throw up.

"If you don't speak up, we can only go by what your husband said. You okay with that?" She drums her fingers on the counter.

Still, I don't answer.

"Fine, have it your way." She sighs as she stomps over to the doorway. "Time for a haircut."

The nurse brings me down a hallway to a room filled with chairs. Two women are already there, both staring into space.

One is an older lady, with thinning gray hair; the freshly cut short bob cleans her up a bit. Next to her is a teenage girl—too young, in my opinion, to be in a place like this—with gorgeous black hair that cascades down her back. The man with the scissors takes one whack and then another. Her jaw clenches with each tress that drops to the floor.

The man with the scissors tells me to sit down, that he'll be with me in a minute, and I follow his orders. The second the girl's last piece of hair hits the floor, she starts bawling. Then the barber starts on me, murdering my hair, stealing one of the only things I have left that makes me feel like myself.

I've never been the prettiest one in the room, but I've always loved my thick, brownish-auburn hair that sets me apart from the other girls. My friends have to get permanents, go to the beauty salon, hassle with rollers, fluff each cluster of curls with a pick. But I just wash mine and let it dry naturally, and voilà, it falls right into place.

"There you go, pretty as a picture," he says, scrutinizing me.

He snatches our smocks off and shakes our shunned strands onto the floor.

I reach up and finger my frayed ends; at least six inches are gone—poof, just like that. I blink once, twice, three times. I scan the room for a mirror. Sometimes a person's imagination can be harsher than reality.

"No mirrors in here," the man with the scissors says. "Besides, ain't like you got a man to primp for anymore."

The hospital attendant shuttles me out of the building and across the street. Her white skirt is wrinkled and fits snug around her thick waist, and her dark shirt digs into the flab of her bicep.

I keep my eyes fixed on the sidewalk until she stops in front of the biggest building I've ever seen. The windows, all perfectly positioned one after the other, glower at me. I can almost hear them cackling, *You'll never make it here.* I feel as if I'm being thrust into a fairy tale—one in which the Big Bad Wolf could never blow the place down, and Little Red Riding Hood would never be able to find her grandmother in the labyrinth of rooms. I breathe in and out slowly as I count the floors . . . one, two, three. A woman on the top floor grins and waves through a window, while the woman beside her pounds on the pane. My eyes move down to the second floor where a group of women gathered in the window hover like buzzards about to devour their prey.

I softly hum my lullaby. This time, Daniel Mitchell can't make me stop.

The attendant pokes out her chest. "This is the Culpepper Building. You'll be staying on the second floor." Her lips are so chapped, I imagine they'd crack and bleed if she smiled. "For your safety, men and women are housed separately. I suggest you lay low and do as you're told. We have about ten thousand patients, and sometimes you can get lost in the hoopla, stay for longer than you intended, or end up crazier than when you got here. Remember, just stay focused on getting better, and you'll be fine." She leads me up the stairs. Her skirt swooshes as I huff and puff, my thighs stinging with every step. When we finally reach our destination, she says, "Welcome to Ward 23." She slides her key into the lock and opens the door. "After you, my dear."

I step into the crowded room. The air is stale and women are everywhere, crashed in chairs, resting against white walls in need of a good scrubbing. A few wear gowns while others wear dresses like mine. One of them reads the newspaper. Two are sprawled out on the floor. Others stare outside with dazed expressions on their faces. The collective sounds of sobbing, pacing, cursing, praying, and mumbling fill the room. I wish I could clamp my hands over my ears without offending them. At the very least, I wish they would open the windows for a few hours.

A handful of women glance up when I walk in. They all have dark circles under their eyes, sullen skin, wrinkled faces, and unruly hair.

"This is the dayroom," the attendant says. "It's where you'll be spending your free time."

I place my hand over my heart, massaging the corner of the girls' picture tucked into my bra. It's the only thing besides my money I got to keep. My belly grumbles and the attendant hears it.

"You hungry?"

I cross my arms. I still feel nauseous; I don't think I could eat even if a plate of fried chicken and mashed potatoes were in front of me.

"Well, it's gonna be a few hours. Supper's at six." She's wearing a watch, but she doesn't bother to tell me the time.

A lady with a mop in her hand peeps out from what appears to be a supply closet near the back of the room. When she sees me, she smiles and walks over.

"Hi, welcome. I'm Rose." She stretches out her hand.

I plant my fingertips on my hips, my face warming.

"What's your name?" she asks.

I step back and wait for the attendant who has my chart to answer for me.

"Well? What's your name? You can talk, I know you can."

"Kora," I whisper, gazing into her kind, chestnut eyes.

She smiles again, this time wider. "Nice to meet you, Kora. I'm the nurse for this ward. I'm almost always here. If you need anything, let me know, okay?"

"Thanks," I mumble.

The attendant taps her pencil on the clipboard. "Well, ladies, I'll leave you to it. Best of luck to you." Her words are amicable, but her tone is sharp. The brown metal door slams behind her.

I suck in the smell that reminds me of diapers when they've sat by the washing machine for too long. My eyelid twitches and a whimper slips out of my mouth as the reality of my situation sinks in. *I am now the property of Hamilton Meadow, and there's not a damn thing I can do about it.* Gone are the days when I could eat a piece of apple pie with a scoop of vanilla ice cream on top whenever I felt like it. Tuck my girls into bed. Listen to music on the radio. Sleep in on the occasional Saturday morning. Go to church, sing in the choir.

I maneuver myself around the bodies to a window and rub my bloated stomach as a pang of grief washes over me. The open arms of the pecan trees across the street shiver with each gust of wind and remind me of the ones at my grandmother's house. When I was a little girl, we'd hunt for nuts on the ground and I'd squeal with delight when Grandma would crack one open, slide out the bitter with her fingernail, and hand it over for me to gobble up.

I want to experience moments like this with my girls, but time has always seemed to get away from me. I squeeze my eyes shut. *Will I ever see my munchkins again? Experience simple pleasures with them?* Sweat beads up on my forehead as my head begins to spin. I grab on to the sill to keep from falling.

A hand cups my shoulder. It's Rose.

"The first day here is always the hardest. Don't worry, spring will be here before we know it and you'll be able to go outside. I personally hate winter. So drab . . . hard to get yourself up and moving each day, don't you think?"

Her voice soothes me like tobacco on a bee sting. For a split second, I lean into her words, almost share with her that winter is also my least favorite season, but then I jerk away.

"So, it's three o'clock now," she continues. "Tonight, after you eat, you'll go to the sleeping ward and hopefully get a little rest."

I reach down to the spot on my arm where they drew blood earlier and rip the gauze off. Rose bustles off, her rubber soles squeaking on the floor. A moment later she plunks a chair down beside me. "Here you go, make yourself comfortable. The temperature's not going to get above freezing today, but the afternoon sun will do you some good."

A girl suddenly bangs on the door and I jump. "I want to go home!" she wails.

Rose rubs my back. "Don't worry about her. She's been here too long. Her family came to see her today, and she's not taking it too well. Nothing that a little tranquilizer can't fix, though." She hustles over to the woman, whispers something in her ear, then guides her over to the couch.

I look out the window again. Men are working outside, clasping their hands around withering blooms of purple and yellow pansies, pinching off their dead leaves. One of the workers is short, skinny, and maneuvers around easily, careful not to step on the healthy flowers. The other is a giant of a man, probably over six feet tall. He pants and his face drips with sweat even though it's cold outside. He wipes it away with a gloved hand and leaves a smear of black dirt. Over and over again, his clunky foot carelessly smashes huddled groups of flowers to the ground. But this man doesn't care. He doesn't know that pansies thrive in the winter when the other flowers die. He just rips up the damaged petals by their roots and chucks them into a five-gallon bucket with the other unwanted sprigs. Then he smooths the dirt over with the sole of his shoe and goes about his business.

I suppose to him it's just another dead flower. And who cares about those old things?

chapter eight

❦

EMILY

The mystery behind my grandmother nags at me like the rain that's been pelting my windowsill all night. After a week of perfect fall weather, it came out of nowhere in sheets.

I glance over at my clock radio that's resting on a pile of chick-lit books on my nightstand. *No need for the alarm this morning.* I switch it off and nestle my cheek against the silk hem of my pillowcase, reflecting on my conversation with Mom last night.

I saw her trying to hide it, but I could tell her nerves were rattled by the way her hands were shaking. I wonder why she was so nervous. And why did she wait all these years to finally show me a picture of her mother? She's so passionate about scavenging the tangled details of other people's lives, yet she's kept her mother's life in a vault. It doesn't make sense. What's even stranger is that she doesn't know why her mother was committed or how she died.

I would love to stay here under the covers contemplating it all, but I have an appointment at the Museum of Art at nine to discuss their latest exhibit. As much as I don't want to go, it's already past seven. I reluctantly slide on my fur slippers and head into the kitchen to put on a pot of coffee.

As I wait for it to brew, I inspect my grandparents' picture again. When I got home last night, I posted it on the fridge like Mom used to do with my straight-A report cards.

I hypothesize who's behind the camera lens capturing Kora's sexy smirk. A friend or a family member? A photographer on the street? And who put that sparkle in her eyes? Papa, who she's cozied up to? Or maybe she's amused because her children are peeking out from behind the photographer's back, making silly faces. It appears Kora is genuinely happy in this picture, so what could have happened to change all that?

The doorbell rings and startles me out of my thoughts. *Who would be out this early on a nasty morning like this?* I pour myself a quick cup of coffee, dump some creamer in, and shuffle to the door. Through the peephole, I see Erin with Sophie in her sling and two white trash bags on the ground beside her. Her blonde bob hangs in dark, wet strands against her head.

I open the door. "Hey . . . what are you doing here?"

She picks up the bags and tromps in.

"This child," she points to Sophie, "has been up since three o'clock screaming. I nurse her about that time, and usually, she falls right back to sleep. I can't imagine what could be wrong with her."

"Maybe she's teething?" I shrug. "She seems fine now."

"Yeah, she finally fell asleep on the way over here. My mom said colic runs in her family, so who knows, maybe it's that." She sets the bags down. "Anyway . . . since she was awake, I figured I'd be productive, so I put her in the swing and cleaned out my closet. Which is why I'm here."

"You cleaned out your closet in the middle of the night?"

"Yep. I am so over all my clothes not fitting. I guess I'm stuck wearing this for now." She swipes her hand, like a game show model, across the flared, black yoga pants she's dressed up with a cardigan.

I let out a half laugh. "You just had a baby. Don't be so hard on yourself. What are you now, a size eight instead of a four?"

"I don't even know what size I am anymore. All I know is I can't wear these clothes." Erin shifts Sophie. "Do you want them? At least I can live vicariously through you until I get my figure back."

I shoot her a look of sympathy. "Thanks, that's really sweet of you."

I move the bags next to Mom's old sofa that's been refurbished with a slipcover and notice that my plant is crying for a drink.

"Be right back," I say.

As I fetch a glass of water, I contemplate telling Erin about running into Colin last night. She's the only person I can talk to about him—but I decide not to. She's got enough going on right now without adding my drama to the mix.

"Mind if I have some coffee?" she asks, moseying into the kitchen.

"Go right ahead. It's dark roast, your favorite. I didn't put the creamer away yet."

She slides a mug out of my cabinet. "So, what do you think about the Hamilton Meadow article? Pretty creepy, right?"

I pop back into the living room and pour the water into the plant. "Oh . . . Bernadette told you?"

"Yeah, she said I might need to cover for you while you're out of town."

I return to the kitchen and swap the glass for my coffee cup. "Hmm . . . that's odd."

"She must've wanted to give me a heads up since I've been flaking out lately."

"Whatever . . . she knows you're doing the best you can." I take a sip. "I'm ready to get out of here, though. I'm in desperate need of a change in scenery."

She meanders past the refrigerator and stops mid-stride. "Hey, cool picture."

"Yeah, it's my grandparents."

"Oh yeah? Your mom's side or your dad's?"

"Mom's." I pick up my laptop bag and sling the strap over the shoulder of my plaid pajama top.

"Is this the same grandfather who passed away a few months ago?"

"Yep. That's him."

"Your grandmother's really pretty. You have her cheek-bones . . . and her eyes are light. I bet they were green like yours." She swivels around. "I've never heard you talk about her before."

"Actually, it's pretty ironic, but she was a patient at the mental hospital I'm going to. She died there when my mom was a baby. I thought about doing a little research on her while I'm there."

"Ooh, how exciting." Her veneers light up her pale face.

"I don't know, though. Mom doesn't seem too thrilled. I may just play it safe and forget about it. I haven't officially decided what I'm going to do. How about you? What do you have going on for the rest of this week?"

She shrugs. "I'm just in survival mode these days. I have to take it one day at a time."

Sophie stretches her fingers and yawns as Erin looks down at her and forces a smile. Purple rims bleed through the ivory concealer caked underneath her puffy eyes. "You know, no one tells you how much work being a mother is when you're pregnant. It's hard, Emily. Really, really hard. You'll see when you have kids of your own."

She glances back up and her eyes cling to mine.

"Are you okay?" I ask. "Maybe you could take a day off from work this week. Let Michael take care of Sophie so you can have a break."

"That would be nice, but I doubt it's possible. His schedule isn't as flexible as mine. Since he just opened his practice, it seems like he has to spend every waking moment at the office." She lets out a sigh. "So, one of us has to sacrifice, right?"

"Well, maybe when I get back in town, I can watch Sophie for you. And you can sleep . . . or have a date night with Michael."

"Really?" she says, her voice breaking. "That would be nice."

"Don't worry, it'll get better." I fix my eyes on the expensive diaper bag I gave her—the one that already has a stain on the front pocket. "Besides, you're lucky," I add with enthusiasm. "Things always work out for you."

chapter nine

🦋

PAM

I descend into Warrior Two, extend my fingertips, and imagine I'm pushing oxygen into the crevices of my body that need the most healing: my lower back, the ACL I ripped when I was training for a half-marathon five years ago, my heart for the frigid way I continue to be so guarded with John, my mind for dwelling on Emily's innocent inquiry about my mother last night.

I press my bare feet into the yoga mat, hold the position until my limbs begin to shake, coerce my brain into silence.

Once class is over, I am the first one into the locker room. I like coming to the seven a.m. class because it's not crowded—and since it's only two doors down from my office, it's convenient. Emily suggested I give yoga a try when I got diagnosed with arthritis a couple years ago, and I decided to take her up on it, mainly to see what all the rage was about. Little did I know, the end result would be coercing my pissed off, aging body into positions I never knew existed.

Young girls float in after me, chatting amongst themselves as they swig on their overpriced water and haul their designer bags out of their lockers. I drag myself over to the chenille chair in the corner and rest for a few minutes. I'm sluggish this morning. I was beat last night after Emily left, but I still resorted to taking an Ambien to relax.

As the gongs and wind chimes signal the next class into the studio, I think about Emily. *Should I check on her? Or should I just let it go, let some time pass, and hope she moves on?*

In the light of day, having had some time to think about it, I regret giving Emily the picture. It will likely stoke her curiosity rather than satisfy it. She caught me so off guard last night. Once she challenged me, I should have just told her no, that I don't want her snooping around that old mental hospital. She usually heeds my wishes if I'm adamant about something. Instead, I'm sitting here with my hands trembling. I sandwich them between my thighs and the chair, hoping they'll calm down, as I wonder, *What if Emily finds out something terrible happened to my mother? How will that make me feel knowing I never cared enough about her to find out for myself? What if Dad was right all those years? What if my birth did push her into a depression?*

The guilt I thought I buried a long time ago surfaces again—an emotion I'm all too familiar with. I even memorized the definition in the third grade after I heard Sadie whispering to Dad one night before bedtime. "Daniel, the moment I became the girls' nanny, I took it upon myself to love and raise them as if they were my own. And I've done everything in my power to make this transition as normal as possible for them. Especially Pam." I had peeked around the corner and saw Dad towering over Sadie's blonde head. "Don't you see what you're doing to her? Pam's heart needs protecting. She needs you just like your other daughters do. For the love of God, it's just not right for you to make her feel so much guilt about her mama passing."

Later that night, when I looked up the word *guilt*, the dictionary said: *1. Responsible for committing a crime or doing something bad or wrong. 2. Feeling bad because you believe you have done something wrong.*

That's why Sadie gave me the picture. To soothe my soul. But that photo, with my mother's exquisite smile and her curls blowing in the wind, only showed me that at some point in her life, before I came along, she was happy.

I exhale and go to my locker. As I'm sliding my chocolate Ann Taylor suit off the hanger, my phone vibrates. My sister's name shows on the display; she's already left two messages this week and I haven't called her back. *What could Ivy possibly want?* I let out a loud sigh. *Haven't we interacted enough in the past two months to last us for the rest of our lives?*

I swipe to answer. "Hi, Ivy, what's going on?"

Ivy booms out a Southern drawl that makes me want to clamp my hand over her mouth. "Thank the Lord up in the big, blue sky I caught you. I thought I was gonna get your darn voicemail again."

I pour myself a glass of lemon water and sit back down. "I guess it's your lucky day then. Is something wrong?"

"No . . . not really."

"Ivy, I know you're calling for a reason. What is it?"

She blows her nose, and I hold the phone away from my ear. Her persistent ragweed allergy must be acting up again. "It's . . . it's Daddy's house. I don't know if I'll *ever* finish cleaning it out."

"I told you to hire someone to do that for you. Didn't you get my email?"

"Yeah . . . but I just can't bring myself to let someone else go through his things."

"I said I'd pay for it." I tap my fingers on the arm of the chair.

"Don't you feel like it's our responsibility to do that and not some stranger's?"

"No, it's not *my* responsibility. What about Fern? Is she able to help?"

"No, she's babysitting for Charlotte this week and next. There's no way she can make it up here right now."

"Charlotte needs to put those kids in daycare. Fern is too old to still be helping her so much. Maybe if there were some consequences for her actions, she'd stop making such poor choices."

"Well, she can't just turn her back on her daughter and her grandbabies. Surely if Emily were going through a divorce, you'd do the same thing."

I study the yoga schedule I picked up on the way in this morning. "Well, things are upside down for me too right now. What about Sadie Johnson? I bet she'd help. Y'all still keep in touch, right?"

"Of course, but she didn't even come to Daddy's funeral."

"Yeah, but she knows every inch of that house. It's not like that man changed anything once she left."

"Pam, that was forever ago—it's been at least forty years since she lived there."

"Then hire out the manual labor and throw everything away or donate it. You're making this harder than it needs to be." I stand up, start to pace.

"Is there nothing in that house you want?"

"No, you know I abhor that place."

She sniffles. "Well, it's hard for me. I get in there, and I start in one place—someplace I think can't stir up memories—like cleaning out the plastic bags from underneath the sink or the pots and pans in the kitchen. And then I'll see something like a case of cigarettes and just lose it. I think back to him watching *Fox News* in his recliner, having his afternoon smoke. Or sitting on the back porch at night in the summertime."

I finally permit myself to sigh heavily into the receiver. "The longer that house sits, the harder it's going to be to sell. Have you at least gotten someone to clean up the yard?"

"Yes, that much I've done. Someone's coming out the first of next week." She clears her throat. "How are you coping, Pam? You know . . . with Daddy's death?"

"Fine."

"You always say that, but are you really? You don't have to be a rock, honey. Mourning is part of the healing process. My therapist said—"

"I said I'm fine, Ivy."

"Okay . . . well . . . maybe you could just tell me what's your favorite memory of Daddy?"

"You sound like *my* therapist now."

She doesn't miss a beat. "*I* have a favorite memory. It's that Easter weekend when he woke us up in the middle of the night to show us that cute, little yellow chick he brought home. Then he let it stay inside with us and sleep in my bed since I was the oldest. Do you remember that?"

"Yeah, I remember. He was drunk."

"You think so? Well, even if he was, you shouldn't judge those who've passed and can't defend themselves." I roll my eyes. "Anyway, we named that little thing Shortcake because Sadie had been gorging us on cake with the first strawberries of the season. That next day Daddy built a coop out of chicken wire, and we all held it and let it run between us. Then we set up a schedule where we'd all take turns feeding it and giving it water. We treated that chick just like it was our own sweet baby."

I bite my lip. "You know what I remember?"

"What, honey?"

"I remember that once that baby chicken got bigger and we got really attached to it . . . feeding it every day, sometimes sneaking it into our room, playing with it . . . a fox jumped the fence and killed it. It punctured its neck, ripped off one of its wings, and left feathers all over the place."

"Oh, Pam, that's what you remember about that little thing?"

"Yeah, and I also remember that when we told Dad, he yanked it up by its feet, walked across the yard with its limp body swaying from side to side, and chucked it into the trashcan. The way I recall it, our father didn't care a thing about that animal."

❦

chapter ten

KORA

A bell rings and the lights flick on.

I survived my first night at Hamilton Meadow Hospital.

I'm already awake; in fact, I never went to sleep because the women were so rambunctious. The things they say and do, their blank expressions, the way they stir around, scares me out of my mind. I spent most of the night with my face under the covers, the springs of the mattress jutting into my back and my body trembling, waiting as each one of them simmered down.

"Time to get moving, ladies!"

It's the nurse from yesterday, and I'm glad to see her. I didn't like the night attendant; she has arms bigger than Daniel Mitchell's. I bet she'd be good at splitting firewood.

The nurse claps her hands and scurries down the middle of the room, rustling bodies one after the other. Voices spring up here and there along with moans and sobs.

The sun blinds me, and I cover my face with the pillow.

"Good morning, Kora," the nurse says.

I don't budge.

She jerks away my pillow. "Time to get dressed. I'm not gonna do it for you. You won't get stronger if you got somebody else doing the work for you." Tears pool up in my eyes. "Oh honey, don't cry." She sits down beside me. "Listen to me. You are still in there. I can tell. You're not like most of the girls here. And trust me, I've seen plenty of insane women walk through these doors. I've only been training for two years, but most of the time I know what's wrong with them before they even open their mouth. And for the record, I think you got a real shot at making it out of here."

I gaze at the other girls. Nightgowns flying off their bodies, saggy bottoms, thighs jellied with cellulite, breasts in all shapes and sizes. They are like little girls in women's bodies, bustling around, talking, laughing, acting as if they're not naked at all.

The nurse snaps her fingers and I shift my attention back to her. "Let me ask you something, Kora. Do you remember my name?"

"No," I mumble.

"It's Rose . . . like the flower. Your husband ever get you flowers?"

I shake my head and bring my hand to my face. *I'm pretty sure that thought never crossed his mind.*

"Well, isn't that a shame. We all deserve a little something nice every now and then." She pats my knee through the sheets. "My advice is to go through the motions even if you don't feel like it. Get dressed, even if you'd rather stay in your gown. Eat, chew, swallow, even if you feel queasy. And last, make an effort to speak . . . at least to me. You gotta talk to somebody in here or else you *will* wind up crazy."

I wipe my wet cheeks with the sleeve of my gown.

"I've got one more thing for you," she says. "You ever drive a car before?"

I slowly nod.

"The first time you tried, were you any good?"

"No. I ran my husband's Chevy into a ditch." My mouth is dry and the words feel stuck, but they tumble out anyway.

"What about the next time and the time after that?"

"I got better and better."

"How long did it take you to learn how to drive that truck?"

I shrug. "I don't know. A month?"

"Right. Repetition. You had to train your brain to learn how to drive an automobile. Now you have to train it to get back to day-to-day living. It's not going to be easy, but you can do it. I know you can."

I nod again to show her that I understand, that I'm listening, because deep down inside there's a piece of my soul that appreciates what she's saying and doing to encourage me.

"So, just keep moving forward. Bit by bit each day. As long as you're doing that, you're making progress, and you'll be back home to those girls in no time."

I tilt my head, wondering how she knows about my girls.

"Your file," she answers without me having to ask. "I like to learn about my patients, know what kind of people I'm dealing with, what I'm up against." She smiles then shakes the girl an arm's length away from me who's still asleep.

Slowly, I push myself up and throw my feet over the side of the bed. I slip my bra on underneath my nightgown, moving in slow motion to get dressed, then make my way over to the bathroom line.

The second I'm close enough to smell the stench of the toilets, bile begins to bubble in my belly and I flatten my hand over my mouth to keep from throwing up. I turn toward the window on the other side of the room and tap my foot, pretending I'm in the fresh air of my pink-tiled bathroom at home, about to take a tinkle and slather my face in Oil of Olay.

But it doesn't work. I run to the toilet and hurl my head into the bowl, vomiting as urine splatters onto my cheeks and blends with my tears. Somehow, I manage not to pee on myself, but judging from the floor, accidents don't seem to matter too much around here.

Once all the poison from last night's dinner is out of me, I sit on the toilet to finish up. After I flush, I go over to the sink to soap up my hands and face. When I glance up, expecting to see my haggard self in the mirror, there are only yellow-painted cinder blocks. Staring at the wall, I run my fingers through my hair from the roots to the tips, as if I can see what I'm doing in my nonexistent reflection.

"Hurry up," the girl behind me says, leaning over my shoulder. Her breath smells like Daniel Mitchell's morning breath after a long night of drinking.

I dry my hands on my dress and catch myself gawking at her. She is skin and bones, collarbone jutting out, well-defined cheeks, deep crow's feet, ebony eyes wide awake and bloodshot.

Out of desperation and habit, I speak silently to the Great and Holy One.

Dear Lord, I'll do anything. Just please, oh please, don't let me wind up like her.

ROSE ESCORTS US to the first floor where the cafeteria is. The tables are long and rectangular with chairs set up around them. It reminds me of the fellowship hall at church on Homecoming Sunday, but it certainly doesn't smell like it. I am seventh in line and a song echoes through my brain. I sang this a few months ago to the girls as they marched around the yard giggling, pausing when they went past me to wrap their arms around my pregnant belly.

The ants go marching seven by seven, hurrah, hurrah.
The ants go marching seven by seven,
the little one stops to go to heaven.
And they all go marching down in the ground
to get out of the rain.

Rose claps and I gasp. "Get a tray, ladies, and keep moving! We don't have all day!"

The women behind the counter serving the food are wearing plain dresses and have homely haircuts like mine. The one who dumps oatmeal into my bowl is wearing lipstick, and the girl pouring the coffee has a pack of Marlboros sticking out of her pocket.

At home, my girls and I would rather go without than eat oatmeal, but after throwing up, I have a little bit of an appetite now. My hands tremble as I put a smidge on the tip of my spoon and poke it into my mouth. The coffee makes me shudder it's so bitter, but I keep sipping from the white, ceramic mug anyway and taking bites of the clumpy oats.

Suddenly, the old lady across from me starts cussing for no reason and spit flies across the table. The girls around me don't even react. Many of them haven't touched their food and continue gabbing like schoolgirls. The one sitting next to me devours her oatmeal like a kitten drinking a bowl of milk.

As I watch this scene, I am certain I have no desire to make friends with anyone here. I already have my own friends back home—Ethyl, Barbara, Joanne—and I don't care to make any new ones.

I push my almost-empty bowl to the center of the table so I can't smell it anymore and hug my stomach. I wait for everyone to finish up as the staff skirts around, wiping down tables, emptying the trash, carting the dirty dishes away.

"You seem curious." Rose stacks her bowl into mine. "In case you're wondering, those women are patients who work around the hospital."

"Do they get paid?" I ask.

"No, but we usually try to make sure it's a good fit, something they'd enjoy doing. Their work here is important. There's no way the institution could afford to hire out all these jobs. We'd fall apart for sure if it wasn't for the help-patients."

Maybe I'd be qualified for a job in the kitchen, I think. *The one thing Daniel Mitchell still likes about me is my cooking.* "What other jobs do they do?"

"Oh, all sorts of things. They work in the laundry room, sew, clean, farm, cook. We've even got a few working in the administrators' homes as housekeepers. Most of the patients, if they're well enough, usually want to do something to help pass the time. I personally believe it speeds their recovery. Everyone needs to feel like they've got a purpose in life. Don't you agree, honey?"

I nod timidly, wondering if that will ever be true for me again.

THE REST OF the day we move from place to place thanks to monotonous bells and attendants adept at barking out commands and enforcing rules.

The women here are different from the ones back home. They don't wear fake smiles, pat your back, hug you and say "Bless your heart," or "I'm praying for you." Their emotions are raw like ripples on the water for everyone to see.

I tune them out and sit in the dayroom, gazing out the window. The wire mesh that lines it blurs my view, but I can still make out the landscape—a veil of clouds covering the sky, bald hardwoods, dull grass, and ample buildings scattered around.

I spend my first day here planted in this chair, thinking and periodically dozing as my lower back aches and my head throbs. At some point, I take time to consider what Rose said this morning about training my brain to get back to the business of living, but my misery taunts me no matter how hard I try to cheer myself up.

I dread going back to the sleeping ward tonight; it's the same apprehension I have when I'm waiting up for Daniel Mitchell to come home. I also worry that the girls won't be properly fed or go to sleep at a decent hour. I hate my husband for leaving me here instead of loving me. I'm hurt that my parents let him cart me off without a solitary objection. I'm angry at the Lord because I'm not holding and nursing my baby right now. I'm embarrassed that my friends from church will find out I'm here and snub me when I get back home. I'm ashamed that I've allowed my feelings to disrupt my life like this. I feel guilty that I'm not at home to raise my daughters. I miss their sweet hugs, but at the same time, I'm relieved that the pressure of being a good mother and wife have been lifted off me, at least for a while.

Maybe I was never meant to be a mama and that's why all of this happened. Maybe I should've kept writing, not given up on my dreams, not settled for a jackass like Daniel Mitchell.

Maybe I do need one of those tranquilizers.

After a dinner of meatloaf, potatoes, and peas, and after the sun has set, Rose leads us back to the ward. When we reach the doorway, she pulls me aside, letting the other girls go in ahead of me. Her short and stylish blonde hair is a mess, her lipstick is wiped away, and mascara is smudged under her bottom lashes. I'm not sure what to make of her unkempt appearance.

"I picked up a little something for you today," she whispers, handing me a simple beige book with spiral rings going down the side. "There's a note in the front flap that explains everything. I've got to get going, though. Try to get some sleep tonight, okay? Remember, when a body like yours is truly exhausted, rest comes easy, no matter where you are. You, Kora Mitchell, control your thoughts, feelings, and actions. No one else. Got it?"

I'm taken aback by her kindness and generosity. For some reason, Rose has chosen to take me under her wing, and I'm not sure how to respond.

I manage a smile. "Thanks."

She returns the smile and disappears down the hallway.

I change into my gown and fold my pillow in half to prop up in bed. When I open the notebook, Rose's elegant script greets me on the inside cover along with two yellow rose petals. I hold one of the petals to my nose and breathe in the sweet aroma as I read what she's written.

Dear Kora,

Your husband wrote on your paperwork that your hobbies are reading and writing. Good for him for sharing this little tidbit of information! Here's a special gift from me to you. Something to get you through your days until you're well enough to go home. I can't give you a pen or pencil until a doctor clears it, but you can write during the day when I'm with you. What you write is up to you. Just make sure your words make you feel better.

Wishing you a speedy recovery, Rose

Rose's note blurs as tears dam up in my eyes. I clutch the gift to my chest and ignore the clatter of the girls around me. Mean Jean, the attendant from last night, is back. Her shrill voice makes my ears ache, my heart pound. She stomps around the room, points her finger, and commands the girls to get into bed. She doesn't tuck them in or fluff their pillows like I'm sure Rose would do. Daniel Mitchell would be thrilled to have Mean Jean as a soldier in his army. He wouldn't even have to give her weapons because she's already got her own supply of tranquilizers, shock therapy, ice baths, and straitjackets.

Outside, a sliver of a moon hangs in the sky. I lay my pillow flat and curl up on my side, placing the girls' picture and the book beside me. My munchkins are probably in a deep sleep by now, in the full bed they share, arms slung over one another. Ivy, snoring with her mouth open, and Fern with the covers kicked off.

But the baby . . .

The baby is . . . where again?

My stomach cramps and I slide the pillow out from under my head and press it against my body. I squeeze my breast to express my milk, but nothing comes out.

I'm all dried up.

How am I going to be able to take care of the baby if I'm locked up in here?

chapter eleven

✤

EMILY

Since it stopped raining and the sun came out, I decided to walk to my appointment at the art museum. I'm on my way back, meandering a little slower than usual and still caught up in the impressionist exhibit I just left, when my phone chirps.

I reach into my bag and rummage past the gum wrappers, orange lip balm, and ponytail holders until I finally find my phone face-down in the bottom. I slide it out and see a text from Bernadette asking me when I'm going to Hamilton Meadow.

I don't respond. Instead I scroll through my missed calls and texts to see if Mom has tried to get in touch with me. *Nothing.* I throw my phone back into my purse and pick up my pace, weaving in and out of the people on the sidewalk. At the corner of Broad and Washington, I stop next to a young mom with a stroller and wait for the light to turn. Her little girl is probably about two years old, snuggling a doll in the crook of her arm and jibbering while stuffing handfuls of cereal into her mouth.

Squatting down, I wave hello to her. The mom smiles at me and says she's glad the weather has cleared up because she gets a little stir-crazy when she's trapped inside with a toddler for too long. When the cars stop, we dodge the puddles as we cross the street, and the mom power-walks ahead of me. A year ago, I would have been dying with envy to be that girl, but now, not so much. I've almost gotten used to being alone. No conflicts, no sacrifices, no forgiving, no give and take, and certainly no expectations.

When I pass by the coffee shop, I decide to get a latte. I find a table by the window and think more about my grandmother.

What if Kora checked into that hospital the way people nowadays go to rehab, and then after a few weeks or months, she was discharged? What if she received therapy and learned better coping mechanisms? Or, what if she had a chemical imbalance that could have easily been treated with medication or nutritional supplements? How much different would my life look? Would Mom still be married to Dad? Would she still be a workaholic attorney, or would she have chosen a slower-paced career, maybe even been a stay-at-home mom? Would I have grown up with brothers and sisters? Would Mom have spent more time accepting who I was instead of pushing me to be someone I wasn't?

When I was little, I was always begging Mom for a doll, or one of those sparkly pink vacuum cleaners, or a Barbie house. But she always said no. She was adamant about me playing with something more "stimulating," toys that were designed for girls as well as for boys.

But one year, much to Mom's dismay, Aunt Ivy gave me a doll for my birthday. It was shortly after Dad left, so maybe she thought something special would be good for me. I remember being ecstatic. A minute or two after I'd feed the doll her bottle, her diaper would be wet, and I'd have to change it. I swaddled her in a blanket, named her Kaitlyn.

The next morning when we left for school, Mom told me to

bring her with us. I strapped her into the seatbelt beside me and said goodbye to her when I got out of the car. That night when Mom got home, she said, "Kaitlyn's gone. I donated her to the woman's shelter. But don't worry, she'll go to a little girl who needs her a lot more than you do."

I still want to cry thinking about it.

I take the lid off my cup and swirl around the flat, frothy milk left over in the bottom, drinking it down in one swig. I get out my laptop and a notepad, doodling a chain of flowers around the top of the paper as I wait for the computer to power up. I'm eager to get started on the preliminary research for my Hamilton Meadow article.

I look up the hospital's real estate page and read that their goals for the future are to revitalize the area and create jobs. I click on the interactive map and tour the computer-generated view of the empty buildings, writing down the addresses of the three properties that have already sold and are currently under construction. I read press releases, browse the other media links, and then slide on my headphones so I can watch local news clips about the project on YouTube.

Three pages of handwritten notes and a slice of pumpkin bread later, I take a break and see what I can find on Kora. From the search engine's home page, I type "Hamilton Meadow Hospital" and click on the first link that pops up. It takes me to the home page of the State Department of Developmental Disabilities, where I select "Genealogy FAQs" from their main menu. As I read, it appears as though obtaining Kora's medical records might be a real possibility. I just need to go to the probate court in Sparrow to begin the process.

At the top of my notes, I do a quick calculation and subtract my mother's age from the year, which would put Kora at the institution sometime in the early sixties. I narrow the search to this date and links to articles flood the screen.

As I read through a few of them, I am in awe of this era and the institution I never knew existed. Besides broad topics discussed in the Psychology 101 class I took my freshman year of college, I don't know anything about mental illness. From reading, I learn that Kora's stay at Hamilton Meadow was likely not a pleasant one.

The hospital was overcrowded—filled to the brim not only with the mentally ill, but also with the homeless, alcoholics, special needs children, religious fanatics, and victims of tuberculosis. I click on "Images" and am assaulted by pictures of patients being jolted with electroshock and insulin therapy. Other thumbnails show the Sparrow patients lined up with weary faces in ice baths or sealed up in straightjackets; kids in cages; twin beds crammed in rooms with barely enough space to walk between each one.

One article links me to a video clip of a 1950s movie about the actress Frances Farmer who was institutionalized in California. The black-and-white film shows a mock lobotomy where a doctor inserts a pick into a person's eye and manipulates her brain.

The latte sours in my stomach.

I wipe my sweaty hands on my jeans, take a deep breath, and begin looking for hotels. There's plenty to choose from outside the Sparrow city limits, but a yellow, antebellum-style B&B seems like the perfect fit for me. It's downtown and appears to be within walking distance of everything. I could leave tomorrow, spend the night, then take a vacation day on Friday to research.

I call the number and a lady with a thick southern accent answers the phone. "Good morning, Magnolia Inn. How may I help you?"

I tap my finger against my now-empty coffee cup. "Um . . . yes. I wanted to see if you had any rooms available for tomorrow night."

"I most certainly do. Would you like to reserve one?"

Watching the people outside, I reflect on where Kora would fit into society today. There's a girl wearing headphones, rapping her hand against the thigh of her ripped jeans; a middle-aged man in a sleeveless shirt with tattoos covering his arm; a professor-type with a beard, drinking a cup of coffee; a homeless person on a bicycle with a little dog and a bottle of liquor resting in the basket.

I close my eyes and take a deep breath. "Yes, I'd like to go ahead and book it."

"Well, I can't wait to meet you," she drawls. "And I gotta ask, what brings you to Sparrow, sugar?"

chapter twelve

PAM

J ohn is standing in the doorway of my office, holding a dozen red roses.

"Let's go to the mountains this weekend." He smiles, exuding the same confidence I fell in love with when I met him at a charity golf tournament three years ago.

"Bribing me with flowers, are you?" I say.

"No, they're a gift. No strings attached." He walks over and puts the flowers in their usual place: the cluttered table across the room I never get around to straightening up. "The leaves are beautiful right now. We should take a road trip—the weather's supposed to be perfect."

"I don't know. It's kind of last minute." I point to the pile of manila folders sitting on the corner of my desk. "I've already started prepping for my next case, and I was planning on working from home this weekend."

"So, we'll go on Saturday, and you can work on Sunday. Maybe we could hit a winery up there. Sit in a rocking chair on a back porch somewhere and take it easy."

"You're making this tempting, you know. Can I think about it and get back to you?"

He sits down across from me and strokes the stubble on his

cheeks that just turned gray this year, a nice complement to his salt-and-pepper hair. "Okay, I can live with that."

I lean back in my chair and fold my arms. "You know you're the only man who's ever given me flowers on a regular basis, right?"

"Yeah, you've told me that a time or two. I have a lot to live up to now. You keep me on my toes by winning all these cases." Appearing amused, he studies my dim office and sniffs, pointing to the lavender candle Emily got me for my birthday last year. I lit it after my conversation with Ivy. "Nice ambiance. Trying something new?"

"Just trying to take the edge off."

"Why? Did something happen with Emily last night?"

I study my bookshelf on the other side of the room that's lined with thick law books, a scattering of pictures of me with my favorite clients, and a print that says, *Anything you say can and will be used against you in a court of law.*

"Where should I begin?" I sigh. "My latest dilemma is Ivy's been hounding me again about helping her clean out Dad's house. And then last night, Emily was asking me questions about my mother."

John pauses, inspecting the flowers he brought. I notice now the edges of the petals are already turning black. "If I know Pam Sharp, I know there's no way you're going to let Ivy talk you into doing something you don't want to do. So, just go with your gut on that one and everything will resolve itself. And don't take this the wrong way, but the thing with Emily doesn't sound like that big of a deal."

"Seriously? You and Emily both know talking about my mother is off limits."

"Okay . . . you've said that more than once. But what brought it up?"

"She's writing an article about Hamilton Meadow for her magazine. The property's for sale, so she wants to play detective while she's in town."

He laughs as he squirms out of his red-striped tie. "Of course she does. That's Emily."

"I know. And I told her that was fine, I just didn't want to be bothered. I don't know, we'll see what happens."

"Have you talked to her today?"

I knead my hands in my lap. "No, I decided to give her a little space. I'm hoping if I don't make a big deal out of it, it'll blow over. And if I'm lucky, all this with Ivy will pass too. Surely my sister can put her big girl panties on and deal with this without involving me. She always was Dad's favorite. It's time for her to own up to that responsibility."

I swivel in my chair and look out the window at the train zooming behind the old warehouse across the street. I think about the last time I went out of town. Two years ago, John and I traveled to Amelia Island and stayed in one of those quaint cottages on the beach. Nothing fancy, just a couple of bedrooms with outdated decor and a splintered boardwalk that led down to the ocean. It was a last-minute trip, but it was one of the first seventy-degree weekends in the spring, so how could I say no? We left on a Thursday and came back on Sunday. We spent our days walking on the beach, lying out in the sun, reading books, drinking cocktails, and eating our fill of boiled shrimp and raw oysters.

I didn't even tell Emily I was going. Just snuck away. For the first time in my adult life, I wanted a break from my career.

Maybe I also wanted to see what it was like to live a life of adventure, to fall deeper in love. Time off to get to know the person I'd become—the woman underneath the makeup and designer clothes, the quick wit in the courtroom, the uncanny intuition.

But on our last night, John got down on one knee in the sand with the remnants of Fort Clinch pier in the background and asked me to marry him. He wanted me to not only give all of myself to him, but he promised that he would love me unconditionally and never leave. But I said no. Rather quickly, in fact. Without even considering it. And instead of finding myself on that trip, I came back more confused than ever.

John is suddenly behind me, massaging my shoulders. "If you need anything, just let me know."

I slowly nod. "I'll let you know today or tomorrow about going away this weekend, okay?"

"Sounds good," he says, patting my back. "Don't let all this get you down. It'll pass, I promise."

I smile, knowing how lucky I am to have this man in my life, yet still uncertain about what our future holds.

chapter thirteen

✠

KORA

I sit in the dayroom, stroking one of the wilted, velvet petals my new friend Rose gave me. After being here for about a week, I've determined the women here are like caged dogs. They sit, lie down, and whimper for attention. Some obey while others have a mind of their own. A few have sad, droopy eyes like bloodhounds, and several have hair that hangs in their eyes like sheepdogs. Some are puppies, young and energetic, while others are old and tired. A handful of them are eager to escape, roam the land, see what adventures await. The rest are content to stay where they are, grateful to have a fence that keeps them safe from the outside world.

The sun shines in long streaks across the cream-colored vinyl tile that's stained with scuff marks, dirty footprints, and grime accumulated from too many feet shuffling over it each day. I slide off my shoes and position my feet side by side in one of the few clean, cool squares. *Step on a crack, break your husband's back. Don't have to listen to his smack.* I sprawl out my toes and move my foot halfway into the other square on the thin, black line.

Rose startles me. "How are you feeling this morning, Kora?"

I look up at her. "Fine, I suppose."

"You ready to start writing in that notebook yet?"

Shamefully, I shake my head. I hid her gift under my mattress the night she gave it to me, along with the girls' picture, and haven't touched either one of them since.

"You could always start with a smaller task," she says. "Maybe you could write a letter to your girls and send it to your parents' address. I'm sure they'd like to hear from you." She rubs my shoulder.

"I don't know. Maybe."

"Well, you never know until you try. I don't want to push you, though. You'll know when the time is right. Besides, I'm not even here to talk to you about that." Her face lights up. "I'm taking you to see Dr. Eugene Hunter this morning. I was able to pull some strings and get you an appointment. He's one of the best physicians we have here."

I knit my brow. "What will he do? I don't want any medication."

"Oh, you'll just talk to him about your problems. That's it, no big deal."

My throat stings like I've just had a shot of whiskey. "I don't want to talk to a man about my problems."

She squats down to my level. "I know, honey, but there are only two female physicians on staff, and they're clear on the other side of campus. I think you'll like him. Not everyone here truly cares about the patients, but I think he really does." She pats my knee. "All I'm asking is for you to give him a chance."

WHEN ROSE AND I step into Dr. Hunter's office, a pale man with thin-rimmed wire glasses glances up from his desk and smiles. He's younger than me and must be fresh out of college.

"Why, hello, you two." He comes over and gives Rose a hug. "I'm almost done with the book you let me borrow. I promise to get it back to you in the next week or so."

"Oh, keep it as long as you'd like." She leans in closer to him. "Do you like it?"

"I do, it's very intriguing." He raises his bushy clumps of brown eyebrows. "Are we still on for dinner Thursday night?"

She smiles coquettishly. "Sure."

I'm about to become singed from the romantic tension between the two of them when Rose finally decides to introduce me. "Oh! This is Kora Mitchell. The one I've been telling you about."

"Nice to meet you," he says with a smile, sliding his hands into the pockets of his dress pants. He looks at Rose. "I won't be long. You can come back in, say, fifteen minutes."

Rose nods then turns to me. "I'm going to run to the administrative building. See you in a bit, okay?" She puts her hand on my arm. "Don't worry. Dr. Hunter's really nice." Then she spins on her heel and scurries down the hallway.

Dr. Hunter's office smells better than the rest of the hospital—like the perfect concoction of lemon oil, vinegar, and water. Golf clubs are stashed in the corner, and a college diploma hangs on the wall. I follow the doctor's orders and sit down in the chair across from him. He leans forward on his desk that's scattered with papers and places his arms on top.

"Now, you and I are going to have us a little chitchat, and I don't want you to be nervous. I need to learn more about your condition, and then I'll write up your treatment care plan. How does that sound?"

I shrug as my eyes travel to the window. A woman's family is visiting her. She sits on the bench with her husband. They're snacking on angel food cake as their three boys run around them, throwing the football, stopping occasionally to snag a piece of the sweet treat. The younger one starts to wiggle out of his coat, but the mother shakes her head no, zips it back up.

"Does seeing that family make you think about your own husband and children?" he asks.

"No. That family's nothing like mine." I turn back to him. His eyes are beady like that copperhead Daniel Mitchell whacked in half with a machete last spring.

He licks his lips and purses them, becoming serious. "How are things with your husband?"

"Fine and dandy."

"Do you think your husband made the right decision committing you?"

The steam builds in me like a pressure cooker boiling collards, but I force myself to answer politely. "No, doctor. I *don't* think he made the right decision."

"Well, I'm sure he was just doing the best he could. No reason to hold on to that anger now. It will only prolong your sickness." He writes something on his notepad then gives me a sly smile. "Before you came here, did you clean house and take care of your children? I mean, were you able to fulfill your duties as a housewife?"

"Not for the last few months."

"What do you think changed?"

I fall silent. Then I start humming the lullaby. I don't like being interrogated by Dr. Hunter, the same way I don't like being drilled by Daniel Mitchell.

"Kora, you need to answer my questions. I need to know these things so I can help you."

"No, doctor, I don't *need* to do anything. You seem like a smart man. Surely between you and my husband, y'all would be able to figure out why I'm not feeling like myself."

He leans back in his chair and folds his hands behind his head. "Do you believe you're sick?"

My right eyelid twitches and I start to twiddle my thumbs.

"Let me ask you in another fashion. How do you feel right now?"

A tear slides down my cheek, and I swipe it away. "How do you *think* I feel?"

"Well, sad obviously, because you're crying. And your eyes are a little swollen. Are you sleeping at night?"

"A little here and there, but I can't sleep in my ward. It's too noisy."

"Are you eating? I see you've got a little meat on your bones."

My face warms as I notice the pleats of my dress hugging my pudgy belly.

"Nothing to be embarrassed about. Proper nourishment will help you recover quicker." He pushes his glasses up. "Do you have any aches and pains? I noticed you seemed a little stiff when you came in."

"I've been having a lot of headaches, and I'm achy all over."

"I see." He takes his hands from behind his head and scribbles down my answers.

"What have you been doing during the day since you've been here? Perhaps you're stiff from sitting all day."

"What else is there to do in the dayroom, doctor? It's not like I'm at the county fair or anything. In case you've forgotten,

I'm locked up in here. I'm a little limited with what I can do." I speak without thinking and it feels good to stand up for myself for a change.

He looks me up and down, and I cross my arms tightly against my chest.

"Many activities are available to the women here. Square dancing, crafts, ceramics, sewing, needlepoint. Why, I've heard the occupational therapy department can't make enough linen tablecloths these days because the demand is so high. Do any of those things interest you?"

I sigh. "No, sir."

"Well, what do you think would make you feel better while you're here? We've had some success with the new drug Thorazine. There are also other tranquilizers available, medication that would help you rest. Electric shock therapy and a few other things are also good alternatives."

"No, I don't want anything like that." I think about my suitcase the attendant took last week. "I like to read. It might be nice to have a book to pass the time with. I brought my Bible with me, but they took it away when I checked in. It would be nice to have it back."

"I could permit that as long as you don't get too overzealous with religion. I could also allow you to go to the library once a week. Would you like that?" He smiles like he's the hero who's just rescued the damsel in distress.

"Sure."

"Okay." He writes more down then takes in a breath. "Well, Kora, I believe you have a severe case of depression. It's simply a nervous condition that's always been present in society, and it's especially common in women. The female's nervous system can be quite complicated, so I don't want you to feel like any of this is your fault." He takes off his glasses. "We'll continue with these sessions when I can fit you in, and I'll give you strategies to help you cope better."

I glare at him and cross my legs.

"I think after a few months of treatment, you'll be able to go back home where you belong."

I glance at the floor, then back up at him. "Doctor, going home doesn't matter. My family is getting along just fine without me."

He sits up a little straighter. "Oh, I'm sure that's not true. A housewife plays an immensely influential role in childrearing, management of the household, taking care of the husband . . . many important things."

I look back outside again. The family is gone now. The wife must be back behind bars, the husband and sons permitted to go free, fend for themselves. Squirrels scurry around and eat crumbs from the bench while the birds wait above on a branch, anxious to swipe their leftovers.

Oh, how I wish I could be free like those animals.

But instead, I'm caged up in here with the damn dogs.

IN THE AFTERNOON, I sit on my usual perch at the window, thinking about everything in my life that's gone wrong.

The girl beside me is sucking on a cigarette and blowing smoke right in front of my face. In my mind, I pretend I punch her, crumple up each of my problems, then yank her cigarette away and set the problems on fire. I watch the flame of each memory—searing, gorgeous, dangerous—stretch like a tower up to the sky. I hold each one until the ends of my fingernails begin to singe and then at the last second, I throw the embers into a bucket of water. The memories sizzle as the smoke drifts into the air.

The girl moves on to her afternoon activity, but I stay put, setting my hang-ups on fire one after the other, over and over again. I think of Daniel Mitchell coming home drunk in the wee hours of the morning. The slap across my cheek if I asked too many questions. The fist against the counter if dinner wasn't ready when he got home from work. The suffocating pressure for everything to always be perfect. The nights I had to sit there, not talk back, pretend like my feelings didn't exist. The wretchedness I felt delivering my second baby when I had no idea where my husband was. All those I-told-you-so looks from Mother. The precious baby that was snatched away from me.

I continue with this mind game every day for the next few weeks. I don't see Dr. Hunter again. Instead, I merely spend my time napping, crying, and going through the motions of living—dressing, eating, speaking—like Rose suggested. I adapt somewhat to the institution's routine and try my best to block out the racket that comes from living with a group of women whose feelings flail around unsupervised. But I don't write in the notebook Rose gave me and I don't go to the library. I don't do anything productive; I focus only on healing.

I mourn not only certain events of my past but also everything I have lost as a result of my commitment: my children, my home, delicious food, privacy, conveniences, friendships. I try not to worry about the future as the days pass by one after the other in a blur.

But one day, I wake up and for a reason I can't explain, I

don't feel so miserable anymore. The darkness left just as quickly as it came on. Maybe being away from Daniel Mitchell *has* given me back my strength.

Rose slides in next to me at breakfast. "My, my, Kora, aren't you looking extra pretty today?"

I smile. "Thank you." I inhale a big bite of eggs and take a swig of coffee. "I don't know why, but I'm feeling better all of a sudden."

Rose lifts her coffee mug and clinks it against mine. "That's great!"

I nod as I devour my breakfast.

"It's a little warmer today," Rose adds. "You know the groundhog didn't see its shadow a couple weeks ago, so hopefully spring's right around the corner. Would you like to sit outside for a bit?"

The bright morning sun gleams from the back wall of windows encouraging me to shine again. "Yeah, I'd like that . . . and Rose—"

"Yes?"

"I think I'm ready to start writing."

chapter fourteen

❧

EMILY

It's refreshing not to be stuck in front of a computer pecking out an article with a deadline hovering over me. Instead, I'm doing sixty-five in my white Kia on a two-lane road heading east to Sparrow, the place where a grandmother I've never known spent her final days alive.

The light blue sky is painted with pink and purple swirls as the sun continues to make its way across the sky. It's a little cold outside, but I roll down my window anyway and blast the radio in an attempt to drown out my thoughts.

The land in the country is peaceful: lanky pines are scattered between the colors of fall; kudzu—a stubborn plant that spreads and can't be killed—wraps its vines around trees; flat, grassy fields are outlined with barbed-wire fences and sprinkled with rolled hay bales, cows, cotton, and green John Deeres; old, one-story brick churches have weathered signs that display messages of the week in uneven block letters—JESUS SAVES, PRAY FOR THE NEXT MILE, PRAISE THE LORD, TRUE CHARACTER IS REVEALED OVER TIME.

The two-hour drive goes by quickly thanks to eighties music, an oversized coffee from the gas station, and a bag of chocolate-covered almonds. I turn up the radio a few notches higher and shake out my ponytail. My hair flies in front of my face as the highway widens to five lanes and commercialized strip malls, discount stores, and fast-food chains clutter up both sides of the road. After a few miles of red lights and traffic, the road narrows as I veer off to make my way downtown.

Sparrow reminds me a lot of Baxter: antebellum homes, tree-lined streets gridded out in neat squares, quaint shops and restaurants. College students stroll around on the sidewalks, groups of friends meet for coffee or an early lunch, and a jeep packed with boys cruises by.

When I see the visitor's center, I make a quick stop to grab some brochures and a map of the city from the wall display, then hustle back to my car and pull out the address of the hospital's administration building. My plan for today is to get a comprehensive view of the campus, check out the buildings for sale and any new construction going on, and if there's any time left, start my quest to find out more about Kora.

The GPS on my phone guides me out of the city and down side roads that feel like they lead to nowhere. On each street of the neighborhood, women sit on dilapidated front porches, men hang out on curbs in dirty ribbed tanks, and girls too young to be mothers stand around chatting with babies propped on their hips. Just when I'm about to pull over to make sure I'm going the right way, the pulse of the city, which has been fading since I left, flatlines. There are no cars, no people, no signs of life anywhere.

Instead, the institution buildings appear one by one and are separated by acres of weeds and trees. Some buildings seem like they were built in the last couple of decades, tidied up for a new occupant to arrive. Others are grand, archaic structures in complete ruin that scream for attention: *Hey, remember me? You used to appreciate me, show me love, take care of me.* Other places look as though a landlord barked out a day's notice to evacuate and the tenants gathered up everything they could in a suitcase and fled, leaving the swags of the curtains to yellow with age.

Even if I wanted to get out of my car and snoop around, I can't. Bernadette was right, NO TRESPASSING signs are everywhere, and security guards in white vans stare me down when we pass on the road.

My heart races as the bass of a song I don't know thumps through the speakers of my car. Finally, the GPS leads me to the front of the administration building. Although it's closed, people must still be employed here because there are a few cars in the parking lot and the outside lights are on. It has a regal presence—tall, white columns in the front, with fancy trim—but the windows are cloudy, the paint is flaking, and black mildew collects in patches and runs in streaks down the columns.

Finding a parking space near the back, I pop a piece of gum into my mouth and get out of the car with my camera. From here, I can see four prominent buildings and grassy, rolling hills scattered with trees. Out on the lawn, college girls are doing yoga, an elderly man is out for a morning walk, and a woman sits on a bench engrossed in her phone.

I snap pictures of the buildings along with other things that would capture a reader's attention: a covered walkway leading to the back admissions door; screens ripped off the windows and lying on the ground; a sign speckled with black mold—WELCOME, COME ON IN AND MAKE YOURSELF AT HOME.

Once I get a couple dozen shots, I head back to my car. My hand is on the door handle when an elderly man with deep wrinkles pulls up. His arm dangles out of his pickup, and he's gnawing on a toothpick. "This place is crawling with ghosts, ya know," he says.

"I'm sure," I reply, forcing a smile.

"You get any pictures of them yet?"

"Oh, no sir. Not looking for ghosts."

"Well yeah, you may have to go a little deeper in. They like to keep to themselves, don't like people too much. Especially don't like the folks in fancy buildings like these."

"I'll keep that in mind." I turn my back to him as I open the door.

"Yeah, I used to work at this place. Lots of good memories."

I swivel again to face him. "Oh really? When were you here?"

He pauses for a moment, stroking his chin. "I slaved at this place for twenty years. Started right when I graduated high school in '55."

"My grandmother was actually a patient here back then."

"Well, that don't surprise me none. There sure were a lot of them. Most everybody knew someone that was at Hamilton Meadow at one time or another."

"My grandmother . . . she died here. I'd like to know what happened to her or at least find out what her diagnosis was. Any suggestions on where I should start?"

"That's not always an easy thing to do. This place has a lot of secrets. Some think they'd like to keep it that way."

"Oh? Why is that?"

"No particular reason. Just a different time back then."

I nod. "Well, I better get going. It was nice talking to you." I wave goodbye and stoop to get into my car.

"Yep, you too." He rolls his window halfway up, but then rolls it back down and points his toothpick at me. "You sure are a pretty little thing. You better be careful out here all by yourself."

I nod and smile politely. "Thanks for your help." I close my door and lock it. My phone's at ten percent, so I crank my car and plug it in to charge.

As I watch the man putter back down the empty road, I wonder, *What if my grandmother was one of those secrets?*

❦

chapter fifteen

PAM

What's the first thing a perpetrator does when he doesn't want to be exposed? He lies about where he was, denies he did anything wrong, and stalls to provide admissible evidence.

I scroll through the Facebook profile of the man my latest client is suing for sexual harassment. You'd never know he was a scumbag. I'm sure his pictures on social media make all his friends envious: playing golf with his teenage son, smiling with his elementary-aged daughter and her science fair project, his children sleeping when they were little, posing with his tan, bikini-clad wife on the beach.

He has everything life has to offer—and yet an earthquake rumbles outside his picturesque dollhouse, a place where smiles are painted on and furniture fits just right in all the nooks and crannies. He clamps onto an abuse of power, grasping for the one thing he can't have, obsessing, until finally, he snaps. When there's backlash, he suddenly realizes his success has no value. There's no way to buy back what's been destroyed.

And what's his response to this claim from his twenty-eight-year-old secretary?

"I didn't do it. She's fabricating the truth. I was downtown at a steakhouse with my wife that night, sipping on a dirty martini, eating a ribeye. Not working late and not abusing my authority like that shallow, money-hungry woman said."

Well, we shall see. *There's always that possibility, innocent until proven—*

My cell vibrates and I jump.

It's Ivy again. On purpose, I let out an irritated sigh the second I swipe to answer. She's going to have to learn I can't drop everything I'm doing every time she's feeling emotionally distressed.

"Pam, honey," she pants into the receiver, "I'm so sorry to bother you again, but it's an emergency."

"What?" I switch her to speakerphone. If I'm hands-free, I can multitask and tidy up my desk.

"A contractor just called me and offered to buy Daddy's house as-is. All we'd have to do is get everything out of there."

"How much did he offer you?"

"$160,000."

I tap my pencil on the desk. "Well, that's a little low, but I guess it really doesn't matter. It's worth taking less just so we don't have to deal with it anymore."

Ivy sniffs.

"Why do you sound so upset? This is a good thing."

"Well, I'm just fit to be tied because he wants to do it pronto. Just as soon as I can get the paperwork drawn up. I know a good real estate agent who could help us, but like I said, that house has got to be cleaned out. There's no way around it. And I don't care what you say, I'm not hiring it out."

"Did you get in touch with Sadie?"

"I called her, but she says she doesn't have time. Pam, whether you like it or not, this is our responsibility and nobody else's. Besides, I made a lot of headway after we got off the phone yesterday. I'd probably only need your help for a day—two at the most."

I study the penciled-in appointments on my desk calendar. Technically, I could go Friday, but I wouldn't be able to go away with John for the weekend—not that I was seriously considering it. I pause for a moment, take a swig of water. "I guess I could come this weekend, get it over with. Maybe come down tomorrow and stay until Saturday or Sunday?"

"Would you really do that for me?"

"Jesus, Ivy. What choice are you giving me?"

"I don't want to force you into doing something you don't want to do."

Ha, like you really mean that. "You're not forcing me. I just want to be done with this. I'm starting a new case on Monday, and I won't have an ounce of spare time after that. Anyway, you're the executor of his will. Dad trusted *you* with that responsibility, so you'll have to handle the closing by yourself."

Ivy sighs. "Thank you. And for what it's worth, I want to put all this behind me too."

After a few more minutes of small talk, we hang up.

I slide my heels off, bury my toes into the carpet, and consider moving John's roses over to my desk. After all, the average woman would want to show them off instead of treating them like they're in the way.

But I don't budge.

I recline in my chair and think about my last encounter with Dad. He had been in the hospital for two weeks, but I didn't go see him until Ivy called and said he likely wouldn't make it through the night. I will never forget how he looked at me that day, the sense of desperation, fear—maybe even a tinge of re-gret?—that seemed to seep from his wrinkled, morphine-laced eyes. He finally professed the words I'd waited a lifetime to hear: "I'm sorry." I contemplated reaching out to touch his hand, express my own forgiveness. But I couldn't. Instead, I glared at him, pressed my lips together, and said, "It's too late for that." Then I slipped out.

And thirty minutes later he was gone.

☙

chapter sixteen

KORA

Each day I improve, but when it's dark, an evil voice lurks inside my head.

Give up, you'll never make it out of this hell hole alive.

You're a disgraceful mother.

You deserve to be apart from your girls and have your baby taken away.

It doesn't matter what you do, you'll never be good enough.

Of course your husband dumped you here. What other choice did you give him?

My heart pounds and my right eyelid twitches. I pull the extra blanket that Rose gave me a few weeks ago under my chin, and when the moon peeps through the top limbs of the oaks, the heat comes on. I tell the voice in my head to shush up and go away. *You've got plenty of other people to harass in here without wasting your time on me.*

Even though I try not to dwell on the bad things that happen here, it's challenging to get back to the business of living when agony surrounds me. Like my new friend Bernice who is howling by the window. Or, Sally, the eighteen-year-old in the bed next to me, who sobs as she belts out the hymn "I'll Fly Away." Or Sheila, who stands on top of her bed, pointing both her index fingers at the attendant, demanding a sloe gin fizz *now*.

All this noise is not going to fly with Mean Jean. She likes it quiet; the patients get one warning from her and then it's full-on attack mode. She's outnumbered but always manages to defeat the enemy without calling for backup. It's like she's got a machine gun cocked and ready to go, while poor Bernice, Sally, and Sheila are armed only with butter knives, fists up, with tongues sticking out.

It takes her a while, but Mean Jean finally gets it quiet in here. The raspy voice inside my head is gone, and my heart now flutters in the distance as my breath slows. The moon has shifted its place in the sky, and it's darker in the room now. I stare at the ceiling as I slide my hand under the thin mattress and touch the girls' picture. I hope they're doing okay and that they understand it was their father's decision for me to leave, not mine. I hope they remember me when I get back and won't get too comfortable with me being gone.

I blink once, twice, three times until my eyes are so heavy, I can barely keep them open.

I hope those sweet babies know how much I love them.

MORNING SEEMS TO come quickly. It's bright outside, and a blanket of frost covers the rolling pasture outside my window. The girls groan and grumble as they emerge from their toasty beds.

I reek of BO and my hair is greasy, so I shower, scrub my teeth, and force a brush through my short curls. Then I head down to the cafeteria with the other girls and eat every bite of my breakfast. Afterward, I settle into a hard-backed chair in front of a window in the dayroom, prop my feet up on the sill, and begin writing in my journal.

But I can't even get a full sentence out without being interrupted—not by my fellow inmates, but by a voice in my head.

Whatever is true, whatever is noble, whatever is pure and lovely, focus on such things.

The Great and Holy One repeats this Bible verse over and over in my head, even though I haven't bothered to get this sacred book out from under my mattress since Dr. Hunter returned it to me.

I'm doing just fine without you, I say to Him. *I didn't ask for your help.*

And yet, the words boom repeatedly, even louder than the patients, dismembering the sentences I'm attempting to write.

"Fine, I'll play your game," I whisper.

Whatever is pure . . .

My girls' hands wrapped around mine as we stir chocolate cake batter.

Whatever is noble . . .

Rose, the saint who is nursing me back to health, and Mother for watching the girls while I'm away.

Whatever is true . . .

This one takes a bit longer. Because really, what is true in this life? What is a definitive true or false? Something you can count on no matter what?

Finally, the answer comes to me.

When I was a young girl, polio crippled me and threatened to destroy every dream I had for myself. But my neighbor, Sam, helped me to rise from the rubble and believe in myself again.

It was June of 1945 and school had just let out. I was twelve years old. Daddy was finally home from the war, and there was a dance scheduled downtown to kick off the summer. More than anything, I wanted to go, but Mother said I couldn't because I wasn't old enough and had no business gallivanting around the city. She didn't care that I needed to feel happy again. She didn't know how badly I wanted to forget the cornbread and milk dinners we were forced to eat because there was nothing else, or how much it worried me that our once thriving farm was now red mud and weeds.

So that Saturday after dinner, even though I had a headache and sore throat, I went to bed early and then jumped out my bedroom window. My best friend Callie met me in the woods, and we took our pretty selves to the downtown square. It was the perfect evening. The dance was outside, and the air was crisp, refreshing, and buzzing with excitement. Until eleven o'clock, I twirled around on the stone courtyard with any teenage boy who asked me to dance. It was the best night of my life, and I hated to see it end.

Callie and I ran home through the fields, holding hands and laughing under a black sky filled with a million stars. When I arrived home, all the lights were out, and I jumped back through the window and slid on my nightgown. That night in bed as my fever rose, I thought my head was going to explode, and my legs cramped something terrible. I would've woken up Mother, but I was afraid she would know what I had done, and besides, I didn't think I could make it to her bedroom. I've never felt so miserable in my whole life, not even now, with this depression. I cried and prayed the Lord would heal me and grant me mercy for disobeying Mother.

The next morning, when I didn't come out for breakfast, Mother found me delirious and immediately called the doctor. That afternoon, Dr. Smith came to examine me, and with his eyes planted on the floor, he said I had polio—an intestinal disease that causes paralysis. At that moment, just as I was blossoming into a young woman, I realized how quickly things can change. I was terrified I was going to die. Privileges I never thought twice about were snatched away from me—walking to school, running through the feathery weeds of the pasture next to my house, jumping from one smooth stone to another in the river.

I was sick for a few weeks, and then one day my fever broke. The pain was gone, but my strong, gorgeous left leg was bent backward, contorted at the knee, and pinned underneath me. I tried to straighten it out, but it wouldn't move. I screamed for Daddy, but there was nothing he could do.

Over the next three years, the doctor let my parents pay what they could for my treatment. I wore casts and braces and did stretching exercises. Fortunately, I never had problems breathing, and I never had to have surgery. Since I was confined to my bed, I had to quit school, but my neighbor Sam made sure I didn't fall behind in my studies.

He knew I loved to read and write, so every day he came by my house and dropped off my homework. He also brought stacks of books and paper each week, repeatedly telling me there was no way polio was going to beat me. His confidence inspired me, and I wrote story after story, read every piece of fiction in the county, and did everything the doctors told me to.

I finally walked again on a spring day in April when I was fifteen. Sam was with me, standing in our yard with a picnic basket filled with fried pork chops and sweet potato soufflé that his mama made. And when I made the twenty-seven steps across that red dirt, he was waiting for me with a wedding band, asking me to marry him.

I look down at my left hand. The wedding ring Daniel Mitchell gave me is at home, in the bottom drawer of my nightstand, wrapped in a handkerchief. I wonder how different my life would've turned out if I hadn't broken off my engagement with Sam to marry Daniel.

Would I be in this hospital right now?

Would I still hear those evil voices inside my head in the middle of the night?

Would I have the life I dreamed about when I was a little girl? A house full of love, laughter, church on Sundays, goodnight kisses, and a houseful of babies?

Sometimes I wish polio would've killed me.

Sometimes I wonder if that would have been for the best.

These thoughts illuminate my mind like candles on a birthday cake. I breathe in so deeply I think my rib cage will crack in two and blow every single one of them out.

I'M ABOUT TO doze off when Bernice squats beside me. Her hands are shaking like they always do. "I need a smoke, Kora. You got any cigarettes?"

I shake my head. "They haven't given me that privilege yet." I rub her shoulder, showing her love just like Rose does for me. "Don't worry, you'll be fine. You don't need those damn cigarettes."

Her words come out in a rush. "But I feel so bad, and I have to go to work in an hour. I just need something to take the edge off before I get any worse. You know I can't get shocked again. I hate that shit."

I lay her head in my lap and stroke her straggly hair. "Here, just take a deep breath and think about something that makes you feel happy."

She begins to whimper. "I don't think anything good has *ever* happened to me. Not like I would know anyway since that shock makes me forget everything."

"Shh, calm down. I'll help you. Just close your eyes and pretend you're on top of a mountain with your children. It's one of those days that's not too hot, not too cold, and a breeze that's just right. The sun is on your face and you can see forever and ever. Your little boy hugs your legs and tells you he loves you. The girls sing their favorite nursery rhyme."

Bernice sniffles and I spot a slight smile soften her face. Her breathing slows like my baby's used to right before she fell asleep.

I drift for a moment to our honeymoon, when Daniel and I went to Black Rock Mountain. Back then, I felt so excited about our future together. Daniel's passionate kisses and the fervor of his arms around me made me feel safe, loved, and happy. I hate how everything changed between us after we'd been married for only a few months.

I gaze out over the grounds and see Rose and Dr. Hunter walking across the lawn holding hands. Her shift must be about to start; her hair is in place, and her uniform is freshly pressed. They pass by two patients playing croquet and Rose waves hello to them. Dr. Hunter must not know them, or he doesn't have time for such fickle conversation, because he picks up his pace and shuffles ahead of Rose. He is almost to the front door of our building when Rose catches up to him. She looks flustered as she gives him an awkward hug goodbye.

I start humming the first few notes of my lullaby.

I finally had another appointment with Dr. Hunter last week. I never told Rose it didn't go very well, because she thinks so highly of him. He said I was making it difficult for him to help me because I refuse to cooperate. I believe the feeling is mutual, though—I think he would just as soon not see me either.

Rose opens the door and bustles toward me, smiling. I stop humming mid-note when she makes a sweet face as she sees Bernice still dozing in my lap. "Good morning, Kora," she whispers. "I'm on my way to the library. Since it's such a pretty day, I thought I'd swing by to see if you wanted to join me."

I yawn and stretch. "Sure, why not. I haven't been yet. Maybe you could show me around."

"I'd love that." She points to my notebook lying on the floor. "How's the writing coming along?"

"Fine until..." I point downward.

Rose grins at Bernice, who is still in a deep sleep.

"But other than *that*, really good. I'd forgotten how much I enjoy it." I pick up my ballpoint pen. "I guess Dr. Hunter thinks I'm stable enough to use a sharp object without doing any harm."

"Oh, I'm sure Eugene would be fine with it. I actually never got around to asking him. He's been so busy lately." She peers out the window, as if she's checking to make sure he's gone. "Besides," she adds in a whisper, "we don't have to tell him everything, now do we?"

chapter seventeen

✤

EMILY

After winding through the roads of the deserted institution, not finding the first two new construction sites, I'm relieved when I finally see a cleared-out piece of land with a massive four-story brick building going up. A yellow permit hangs from a chain-link fence; the ground is trenched with bulldozer tracks and purple wildflowers sprout from the grass near the woods.

I park beside a full-sized black truck and go over my notes. This is the Goldman Center, a rehabilitation facility for children with autism, slated to open in May.

I change out of my clogs and into my boots, then grab my clipboard and pencil. I clomp through the red mud that's starting to harden as the sun beats down on it and lunge onto the stoop. The construction is pretty far along—some of the walls are up, the electrical wires and plumbing are already in place, but the floor is still plywood. Country music blares from the back.

"Hello?" I call out. "Anyone here?"

When no one answers, I walk past the lobby and down one of the hallways. "Hello?" I say a little louder this time, tracking the sound of someone whistling.

A few doors down, a guy with a friendly smile peeks his head out. "Hey, what's up?"

"Hi, my name's Emily, and I'm writing an article for the magazine *Southern Speaks* about the renovations here."

He walks toward me and extends his hand. "Graham Fuller, project manager. Nice to meet you, Emily."

"You too." Graham's hand is warm around mine. He's at least six feet tall with dark hair and light eyes. I take a deep breath. "Any way you could answer a few questions for me?"

I notice his light blue button-up shirt has *Cash Construction* scrolled on the pocket in white letters.

"Yeah, sure. Can we step outside, though? I'm about to leave, but I've got a few minutes."

"I won't take up much of your time." I let him walk ahead of me. "I wasn't expecting this place to be so deserted. I couldn't even find the other two construction sites. Actually, besides some bizarre old man and a few security trucks here and there, you're the first person I've seen."

He glances at me from over his broad shoulder. "Well, it's usually quiet around here, but it's been even more dead than usual because of the two inches of rain we got yesterday. I usually have a full crew working outside, but they had to take the morning off because it's still so muddy. And the other buildings haven't broken ground yet. I guess you're talking about the nursing home going in over on Circle and the center for troubled teens on the west side?"

"Yes. Any proposed start date on those?"

"I thought they were starting this month, but I'm learning things around here tend to happen later rather than sooner." He stops on a patch of grass next to his truck and faces me.

"So, tell me about this place," I say. "I know the autism rates are one in fifty-nine now, so I'm sure the Goldman Center is going to be a tremendous resource."

"I agree. I think it's going to help a lot of kids. I've heard they're going to offer speech, behavior, music, and equine therapy.

Probably more than that, but I don't know all the details. Classes are also going to be available for the parents."

I jot down notes. "Wow, sounds like a lot of jobs."

"Yeah, I think they're projecting around three hundred. Besides therapists and administration, they're going to need doctors, nurses, and a full crew to manage the families who come here from out of town." He points to the half-bricked building beside the one we just came out of. "We've got a hundred small condos going in over there."

"Sounds like they've thought of everything. Do you know how much they're planning to charge for the services?"

"I just know it's government funded . . . children will be accepted on a first come, first serve basis, and everyone else goes on a waiting list. The fee they pay is supposed to be based on their income, so there won't be any discrimination either way. And if this location goes over well, the plan is to expand and put a few more around the country."

"Any idea why this particular property was chosen?"

He shrugs. "I'm not sure. I think the goal is to have this area be an expansion of the medical community downtown. And since the land is just sitting here not being used for anything else, I guess it just made sense."

"I'm blown away by how huge this place is. I saw pictures online, but you can't get a real feel for it unless you're here. It must've been quite the scene when it was at its peak."

"Probably. I can't even imagine what it was like with thousands of people living here." He points to the clearing in the trees. "See that area over there where the dirt's worn around that big oak?"

"Yeah?"

"One of the women's wards was there before we bulldozed it. They say every Sunday afternoon a group of mothers would come out here and sit under that tree and pray for the children they had to leave behind." He sways back and forth. "Anyway, I think they would've liked what the land's being used for."

I nod as I take more notes. "You know, when I think about an old mental asylum, I think of people being insane and not able to take care of themselves. But it sounds like there were definitely some exceptions."

"Maybe. I've heard if you didn't fit into the neat box society created for you, then your family shipped you off to an institution. I'm glad a lot has changed since then."

"Me too. It's about time we've become more accepting of all types of people." I skim my notes. "Well, I guess that's all I need for now. Thanks so much for your help. I really appreciate you taking time out of your day to chat with me."

We shake hands again then both dig into our pockets for our keys.

"Oh," I say, "one more thing . . ."

"Sure."

"Why do you think the state waited so long to sell this land? I mean, it makes no sense why they'd let these buildings just fall into ruin like this."

He shakes his head. "It's hard to say, but it's kind of typical of our arrogant society, don't you think? People work hard to build something special, then take it for granted once they have it. Then they decide it's easier to throw it away and start over instead of fixing what's broken. And if they do happen to have a change of heart, usually by then it's too late, the damage has already been done."

I slowly nod, letting his words swirl around for a moment. Smiling awkwardly, I thank him again then make my way back to my car.

Sitting in the driver's seat, I'm happy I have enough information for my article. Now I can start digging into my grandmother's story.

❦

chapter eighteen

PAM

Being raised in a house with a father who blamed me for my mother's death made me feel like I was found guilty without a trial, like the victim of a deplorable case of being at the wrong place at the wrong time. My "sentence" meant I didn't get the same treatment or rewards as the other girls my age. Making good grades and being obedient didn't earn me a scoop of vanilla ice cream or a Barbie doll.

Over the years, my hurt turned into anger—anger at my mother for being sick, anger at my father for not being the man I desperately needed him to be. And even resentment toward my sisters for not trying harder to keep our mother at home where she belonged, though they were much too young to have that kind of pull.

I hated feeling this way, so I obeyed Sadie when she told me to read three chapters of a book each night and discovered how much I loved the escape. I also began reading the newspaper every day after school and developed a natural love for civil rights. When the KKK would burn a cross in someone's yard, Sadie and I would sneak and bring the family dinner, complete with dessert, even if it meant we'd have to accept less for ourselves.

Sadie left our house when I was thirteen, six years after Martin Luther King, Jr. was assassinated. While things were starting to improve for people of color, there was still a lot of work that needed to be done.

Around that time, I began dreaming and plotting my escape plan. I toyed with the idea of becoming an attorney because I wanted to help victims seek justice for their unfair circumstances. But I didn't know how I'd pay for college or how realistic it was since I was a female.

Sadie was in nursing school but would stop by on holidays or my birthday. "You can do anything you set your mind to, Pam," she said one summer night while we drank lemonade on the front porch. "No one can tell you any different. Especially not your father." Then she offered to help pay for my college education.

So, when I turned eighteen, I left home vowing never to return. I got a job at Rich's department store in the city and rented a one-bedroom apartment with Rebecca, a girl I met at work. Things were going great—I was dating here and there, shutting down any boy who wanted a serious relationship, making good grades, and earning just enough money to scrape by. But then my junior year, Rebecca got pregnant and had to get married. I couldn't afford to live by myself, and with the single female population dwindling at an alarming rate, I couldn't find another roommate.

So, I stayed in school, kept my job, but moved back home.

Dad and I kept our distance and spoke only when it was necessary. He fixed himself country ham, field peas, toast, and sliced tomato almost every night for dinner, and I survived off sandwiches and fruit. I bought myself a television set, so I spent most nights in my room, eating dinner, watching TV or reading, and doing homework.

Once I graduated college with a political science degree, Sadie encouraged me to continue chasing after my dreams. I turned in my application for law school and got accepted on a scholarship. I was still working at Rich's and making a little more money, so I was able to get an apartment by myself. Once again, I packed my bags and promised never to return home.

But there was always something, always some sort of obligation that begged for my attention. Pressure from my sisters. Emily begging to see her cousins at Christmas. Dad's stroke in '94, his broken hip in 2005. And now that he's gone and I've completed a life sentence I never thought would arrive, somehow, I'm still being pulled back home against my will.

AFTER I GOT off the phone with Ivy this morning, I decided to go over to John's office and let him know in person that I can't go out of town this weekend. He works in a building on Washington Street where he rents out space on the second floor. I take the stairs, and when I get to his floor, laughter is drifting down the hallway. I walk warily toward his cracked door and angle myself so I can eavesdrop without him seeing me.

John is with his daughter, Taylor, and cake samples are spread out on his desk. "Seriously, Dad, which one is your favorite? You're the tie-breaker."

"Well, I guess if you're making me pick just one, the raspberry filling is pretty remarkable."

I smile. John is such a good dad. If only I had made a wiser choice with my first marriage, Emily might actually have a father who'd come around every once in a while.

"Aww, that's Mom's favorite too." Taylor pauses, takes a

bite. "Dad, when you and Mom were married, were you happy?"

"Of course, baby. You know that."

"Well then, why did you guys split up? How can I be sure Drew and I won't wind up the same way?"

"Your mom and I got married too young and grew into two different people. We didn't understand the value of marriage. Neither one of us did. She lived her life, and I lived mine, and that's not how a partnership works. Just remember to love each other, baby. Always remember why you got married in the first place . . . work together . . . and you'll be just fine."

"But it's strange to me because you and Mom don't act like you hate each other. I mean, you fixed her washing machine last week."

"It wasn't always that way, though, you know that. It's taken fifteen years to forgive each other since the divorce."

"I guess. But back then, how did you know Mom was 'the one'?"

John goes silent for several seconds. "To be honest, I *didn't* know. I was only nineteen when we met. But I *can* tell you how I know Pam's the one. She just feels like my other half, you know? The perfect complement to me in some unexplainable kind of way. The person I can see spending the rest of my life with. And that's why I stick by her even when she sometimes pushes me away."

I stare at the carpet threads and my heart aches. Suddenly, John jumps back to his case for raspberry filling over dark chocolate, and I take that as my cue to tiptoe away.

I breathe in the fresh air as I cross the street and head in the other direction. My heels clink along the pavement, and my purse slides off my shoulder. I try to prop it back up, but my hand is shaking so badly, my bag slips right back to the crook of my elbow.

I reach into my purse and rest my hand on my cell. I consider calling Emily just to hear her voice and find out when she's going out of town. I also wonder what she decided to do about investigating my mom since I never ended up talking to her yesterday.

But I change my mind.

Right now, I just need to get away from here . . . as far away as possible.

chapter nineteen

KORA

Rose and I sit at a picnic table on the lawn outside the Culpepper Building and eat the brownies she snatched earlier from the cafeteria. The vibrant yellow daffodils stand confident beside us, eager to show off their blooms after a winter spent buried in the dark, dank dirt. A bumblebee hums over them, dipping in every once in a while for a taste of their nectar, and the birds serenade us like a choir.

I've always loved spring. A time for fresh starts and anticipation for what is to come. Rose was on call this weekend and ended up working a twelve-hour shift last night, so she went to her apartment this morning and slept for a few hours. Despite being tired, she's already back, spending her lunch break with me.

"It's a good day for chocolate," she says, and I agree.

She savors the last morsel, then pivots off the bench and lies down on the grass. She fans her freshly ironed white dress around her and closes her eyes. "Oh, Kora, I wish I could just freeze this moment. Sometimes I don't think I'm really cut out for all this nursing business. I mean I'm only twenty, I could still do anything I want with my life."

"But you're so good at what you do. We'd all be lost if it wasn't for you."

"Thanks . . . but . . . I only joined the hospital's nurse training program because it pays halfway decent and I get so many benefits. My father was killed in World War II when I was three, so after the war when all the women left their blue-collar jobs at the factories, my mother had to keep working. That left me to take care of my baby brother. When I got out of high school, nursing was really the only thing I could see myself doing. But now I'm not so sure."

I give her a sympathetic look. "I'm sorry." I lick the chocolate off my fingertips. "Well, for what it's worth, I appreciate all you've done for me."

Rose smiles. "I'm proud of the progress you've made. You're lucky because so many of the people here are at the mercy of the hospital. They don't have a say-so in what treatments they get, and it just breaks my heart. I know Hamilton Meadow's doing the best they can, but sometimes I think surely there's a better way. That's the part of this job that starts wearing on me after a while."

"Is shock therapy terrible?" I ask. "Bernice hates it."

"Yeah, Bernice has been in treatment for a few weeks now." She rolls over and props up on her elbows. "I'm not a proponent of electric shock therapy. When I was training to be a nurse, they let me sit in on a session, and I told them I would work here, but there was no way I was doing *that*. It's just too much for me, not my thing."

My right eyelid starts to twitch.

"So, what have you been writing about? You always seem so deep in thought whenever I'm in the dayroom."

My face warms and I fan myself with my hand. "Um . . . a little bit of everything, I suppose."

"Well, whatever you're doing, keep it up. You're looking like a million bucks these days." I smile as Rose stands up to stretch. "I actually have something I'd like to run by you."

"Oh yeah? What's that?"

"You may be able to start writing even more."

"What do you mean?"

"Have you ever read *The Flare*? They deliver it to the patients on Wednesday mornings."

"No, you know how I am . . . I keep to myself most of the time. Everybody always makes such a ruckus when it comes in. I try and just stay out of their way. By the time things have quieted down, I've usually forgotten about it."

"Well, it's a weekly news bulletin, and it covers things going on around the hospital like activities, therapies, and general news. It's written for the patients, but the staff also reads it. And they even sell issues to other hospitals, and to friends and family too." She plops down next to me. "The best part is, they have an all-female staff—an editor, mimeograph operator, reporters, and artists for the cartoons. It's run by Hazel Valentine, an occupational therapy aide, but it's produced entirely by patients. *And* as luck would have it, a reporter just got discharged, and they're trying to find someone to take her place. I thought you'd be the perfect fit."

My heart swells in my chest. "Me? Really? I assumed I'd be more qualified to work in the kitchen."

"Why? You're a writer. Not everyone is given such a special gift."

I feel like my girls have just hugged me for cooking them pancakes for breakfast. "But, do you think I have enough experience? I worked at the *Daily Chronicle* for a couple months before I got pregnant with Ivy, but I never covered anything newsworthy. Just stories about food or gardening or fashion. And when Ivy was little, I helped with the church bulletin, but otherwise, that's it. All I've written lately are poems and lullabies for the girls."

"Well, I'm not guaranteeing anything, but I think you've got a good shot at it. Overly qualified even."

"Really?"

Rose locks eyes with me. "Yes, really. But I don't want you to feel like you *have* to do this. If you think you're not ready to work, I completely understand."

"No, no . . . it sounds great. Blissful, actually."

"Well, good. Let's go talk to Dr. Hunter about it then. I've still got a few more minutes left before I have to be back to the ward."

"Do you think he'll say yes? The two times I saw him, I wasn't exactly cooperative."

"Oh, he's used to that. Let's be honest, the last thing any of these women here want to do is talk to a man about their problems. Heck, most of them are here *because* of a man. It's like kissing the devil himself."

I stand up and brush the crumbs from my dress. "So, what's up with you two? I guess y'all are courting?"

Rose lowers her voice even though no one else is around. "Yeah, we've been seeing each other for a few months now. You know, I think he may propose. I saw him the other day in town looking at rings."

"Would you say yes if he asked you?"

She shrugs. "Sometimes I think I want to be a housewife and a mother, but other times I don't want anything to do with it. I'm not fond of working here at the hospital by any means, but having a career is important to me. It gives me the freedom to do what I want."

"Even though you're young, you sure are smart."

Rose squeezes my hand. "Oh, honey, you're smart too. You've just spent too much time with that husband of yours. Don't worry, it'll all come back to you. You've just got to start believing in yourself again."

When we reach the hallway of Dr. Hunter's office, a woman is screaming and flailing like a hog about to be slaughtered. A female attendant grabs her and the patient punches her in the face, slamming her against the wall. A male attendant steps in and wraps his burly arms around the patient until she collapses. She pants as her screams fade to whimpers.

"He's going to hurt me," she sobs. "Get me away from him. He sent the crows after me to peck holes in my head."

The attendant picks up the woman and takes her away. Dr. Hunter is standing there with his hair disheveled and the back of his shirt untucked. He diverts his attention to Rose and sighs. "Is Kora here to discuss that job you mentioned?"

"Yes." Rose turns to face me. "Kora, when you're finished— as long as it's okay with Dr. Hunter—you can go back to the ward by yourself."

I nod. "Okay. Thanks, Rose."

As she scurries back down the hallway, I can tell Dr. Hunter finds my timing burdensome. He drags himself into his office and lands hard in his chair.

I smell liquor the second I walk in, and it's obvious Dr. Hunter's been drinking. It doesn't take me long to spot a liter of Bell's whiskey poking its head out from the corner behind his briefcase.

"Sometimes we all need a little something to take the edge off," he explains.

"Does Rose know you're drinking in the middle of the day?"

"No, and we're going to keep it that way." His face contorts, and he taps his pencil on the desk. "Kora, I'm pressed for time, so what do you think about this job Rose found for you?"

I ignore the sarcastic response brewing inside my head. "I think I would enjoy writing for *The Flare*, but I told Rose I didn't know if I was qualified enough."

He smirks. "Well, it's not like you're composing speeches for President Eisenhower or anything. Besides, it's just writing. How hard can it be? I assume you got good marks in school."

"I had to quit school in the eighth grade because I had polio. I was bedridden for a couple of years, but I kept up with my schoolwork. I don't have the certificate, but I'm self-taught. I might as well have graduated. I was always good at reading and writing."

"Well, I'm willing to give you a chance if Hazel Valentine is fine with it. She'll be the one interviewing you, but she may need to get final approval from Mary Robertson, the occupational therapy department supervisor." He jots something down and slides the paper over to me. "This is where you can find her. *The Flare* press is in the basement of the administrative building."

"Okay, thank you, sir."

I'm about to leave when his phone rings. He immediately puts his hand up after answering, signaling me to stay. After he hangs up, he says, "Your husband is here to see you."

I swallow the lump that rises in my throat. "Daniel's here in Sparrow? Right now?"

"Yes. And before you see him, I want you to understand what my role is in all of this."

"Okay," I murmur.

"When your husband had you committed, you became Hamilton Meadow's responsibility. I decide when you get released. So, your husband isn't calling the shots anymore, I am. The problem is, I haven't been able to see you very much because of my heavy patient load. It's hard for me to truly assess psychologically where you are right now. Do you understand?"

"Yes, sir."

"Are you sleeping better now? Crying episodes decreasing?"

"Yes, sir."

"But my guess is, you still have moments where you feel emotionally fragile. Am I correct?" Dr. Hunter peers at me as if he's the know-it-all father and I'm the little girl forced to abide by his rules.

"Yes, sir," I mumble.

"Then I think you should stay for a bit longer. I believe working as a help-patient would benefit you and lessen your chances of relapse." He comes out from behind his desk and helps me up. His hand is hot and sweaty, and he smiles wider than he should. "Come on now, let's go see what that husband of yours wants."

I ALMOST DON'T recognize Daniel Mitchell when I walk into the visitors room. He's grown a beard, brown with specks of white in it. It adds ten years to his face and draws attention to the wrinkles around his eyes. He needs a haircut, so he's got it slicked over to the side with a perfect part down the white of his scalp.

He glances up when I come in and flashes his best smile at me. "Kora!"

He hugs me and his whiskers scratch my cheek. "You're looking good."

He must not have showered this morning because his armpits stink and his hair reeks of cigarettes. My heart pounds and my right eye twitches like it always does. Being close to him makes me queasy and bile burns my throat.

I sit down in one of the chairs and Daniel Mitchell stands over me with his hands planted on his hips.

"The hospital sent me a letter a couple weeks ago and said you might be able to come home soon."

"That's news to me."

"Well, maybe they didn't want you to get your hopes up. Anyway, I wanted to come see for myself, so here I am."

I twirl my thumbs in my lap.

Daniel Mitchell sighs. "You look fine until you start doing *that*. Good God, Kora. Can't you keep it together for five minutes? Unless you're just faking this so you can get out of taking care of your kids."

I glare at him. How dare he throw guilt at me like that. I'm not surprised, though. He's so good at making me feel guilty for doing nothing wrong, for doing something that was his idea to begin with. My icy stare challenges him, lets him know I'm not afraid anymore. In some twisted way, I feel like I'm safe here, free from his grip. I stop circling my thumbs and form a steeple with my index fingers like I used to with the girls. *Here's the church, here's the steeple, open it up and see all the people.*

"How are the girls doing?" I ask.

"Better if you were there," he sneers.

"Is Mother taking good care of them?"

"Yeah." He slinks over to the window. "But she's not you.

She doesn't make eggs for me, and she keeps the biscuits at her house. Only gives those to the girls. She makes me eat corn flakes for breakfast."

That's Mother for you, I smirk. I walk over to him. "Daniel, why did you come here?"

"Because I want you back home."

"Hmm. Sounds like you're rethinking sending me here."

He shrugs.

"Maybe you should've been a little more patient with me. It wasn't my fault that everything turned out the way it did."

"Jesus, you got a smart mouth on you now. Don't try to blame all this bullshit on me."

I move over to the door, my signal that I'm either waiting for the nurse to come back or that I'm ready for this man I can't stand to leave. I understand that there's a right and wrong way to treat my husband; it's a vow of matrimony I learned early on when I promised on my wedding night, exactly twenty-one days after I met Daniel Mitchell, to love and obey him, in sickness and in health, till death do us part. But for me to fulfill my responsibility as a wife, society expects me to treat my husband like a king even though he's never been very good to me. They expect me to compromise my own wants and needs—things that bring me joy, make my own life worth living—to make him happy.

But why?

Why is his happiness as a man more important than mine as a woman? And if we serve a loving, protective God, why would he command that I stay married to a man who has spent years tormenting me? For goodness sake, I'm not Jesus Christ sent here to pay for Daniel Mitchell's sins.

My husband hastily stomps toward me and pushes me out of

the way. "Bitch, I didn't want you back anyway." He slams his fist into the metal door. "Unlock this goddamn door! I'm ready to get the hell outta here!"

I blink slowly once, twice, three times.

Suddenly, it's confirmed.

I'd rather do anything than go back home, anything but share a quilt in the same bed with this man, spit my toothpaste into the same sink, scrape the dried food from his dirty dishes with my fingernails.

Yes, there are currently many unknowns. I don't know where I'll live once I'm released, or how I'll financially support myself. I don't know what life will be like as a single mother. But I do know one thing: if I spend a lifetime with Daniel Mitchell, in the end, there will certainly be nothing—not a solitary thing—left of me.

chapter twenty

EMILY

A s I make the five-minute drive to the probate court in
downtown Sparrow to request my grandmother's medical
records, I roll down my car window and take in the silence of the
orphaned world that surrounds me. I notice details I didn't before: street lights on, even though it's the middle of the day;
concrete picnic tables in front of the buildings; benches knocked
over with jagged cracks in the stone. A dog limps around on a
bald lawn, sides sunken in, ribs poking out, sniffing the ground
as if he's searching for something to eat. When I slow to snap a
picture of him, he doesn't even look up.

It's hard to imagine what it must have been like when the
institution was a thriving community, bustling with doctors,
nurses, and patients. I wonder if Kora was allowed to wander
around the grounds unattended. Could she spend time outside,
have lunch on one of the tables, read a book? Or did she spend
time by herself indoors, lying on a sagging twin bed inside one
of these daunting buildings, attempting to forget about all she
left behind?

I make a left then a right to leave Hamilton Meadow behind.
My GPS winds me through the one-way streets of the city until I
reach the county's two-story brick courthouse.

At the entrance, where I'm required to put my purse on a

conveyer belt and stroll through a metal detector, I have a sense of déjà vu. Growing up, when my babysitter would call in sick or take time off, Mom would take me with her to court. She'd make me wear my nicest clothes, and she would pull my hair back in a low, sophisticated ponytail.

I'd mirror Mom's image as her heels clicked down the hallways of the courtroom—the short staccato beats, arms swinging so fast I thought they might lift her off the ground. But once I got into the courtroom and colored a picture or two, I'd grow bored and find myself wishing I was at home watching television, or doing whatever it is that kids do when their mom is home instead of working.

I glance up at the big-bellied security guard who has his arms crossed against his chest. "Which way is the probate court?" I ask.

He points to a door in the back corner, and I pick up my purse and head that way.

There are only a few people in line ahead of me, and I take out my phone to check my emails while I wait. I'm feeling nervous all of a sudden, and I shift back and forth on my feet.

"May I help you, please?" the lady behind the counter says as she takes a sip from her coffee mug.

I take a deep breath and rest my arms on the counter. "Hi . . . um . . . my grandmother was a patient at Hamilton Meadow. How would I go about getting her medical records if she's already deceased?" I say the words fast so I won't lose my courage.

The lady reaches into her candy dish and unwraps a peppermint. "When did she pass?"

"I'm not sure of the exact date. I just know it would have been sometime in the early sixties. She actually died there shortly after she was committed, I believe."

The peppermint rolls around in the lady's mouth and she smacks her lips. "Well, since she's been deceased for less than seventy-five years, you have to start by getting a court order."

"Really? Even if I'm her granddaughter?"

"Yes, ma'am. And you must be next of kin to make the request." She raises her eyebrows. "Medical records are confidential information. The rules have been put in place to protect the patient's privacy."

"So, when you say, 'next of kin,' does that mean my mother will have to file the court order?"

"If she's still living, she will. We could send her the form electronically if that's more convenient."

"Okay, that would work. Could you send it to me and then I'll forward it to her?"

"Sure. What's your email address?"

After I give her my email, she swivels around in her chair and hands me a form from a manila folder. "Here's you a hard copy, also. This part of the process is pretty easy. We charge a fifty-dollar filing fee, and you just fill this out and bring it back to me. I'll pull her death certificate and give the judge your paperwork so he can sign off on it."

"And then?" I ask as I scan the form that's been photocopied a few too many times.

"And then the real fun begins." She laughs. "You turn the court order into Hamilton Meadow and wait to see if they actually *have* her medical records. They still have a few admin people on staff, so they'll check for you. It's a process, though, because none of those older records are computerized. I don't know all the details, but I've heard through the grapevine it's a mess. Some records have been damaged or thrown away over the years.

I believe some of them are at the state archives on old microfilm or ledgers. Heck, some are probably still scattered in some of those old buildings over there."

"What if I want to find out where she's buried? Is that on public record somewhere?"

She crinkles her nose. "I'm sorry, but first you have to get her patient number from her medical records, and then you match that number up with the grave number. The hospital also handles those requests. The problem is that patient numbers were duplicated based on race and sex. So, one number might have been assigned several times." She shrugs. "Another problem is that the gravesite locations are sketchy. Like it may reference that someone is buried in the woods, next to a certain type of tree, but now that tree isn't there anymore. And to complicate matters further, a lot of the markers were pulled up over the years. So, the patient number can get you close, but it doesn't always offer you a guarantee."

She glances at the people standing in line behind me. "I'm sorry I can't be of more help."

I nod. "That's okay. Thank you."

Disappointed, I amble off, my eyes glued to the white tile floor. *It sounds like it's going to be harder than I thought to figure out what happened to Kora.*

I'm just hoping Mom will be cooperative, and that I'll at least have the opportunity to try.

chapter twenty-one

PAM

The consistency of a steady routine outside of work helps to calm the chaos that comes with being an attorney.

Every day I wake up at five a.m., have a cup of coffee, then settle back into bed with my laptop and *USA Today*. On the days I don't have yoga, I run three miles in thirty-two minutes on the treadmill. Breakfast during the week is a bowl of oatmeal with blueberries and nuts, or a smoothie made with frozen fruit, a banana, and almond milk. Plenty of nutrients to keep my neurons zipping along despite my aging brain. Weekends I give myself a little more freedom. I permit myself to indulge in a few treats here and there, and on Saturdays, I run errands and go to the nail salon.

I also try to hit Starbucks during their lull. But even though I'm here at the same time as always, they're slammed. I tap the pointed toe of my Manolo Blahnik as the college girl in front of me orders five pumpkin spice lattes. I slide my cell out of my purse to check my messages, but still no word from Emily. *You should reach out to her. It'll make you feel better.* John's advice replays in my head as I cross my arms. I just need for Emily to complete her article and for me to get Dad's house taken care of this weekend. Then my life can get back on track.

Maryann, the barista, drags me from my thoughts. "Vinte dark roast for you today, Pam?"

"Yes, ma'am." I grab a banana and a pack of nuts from the metal basket beside the register and toss them onto the counter along with a ten-dollar bill.

She hands me my coffee and change, then winks. "Here you go, lady. Have a good day. Try not to work too hard."

Just as I toss my snacks into my purse, my phone vibrates and I see that it's Emily, only I'm not sure I really want to talk to her right now. I could easily wait until after work to call her back, tell her I was too busy and didn't see the call come in.

By the time I get to the door, the call goes to voicemail. I'm about to zip up my purse and head back to work when she calls again. *Damn Millennials. They have no patience whatsoever.* I set my cup on a table and answer.

"Hey, Mom," she says. "Do you have a few minutes to talk?"

"Sure, what's going on?" I juggle my phone in one hand and my coffee in the other as I push open the door.

The line falls silent like we've been disconnected.

"Emily, what is it?"

"Promise you won't get mad at me for asking this."

"You know I don't make promises. Just tell me."

"Well, I'm here in Sparrow. I left this morning." Her words come out in a rush. "I finished up what I needed for my article, and now I'm at the probate court trying to figure out what's required to pull your mother's medical records. But it turns out I can't make the request. You have to because you're next of kin."

I take a gulp of coffee and burn my tongue. "I thought I made it perfectly clear the other night that I have zero desire to dredge up the past."

"If it's any consolation, they probably won't even be able to find her records."

"Why do you say that?"

"Apparently, the records aren't organized very well. I don't even think they're in one location. They said a lot of them have been lost or damaged, and the ones that are still available aren't in any particular order. None of them from that time were ever scanned in, so all they've got are the original records."

I make my way over to a bench, set my coffee down, and make figure-eights with my fingertip along the slats. "Let me think about it, okay?"

Emily doesn't respond. I can practically hear her eyes rolling over the phone.

A wave of guilt washes over me. "What? I said I would think about it. That doesn't mean I'm *not* going to do it."

"Mom, do you remember when I accidentally ran over our neighbor's cat when I was a senior in high school?"

"Actually, I do. I told you to tell them the truth about what happened because they would understand it was an accident. And I also thought it mattered, so they would know what happened to their pet and could stop worrying about her."

"Yeah, well, I did what you said, even though it wasn't easy and I was scared. But the only reason I did it was because of you. Because I thought what you said made sense . . . that if her owners knew the truth, then they could move on."

I digest what she's said, feeling proud all of a sudden that she's grown into such a wise young woman. "Look, I'm not making any promises, but if you forward me the paperwork, I'll consider it."

"Okay," she says. "I love you."

Her words make my heart heavy. "When are you coming home?"

"Tomorrow, I guess."

"All right, well, drive safely and call me when you get back."

We hang up. It wasn't the time to tell her I'm going to her grandfather's house tomorrow, or how bewildered I am about my relationship with John. Besides, it's not important. I don't need anyone's help. I'll get through it, I always do. Confiding in my daughter would only convolute matters, make her ask more questions, eat up too much of my time. I just want to slink away this weekend without anyone knowing or prying into my business.

Pressing my back into the bench, I contemplate whether or not Emily has the civil right to obtain her grandmother's medical records. I trace my fingers along each charm on my bangle bracelet: my initials, a gavel, a scale of justice, a WEAPON OF CHOICE trinket, and a stiletto. Emily gave me this the year I made partner.

Early on, I learned that in order to get ahead in this business, I had to work harder than everyone around me. It's how I became the first female partner of my law firm. I had to prove myself alongside a team of men that a woman, especially a single mother, could put in the hours necessary to make it to the top.

The year I made partner was the best time of my life. That's why I wear this bracelet every day . . . to remind myself of the turning point when I started winning for a change. Finally beating life instead of always letting it beat me.

chapter twenty-two

KORA

The morning after Daniel's crash landing at Hamilton Meadow, I stroll across campus with Rose, taking slow and steady breaths to try and calm my nerves about my interview with Hazel Valentine.

Even though I'm a little anxious, it's still refreshing to be outside bustling around with the other somebodies—to be granted the privilege of walking free in the sunshine, feeling the gift of fresh air, being able to smile and say hello to friendly faces that pass by.

Rose waits until we get to the lawn of the administrative building to ask me how my visit with Daniel went. She says Dr. Hunter told her about it at dinner last night.

I wonder how that's any of his business as I pick up my pace, fixing my eyes on the grand columns that line the front of the building. If it were anyone but Rose, I'd be pretty upset. "It could've gone better, but my husband's a jackass, so I can't expect much from him, I suppose."

She puts her arm around me. "I'm sorry. Did he say he'd bring the girls to see you?"

I shake my head. "My husband wants only one thing from me right now—for me to be his slave—and I'm over it. I'm here, there's nothing I can do about it, and he's clearly not willing to fight for me. So, I'm not willing to fight for him either."

"Are you going to divorce him when you get out? You should."

No one's ever mentioned the word divorce to me, and I feel a smidge of guilt for talking about Daniel behind his back. If he ever finds out, he'd have my hide for sure. "I tried to leave him a few years ago and move in with my parents, but they believe a woman stands by her man no matter what, so they made me go back to him."

"That's why I don't think I want to get married. Too much at stake and too much to lose. But you could start over with your girls. I know you could find a way to make it work."

I stop at the bottom of the stairs and gaze up. The building is like a white palace of purity that welcomes filthy minds to their new home. Even though this is the building where I checked in, I was so out of it that day, I don't remember much about it. Now, I notice the triangular peak above the portico, the ornate trim and windows, the tall, wooden double doors. My heart gallops inside my chest, and I pull out the paper Dr. Hunter gave me yesterday with Hazel Valentine's office number on it. "Thanks for walking me over, but I think I need to do this by myself."

She squeezes my hand. "Good luck in there, Kora. Hazel's going to love you."

I want to ask her why she's helping me, why she cares so much. But I don't. It's always been hard for me to communicate how I'm feeling. That's why writing helps. On paper, my mouth can't get in the way.

⊷

HAZEL VALENTINE'S OFFICE is in the basement down the hall from the other occupational therapy rooms. Her door is cracked and when I tap on it, she says to come on in. She smiles when she sees me.

Hazel Valentine is pretty, with lips blotted in an orange-red hue and clumps of short, dark curls framing her face. Her office is tidy. A typewriter stacked with paper sits on the table behind her and textbooks are lined up on the shelf in the corner. She closes the folder in front of her and stacks it with the others on the edge of her desk.

"You must be Kora," she says. "Please, have a seat."

I plant myself in the chair across from her, my hands quivering in my lap. My thumbs start tracing an imaginary circle, but I stop them mid-flight when I look into Hazel Valentine's eyes. They ironically match her name: the color that changes from gold to green to brown depending on what hues you're wearing. The same type of eyes my Fern has.

She gets right to it and starts asking me questions, and somehow, I manage to answer each one with confidence I haven't felt since I was a young woman.

"I think you'll be a tremendous asset to our team," Hazel says after our interview. "I'll let Mary, my supervisor, know I found us a new reporter." She winks and stands up, smoothing out her dress that accentuates her pointy bust and narrow waist just perfectly. "Welcome aboard."

"Thank you so much. I really appreciate the opportunity." I push myself out of the chair and we shake hands over her desk. There's a picture of a little girl behind her. "Is that your daughter?" I ask.

"No, that's my niece, Bonnie. My sister also works here at the hospital. She draws blood down in the lab. Bonnie comes here most afternoons, so I'm sure you'll get to meet her."

I point to her wedding ring. "Do you and your husband want children?"

"Sure, but only when the time is right. How about you, Kora, do you have any children?"

"Yes, ma'am. My girls are about Bonnie's age."

"I'm sure it's difficult to be away from them. But don't you worry, you'll be home in a jiff. The vast majority of the patients participating in our occupational therapy program are either furloughed or discharged in a reasonable amount of time."

I nod, suddenly feeling embarrassed that I'm here instead of at home where I belong.

"Now, before I show you around and introduce you to the other girls, I want to give you a little bit of background on us."

"Okay."

Hazel holds the door open for me, and we begin strolling down the hallway.

"We've got something special here—we're up to 2,500 copies a week and expanding our audience every day. And we've recently established a weekly paper for the colored department." Her face lights up. "I don't know how much you know about occupational therapy, but it was originally founded in 1917 by a psychiatrist, a secretary, a teacher, a social worker, and two architects. Of those six people, three were women. A pretty significant accomplishment for those ladies, considering we couldn't even vote back then."

"I'll say."

"The concept of O.T. then and now is simply the belief that patients will recover faster if they're kept busy with activities.

That's why Hamilton Meadow started this publication back in the thirties. It began strictly as a therapeutic service for patients to type, draw, and print. It was actually called 'printing therapy.' But then they began seeing psychological improvements in the patients who busied not only their hands, but also their minds . . . with editing, rewriting, coming up with compelling headlines, arranging the material on the pages, creating artwork . . . that kind of thing. It was also a huge success because the other patients really enjoyed reading the paper. It gave them something to look forward to each week. They were in better spirits, more cooperative."

We stop outside the press room and Hazel Valentine stands up straight.

"I don't have an official degree in occupational therapy, but I've witnessed this publication flourish because of women like you—talented women just put in the wrong circumstance at the wrong time."

My face warms. "So, I have to ask, why is this an all-female staff? Women were few and far between at the *Chronicle*."

She plants her hands on her hips. "Well, for one thing, the bulletin is managed by me, and I think we both know *men* don't want a *woman* telling them what to do. And personally, I take safety into account. We trust each other down here. If it's just us, we don't have to worry about having an attendant on duty for security purposes."

"I see."

"But it wasn't always primarily women. When print therapy in hospitals was first introduced during World War I, plenty of veterans participated. But I've heard sometimes it was met with opposition because women were training the men. I don't know if the men had a problem with it, or if their wives did, or maybe one bad apple spoiled the whole bunch. But regardless, now that the dust has settled and men are back to doing what they do best, we're still here. Pouring our heart and soul into something we can be proud of. Doing what we as women have always been good at—nurturing and supporting others and making the best out of bad situations."

Hazel speaks with a flair of sophistication I've never heard in a woman before; she must not be from the South because she has no accent whatsoever. Each word is pronounced perfectly, and fluid sentences flow effortlessly out of her mouth.

Feeling a little breathless, I'm not sure what to say.

She pats my shoulder. "Come on in, dear. Let me show you around."

The air in the press room reeks of ink and cigarette smoke. There's an overhead light, and the bushes have grown past the windows, so the sun can't shine in. The walls are clean and a pale yellow. The flooring is the same tile that's in the women's building, but cleaner and fresher because it's likely never been peed on. Women in plain dresses like mine sit at oak desks with papers and books scattered around them. There's a shelf in the back of the room where past issues of *The Flare* are stacked, and a hefty brunette stands next to a machine as copies flow out. When we walk in, she glances up and waves hello with a purple-ink-stained hand.

The girl closest to me stops typing on her IBM, grins, and stands. "Hey, welcome to our neck of the woods. We're the sanest bunch of gals at Hamilton Meadow. My name's Lisa. Nice to meet you."

"Hi, I'm Kora," I shout, speaking over the rattle of the copier.

Lisa sits down, and another girl stands. "Good morning, Kora. I'm Deborah." She curtsies with a smirk on her face. "Don't let her fool ya. We got our own kind of crazy going on down here."

Deborah plops back down in her chair, and the homely girl behind her doesn't take the cue that it's her turn to go next. She's hunched over, sketching with a pencil, only pausing to slide the paper around her desk, poring over it from all angles.

"That's Suzette. She's our quiet one. Does all the artwork and cartoons here. See these prints on the walls? She's done all of them." Hazel taps the toe of her white nursing shoe that doesn't go with the dress she's wearing. "We also have an editor. Where's Darcy, ladies?"

Lisa slides her pencil behind her ear. "She finished up her final edit and then high-tailed it out of here. Said she needed a cigarette. She's been gone for a while, though. She might've fallen asleep out there on the grass like she always does."

Hazel points a manicured fingernail that matches her lips toward the machine in the back of the room. "Excuse the noise. It's not always this loud in here, but tomorrow's delivery day. The way it works is, you girls research and type up the articles, and then copies are made on the mimeograph back there. We've recently gotten rid of the hand crank because we were able to buy an electric one with our profit. It's been a lifesaver. We can print a lot of copies at one time, which is why our publication numbers have skyrocketed."

I nod, taking it all in.

"So, once the copies are made, you girls band together and staple the newsletter down the side and bingo, another issue of *The Flare* is ready for distribution. You think you can handle it?"

"Yes ma'am," I say with a smile.

"Well, you can start today if you're up to it, and then report here tomorrow morning after breakfast, and I'll give you your first assignment. When the other women in your ward go to their activities or to the dayroom, you just come here."

I bite my lip to keep from shouting with joy. "Hazel, thank you again. This job . . . it's . . . it's perfect for me. And I promise I won't let you down."

"You're welcome. I know you're going to do a stellar job for us. Just don't make your recovery too quick because I have to admit . . . we've never had a professional working for us before. It'll be good to have your expertise around here."

Hazel takes a few steps toward the door but then swivels back around. "And one more thing . . . Leo Larson, a reporter from the *Daily Chronicle*, has been snooping around here for days. Word from the bird is he's not leaving until he's dug up every secret the hospital's got. We've been given strict orders not to speak with him, so if he happens to make his way down here and starts asking questions, you are not allowed to answer him. Got it?"

Suzette looks up from her drawing and seals her lips with her fingers, then throws away the key.

"Yes, ma'am. Don't worry, Mrs. Valentine, I won't say a thing."

EVEN THOUGH THE sleeping ward is rambunctious tonight because of the full moon, I fall into bed and block out everything around me. I stare at the ceiling, replaying everything that's transpired over the past two days. All of a sudden, I feel like I could explode from the clash of happiness and grief that's boiling inside of me. I place the girls' picture on my pillow and start to hum the lullaby, only this time, the words also seep out.

> *Rock-a-bye baby on the treetop.*
> *When the wind blows, the cradle will rock.*
> *When the bough breaks, the cradle will fall.*
> *And down will come baby, cradle and all.*

I gasp for air and sit up in bed, hugging my knees to my chest as I rock from side to side. I sing it over and over. Each time I get to "down will come baby," Sally, the girl beside me, slaps her hands together so loud I gasp. Then I have to start all over, sing it again until I can get the verse flawless, the way it should be.

If I'm going to be a success at my new job and get back home to my girls, I need to say goodbye to the baby, perhaps even forget that she ever existed. I must say goodbye to this tragedy that's poked holes in my heart and cast it into the dark water of the ocean. It now lies at the bottom, mingling with the sand, rocks, and shells, begging not to be devoured by fish or a shark, or electrocuted by an eel.

The baby.

I must say goodbye to the baby.

And so I get out the book of matches I conveniently store in my brain and strike one. The flame is beautiful, and I close my eyes, holding it just an inch from my face. I don't blow it out, though; the fire burns my fingertips and makes them welt with blisters. I light each match again and again until tears stream down my face.

I can't allow this memory to burn me anymore. I have to throw it where I can't see it, feel it, taste it.

In the darkness, Mother places a grenade in my fingertips. Wrapping her hands over mine, she commands me to do what needs to be done. I massage the exterior, finger each crevice, then pull the fuse. Screaming, I chuck it as high and as far away as I can.

Over the cradle, over the treetops, over the bough.

Until finally . . .

The memory of that sweet little baby explodes.

chapter twenty-three

EMILY

Magnolia Inn, the B&B I'm staying at, is a restored ante-bellum home oozing with southern hospitality. The ceilings are high and trimmed in dark crown molding, and the rooms are decorated with antiques and floral draperies. Mabel and Sissy greet me and take my credit card information, then they invite me to eat shrimp and grits with them and the other guests tonight. Sissy dismisses herself into the kitchen as Mabel gives me my paperwork and points me to my room.

"I'm afraid I'm going to have to say no to dinner," I say to Mabel before I go upstairs. "I wanted to check out the city tonight. Any recommendations on a good place to eat down-town?"

"I should know a young whippersnapper like you wouldn't want to stay home with Sissy and me. Can't say I blame you for wanting to go out and explore." She skims her perfectly mani-cured nails over her chin. "Well, there's Friends . . . that's a good bar and grill type place. And if you like Italian, you can't go wrong with Gianetti's. They've got the best pizza this side of the Mason-Dixon line. And, it's only about a five-minute walk from here."

I smile politely. "Perfect, thanks so much."

"No problem, sugar." She stands up and pats her short white

hair that looks freshly permed. "Well, breakfast is served until 9:30 in the morning, so if you're not eating dinner with us, you better not sneak out of here without letting me feed you a buttered biscuit with some homemade pear preserves."

I laugh. "Yes, ma'am. Don't worry, I'll make sure I stop by in the morning before I leave. There's no way I can pass up homemade biscuits."

ONCE I GET to my room, I pull out my laptop and check my email. The probate court has already sent the court order, so I go ahead and forward it to Mom. I spend the rest of the afternoon writing and proofing my article, then send it to Bernadette so I can have a full day off tomorrow without having to think about work. After I take a short nap, I change into leggings and an oversized sweater, then freshen my makeup and run a brush through my hair.

It's a nice evening for a walk and I decide on Gianetti's for dinner. When I arrive and open the restaurant door, blaring music welcomes me. Cooks' foreheads glisten with sweat as they toss pizza dough into the air and slide the finished products onto metal pans. I take a seat at the bar next to an older man who is sipping on a beer and watching the evening news.

After I order a glass of red wine from the bartender, someone taps me on the shoulder. "Emily?"

I turn around and see Graham, the guy I met earlier.

"Hey, I thought that was you," he says.

"Hi, how are you?" I say, sounding a little too enthusiastic.

"Good, I'm just grabbing some dinner." Graham's wearing dark jeans and a white button-front shirt with the sleeves rolled up. His eyes shift back and forth. "So . . . um, are you from around here? I kind of got the impression earlier that you weren't."

"No, I live in Baxter. It's about a two-hour drive, so I decided to stay the night."

"Ah, Baxter. Such a cool little town. One of my best friends from high school went to college there. Is that where you went to school?"

"Yeah, I was there from 2011 to '15. Once I graduated, I decided to stay because I liked it so much."

"I thought we were about the same age. I graduated from Clemson in 2013."

The bartender hands me my wine, and Graham orders a beer.

"Would you mind if I joined you for dinner?" he asks.

"Sure, that'd be great." I gesture to the empty stool to the right of me. "All yours."

He smiles and slides onto it.

"So, do you come here a lot?" I ask, taking a sip of my merlot.

He shrugs. "Maybe once or twice a week. I just live right around the corner. I can get in and out of here pretty quick."

I pick up the menu sandwiched between the shakers of red pepper flakes and parmesan. "So, what's good here?"

"I usually just get a couple slices of pepperoni pizza. How about you? What are you in the mood for?"

"It looks like they have veggie slices, so I think I'll have two of those." I slide the menu back between the shakers. "So, do the college kids go out here on Thursday nights like they do in Baxter?"

"From what I've seen, yes. But obviously later. You and I are more on senior citizen time." He points to the empty booths donned with red-checkered tablecloths.

The bartender returns with Graham's beer. "What'd y'all decide on for dinner?" he asks.

Graham places our order then leans back in his chair. "So, what's it like living in Baxter?"

"It's pretty cool. I live in an area called Five Points. It's about ten minutes from downtown and the university, so I get the feel of living in a college town, but I'm far enough out that I'm not surrounded by students 24/7. How'd you wind up in Sparrow?"

"I'm actually from South Carolina. I was a business major at Clemson, but once I got out in the real world, I hated being stuck behind a desk all day. When I was a kid, my dad was in construction, and that's what I did part-time when I was in college. I enjoyed it, so I decided to get back into it." He takes a swig of his beer. "I'm just here temporarily, for the next year or so. My job takes me all over the southeast."

"Do you like the diversity of that? I think I might."

"Yeah, so far it's worked out. I don't know if I'd want to do it forever, though. Do you have to travel a lot for your job?"

"No, this is kind of a special occasion for me. I usually just cover local news and events in Baxter. I'm hoping I can eventually get a job writing articles that are a little more thought-provoking, but for now, I'm just getting experience and building up my resume."

"You're piling up sand for the sandcastle you're going to build later."

I smile. "Exactly . . . I like that."

"I can't take credit for it. It's one of my favorite quotes." He leans on one elbow and faces me. "Did you always know you wanted to be a writer?"

I nod. "Ever since I was a little girl. My mom's an attorney, so I'd always write stories about her cases."

"How's your article coming? Did you find everything you needed today?"

"Yeah, I wrote it this afternoon and sent it to my editor."

"Well good, maybe that means you can chill out a little bit tonight." His face relaxes into a smile. "So, your mom's an attorney, how about your dad? What's he like?"

"I don't see him that much. He's a stockbroker, also very much a Type-A personality like my mom. They got a divorce when I was five, and he moved to New York."

"That must've been hard. Your mom must be a strong woman."

I swirl the wine in my glass. "That's an understatement."

"Sounds like my mom. My dad died when I was thirteen. That's one reason I got back into construction. It makes me feel close to him." A nostalgic expression spreads across his face.

"You talk about his death so easily."

He shrugs. "Everything happens for a reason, right?"

"Maybe . . . I don't know. I'm not sure if I buy into all of that." One of my favorite country songs comes on, and I start bobbing my head to the beat.

He leans in a little closer and I get a whiff of his cologne. "You a country music fan?"

"Um . . . just recently. In the past year or two, I guess."

"That surprises me. You know what people say, if you play a country song backward, you get your dog back, your man back, your truck back." He laughs.

I reach for my sapphire necklace, but realize I forgot to put it back on after my nap this afternoon. "Well, then, maybe I should stop listening to country music because I definitely don't want my ex-boyfriend back."

"Sorry, I was just joking. I didn't mean to—"

The bartender swings by. "Either of y'all want another drink?"

"Yes," we say emphatically at the same time.

We both laugh.

"Nice synchronicity," I say, then immediately feel the need to switch topics. "So, I have to ask . . . what's it like working at Hamilton Meadow? It so spooky there. Do you ever get scared?"

"At first it weirded me out, but yeah, I've pretty much gotten used to it by now. Plus, it helps that I've usually got a full crew working with me."

We make small talk about the hospital until our pizza comes and continue chatting through dinner: about Erin and her baby, my other friends, his friends, what we do on the weekends, our favorite movies, the nuances of our jobs, what we loved and hated about being only children. The words pour out of me, and I realize how much I've missed not only going out, but also how easy conversation flows when you have a natural connection with someone.

With Colin, I settled on his level of intellect, and even overlooked how he was always talking about himself. And with Erin, once she became a mother, everything changed between us. We've struggled to find things in common, and I often find myself staring off into space when she complains about Michael leaving the toilet seat up or turning her favorite white shirt pink in the wash, or when she drones on about Sophie.

"What do you have going on tomorrow?" Graham asks as we're signing our credit card bills.

"I'm staying at Magnolia B&B here in town, so I figured I'd sleep in and have breakfast there. I have a couple of things I'd like to get taken care of, but I'll probably be out of here by lunch."

A group of loud frat boys plows through the front door. One guy punches his friend in the bicep then points to a table of attractive girls in the back. Graham ignores them as he stands to leave. "Well, I'll give you my phone number. Shoot me a text if you end up staying. Maybe we could grab lunch or a coffee before you head back to Baxter."

"Yeah, I'll let you know." I feel my face flush and pull my hair over my shoulder, feeling awful that I've just told a lie to the nicest guy I've ever met.

chapter twenty-four

✤

PAM

I lie in bed and stare at my packed suitcase on the other side of the room. Tomorrow morning, I plan to get on the road early. The sooner I get to Dad's, the sooner I can get back home. And as for Emily's email with the court order attached—surprise—I never got around to opening it.

I turn off the lamp and slide my eye mask down. John called three times tonight, but I didn't answer. Instead, I sent him a text saying I couldn't talk because I was working late and would call him back later. I envision his handsome face tightening in a grimace, his eyebrows furrowed when my message popped into the display of his cell.

The soft cotton of my mask comforts my fatigued eyes, and I focus on my breathing like I'm supposed to. A whippoorwill sings its one-word song nearby. I can't remember the last time I heard one of those. Its voice comes in slow and steady intervals. Predictable, melancholy. I match one full breath with the call of the whippoorwill for ten cycles until my mind forgets about my worries of today and fades into a dream.

I'm standing at the end of a dirt road as my pink, flowy silk dress blows in the wind. Sweat runs in streams down my back. My mouth is dry, my armpits sticky. I'm not sure how old I am, but I feel young, hopeless, frantic. My car has run out of gas. I've never seen this car before, but it is exquisite: a red convertible BMW, the kind that can make you feel as free as a bird when you're doing sixty-five with the top down on a summer day.

A black Range Rover speeds around the curve and stirs up the red dirt into a cloud of dust. The car stops and reverses to where I'm standing.

A man is driving alone, and he rolls down his window. He looks like a movie star. Black hair, brown eyes, and a dazzling smile he probably paid thousands of dollars for. *A wolf in sheep's clothing*, Sadie's voice cautions in my head.

"Hey, you need any help?" he asks. "If something's wrong with your car, I'd be glad to check it out for you. Or, if you're out of gas, I could take you to the nearest gas station."

A crystal angel sways on his dashboard like a hula girl.

"I ran out of gas, but I'm fine. My father should be here any minute," I lie.

"You sure about that? The nearest gas station's five miles from here. I'd be happy to give you a ride."

I study his smooth face. I'm usually a good judge of character. He seems to be a nice enough guy, doesn't appear to be a serial killer. "Well, I guess I could call my dad once I get into town."

I open the car door and get in. His car smells like leather and it's freshly vacuumed with the wood-grain interior polished to a shine. He puts the car in drive without telling me his name or asking mine. He turns up the radio. "Hold On Loosely," a 38 Special song from the eighties is playing. It's one of my favorites. *Everything's going to be fine*, I tell myself. *Stop being so paranoid.*

The man stares straight ahead as he drives. There's a bottle of water in one cupholder, and change and a pocketknife in the other. Suddenly, I panic. *What could be in his glove box, or under his seat, or in the trunk? Why did I trust this man?*

There's a loud boom and I gasp. The angel gyrates and the man laughs.

"What was that?" I ask, clutching the door handle.

The man points ahead. "Good thing the station's right there. Sounds like I popped a tire."

My dad walks out of the gas station and I'm relieved. He's a young man again, emptying a pack of peanuts into a Coke bottle. I don't understand why he's here, out in the middle of nowhere. It must be my lucky day. I jump out of the man's car and slam the door behind me. I run to Dad, throw my arms around his neck.

"Daddy, I'm so glad to see you! My car . . . I ran out of gas on that old dirt road off—"

He holds up his palm and stops me mid-sentence, crunching on his peanuts with his mouth open. "Um . . . sorry. You must be mistaking me for someone else. I've never seen you before."

He pushes past me, shuffles toward his truck.

"But you're my father. I know you are," I call out after him. "What am I supposed to do out here all by myself?"

The man who drove me is still in his Range Rover, watching us with a smirk on his face.

When my dad gets to his truck, he sneers at me. His face suddenly becomes blotchy and the whites of his eyes pool with blood. He maliciously laughs. Then, beginning with his head, his body turns to charred pieces of ash. He crumbles away until there's nothing left of him but a pile of gray dust on the pavement next to his Coke bottle.

And then I wake up.

My chest feels like it's going to cave in and I yank my eye mask off, blinking into the darkness.

I let out a sigh of relief. *It's over. I don't have to worry. I'm home, in my bed. Safe. A grown woman. And I sure as hell don't need my father to rescue me anymore.*

chapter twenty-five

KORA

The sun's only been up for a few minutes when I spot her: an exquisitely shaped ebony and aqua blue butterfly with specks of gold, fluttering outside the window. I imagine that her translucent wings are powerful enough to fly against the wind or survive a summer thunderstorm. I also imagine that she is brave enough to travel alone from place to place—responsible for her own happiness. As well as clever enough to dodge a child's cupped hands trying to put her in a jar for Daddy to see when he gets home from work.

I squeeze my eyes shut and envision the butterfly landing on my finger, whispering her secrets about how I, too, can change from an ugly, old caterpillar with feet that keep me trapped on the ground to a gorgeous creature who can soar over the highest blooms of a dogwood tree.

This morning, I am free like her.

I report to my new job after breakfast, just like Hazel Valentine requested. Today Rose doesn't come in until ten, so I make the trek alone. Even though it's been climbing into the sixties in the afternoon, the mornings are still chilly. The wind blows and cuts straight through my sweater, so I fasten the top buttons and hug my arms against my chest. I say hello to a few women who pass by, but they just nod their heads and keep walking. A group of nurses bustle toward me with their faces buried in the *Daily Chronicle*, cupping their hands over their mouths and whispering to each other.

My bicep strains as I open the heavy wooden door of the administrative building and stroll inside. I say hello to the attendant standing guard at the front, then round the corner to the hallway that leads to the stairwell. Suddenly, I hear voices—angry, deep male voices coming from one of the conference rooms with the door ajar. They sound like a yapping pack of coyotes at midnight.

"I can't believe that state legislator, he should've just come to us himself instead of going behind our backs and lighting a fire under that reporter's ass," one gruff voice booms. "Or hell, if he truly believes there's a problem here, why didn't he just go to the state himself? Why'd he get the goddamn *Daily Chronicle* involved?"

Another man speaks up. "It wouldn't surprise me if that son of a bitch Leo Larson was padding his wallet. The government acts like they're all high and mighty, but they're no better than any of us."

I creep to a halt.

"You heard Superintendent Goodwin," says a man who sounds like he's smoked too many cigarettes. "Leo will get his day in the sun, and this will pass just like everything else does."

There's an ambush of silence. Then one man clears his throat and another coughs.

"We're acting like this surprises us. We know how out of control everything is here. Maybe Leo Larson's investigation isn't such a terrible thing after all. Maybe the state will finally give us the money we need to properly support these patients."

"Ha. What are the chances of that happening?" the first voice says. "I think he's out for blood. Plain and simple, he wants to be a hero. Even if the state increases our funding, we'll be damn lucky if any of us have jobs after this."

A fist slams against the table and I gasp. "Fine then, we'll just get other jobs! There're plenty of places that would appreciate what we're doing for these folks. Everyone's quick to point the finger and tell you what a bad job you're doing, but no one wants to step up to the plate to help."

When the next person interjects, I hold my breath and hustle toward the stairs. If they catch me eavesdropping, I'll lose my job at *The Flare* for sure. I huff and puff as I jog down to the press room. When I walk in, all the girls are huddled around Lisa's desk and Deborah's mouth is hanging wide open.

I shuffle over to them. "Hey, good morning. What's going on around here?"

I stand next to the woman I saw yesterday running the mimeograph and peer over her shoulder. Her hand is sprawled out on the cover of the *Daily Chronicle*, purple smudges still on her fingers.

"The newspaper ran a story today about the hospital giving experimental drugs to patients without their consent." Deborah rolls her eyes. "And we've heard through the grapevine this is only the beginning. Apparently, Leo Larson has a lot more mud he's about to start slinging."

Lisa drums her fingers on the desk. "I knew he'd get something on them. I mean, how hard can it be? There's a story slithering around every inch of this place."

"Well, those doctors better not try to force me to do something against *my* will," Deborah says, sashaying back to her desk.

"Remember when I interviewed those nurses a few months ago about their expertise in judo? I even sat in on one of their classes. If they mess with me, I'll karate their ass."

Lisa tosses the paper over to me. "Here ya go, Kora. We're done with this if you'd like to see for yourself."

I go to my desk and read the article. The patient's families were also unaware of what was happening, and one person had died, most likely because of the medication's side effects.

I rub the front page of the newspaper between my fingertips until they turn black, thinking of the weary faces and sometimes convulsing bodies that often haunt me in the sleeping ward. I start to feel queasy.

The story was, of course, leaked by an inside source: another doctor who refused to use the drugs on his patients because he thought it was unethical. I guess this is why those men in the conference room were so upset. They instructed everyone to seal their lips and throw away the key. But one person was smart enough to hide that key in his shirt pocket where he could snag it whenever he pleased.

MY FIRST ARTICLE needs to be three-hundred words, as short as possible to get the point across. It's about two male patients who tried to escape last week. They beat up an attendant and then made a run for it. The employee is still in the hospital, and the patients were caught right outside the city limits.

I'm in Hazel Valentine's office, and she leans back in her chair and takes a sip of her coffee.

"Kora, just so you know, this isn't something we typically cover because we don't want to give patients any ideas or have people from the outside snooping around in our business. The hospital police force didn't even want the county to know, but once again, someone leaked this story to the *Daily Chronicle,* and now we're stuck cleaning up their mess."

"Okay," I tell her, "I'll get right on it."

Hazel slides a legal pad and a pen across the desk to me. "You also need to conclude it by stating if any other patients try to escape, they *will* be held accountable for their actions. Ordinarily, I'd say to get a quote from Superintendent Goodwin, but I've heard he's been a little salty lately because of all this ruckus with Leo Larson. So, let's just make do on this one without bothering him. When you're done with your article, just turn it in to Darcy for her to edit."

She stands up beside her desk and taps her foot—my cue, I assume, that our meeting is over and she's got other, more important things to do. I notice now that Hazel Valentine is looking extra professional today. Her curls are a little tighter, her eyelashes more pronounced. I notice, too, that her high heels are exactly like the pair I donated to the institution a couple of Christmases ago.

In my past life, before all hell broke loose, my friend Joanne came to my house and helped me gather up donations for our Sunday School class to send to the patients here. She was sitting on my bed, fingers wrapped around my china saucer, eating the lemon pound cake I'd just taken out of the oven thirty minutes earlier. I'd already eaten my piece and was standing at the closet sorting through my old dresses.

"Why, I heard the folks at Hamilton Meadow are so crazy that when there's a full moon, they literally howl. Just like animals. I bet no one gets a lick of sleep on those nights." She crinkled her nose as if she'd just eaten a lemon wedge that toppled into the cake batter by accident.

I took four church dresses that I hadn't been able to get back into after having the girls, along with a pair of high heels—the ones that always gave me blisters—and threw them on the bed beside her.

"A pretty dress and shoes will make any woman feel better," I said. "I don't care how crazy you are."

"Yeah, that . . . and lipstick," she added.

"And perfume," I smirked. "I'm glad we're doing this, Joanne. It feels good to do something nice for those less fortunate."

"Honey, we are the hands and feet of Jesus. If we don't help those poor, lost souls, who will?"

"Daniel would kill me if he knew I was giving away perfectly fine clothes." I pulled back the curtains to make sure he hadn't come home for lunch early like he sometimes did.

"But it's Christmas. Surely this time of year the Lord would soften his heart?"

It was easy not to answer her because I was so well trained; I knew better than to gossip about my husband.

Now, in Hazel Valentine's office, noting her shoes that look just like mine, I wonder what happened to those things our Sunday School class sent in that Christmas. Did the employees sort through the donations and take what they wanted? Or, did our things get tossed in the trash? My friends and I didn't know it at the time, but the ladies here certainly didn't need old church dresses and high heels. They needed the basic necessities of life: old smocks, flats that were good and broken in, socks without holes in them, hair brushes. Not our fancy hand-me-downs and perfume.

I wonder if Joanne will still be my friend after all this. Or, if I'd even want her as a friend. Once things started deteriorating with Daniel, she didn't come around as often anymore. Kind of like my neighbors who stood outside on their front porches with their mouths hanging open that time I drank half a bottle of Daniel's whiskey and wound up plumb snockered, stumbling around in the yard as I attempted to make my way to the front door.

Sometimes life changes us, and we can't go back to who we were before. And I think I'm okay with that. I can now appreciate that my soul needs more than a form-fitting sheath dress, blushed lips, and a pair of high heels to be happy.

I'm just grateful I'm finally figuring that out.

WHEN I GET back to the ward that afternoon, the dayroom is buzzing, not only because copies of *The Flare* are flying around the room, but also because Sheila is being furloughed tomorrow. I used some of the money Daddy gave me to chip in with the other girls, and Rose brought us Coca-Colas and peanut butter crackers. A group of us gather around in a circle on the floor with our treats in front of us.

"So, Sheila," I venture once we're all settled, "what's the first thing you're going to do when you get home?"

"Listen to her, she sounds like a real reporter now . . . asking the questions we all want to know the answers to." Rose winks and takes a swig of my drink.

Sheila licks the peanut butter from her fingers. "I think I'm going to eat a three-layer red velvet cake and have it with hot coffee filled to the brim with cream."

"But if you do that, the first thing you'd have to do is slave away in a kitchen baking," says the young girl who refuses to eat. She sticks her finger down her throat and makes a gagging sound.

"Oh no," Sheila giggles, "I'd have my housekeeper bake it."

"Red velvet cake and a housekeeper. What more could a woman ask for?" I say.

Sheila deepens her voice and points her index finger at each of us. "Make me some cake, woman, and when you're done with that, scrub my toilet."

Everyone laughs.

Bernice, who had shock therapy earlier this week and is surprisingly communicating quite well, says, "No offense girls, but I'm going to take a hot shower—alone of course—and then I'm going to put these babies in a red lace bullet bra." She cups her hands over her breasts and squeezes.

The girl to my left laughs so hard she snorts and snot flies out of her nose.

"Gross!" several girls remark.

Sally, the girl who bunks next to me at night, leans over. "What about you, Kora? What are you going to do when you get out of here?"

I start to twiddle my thumbs. "I'll cross that bridge when I come to it."

"You want any more children?" Sally asks.

I open my mouth, but Genevieve throws her hand into the air like a child begging her teacher to answer a question. "My turn, my turn! When I get out of here, I'm going to go home and give my husband the biggest, wettest kiss he's ever had!"

My carefree mood fades away. The truth is, I won't gain anything by leaving Hamilton Meadow Hospital. Here or at home, I'm still in prison.

Only here, shockingly enough, I have a precious little thing called hope.

❦

E M I L Y

I wake up at the B&B just like I went to sleep: thinking about Graham. The way his eyes pulled me in, replaying everything he said, every gesture he made. He offered to walk me back last night, but I declined and told him he didn't need to go out of his way, that I'd be fine by myself. Instead, we exchanged numbers—a spontaneous decision on my part—which I cursed myself for once my wine wore off.

The truth is, I'm feeling emotionally delicate these days, and I'm not sure why. One part of me wants to leave Sparrow and forget I ever met Graham, while at the same time, I want to get to know him better, maybe share another meal with him today. My psyche juggles these opposing desires as I lie in my plush king-size bed, not wanting to ever leave it.

I glance at my phone on the nightstand and see an unread text from Erin that came in after eleven last night, asking me to call her.

Since I have a little over an hour before I need to check out, I give her a call.

"Hey girl," she whispers. The line falls silent, then I hear sucking noises in the background.

"Are you nursing Sophie?"

"Yeah, I can't even go to the bathroom without this kid attached to me. And guess what, I had to call in sick again today.

She has a fever of 101, and she's been pulling at her ears all night. She must've picked up something at daycare again."

"Oh, Erin, I'm sorry." I sink deeper into my pillow, grateful not to be encumbered by a child.

Erin sighs heavily. "Emily, I'm afraid Bernadette's going to fire me. That's what I wanted to talk to you about. She's been acting different toward me for weeks, but yesterday when I stopped by her office, something was off with her."

"Maybe you caught her in the middle of something. With magazine sales down, I'm sure she's had a lot on her mind lately."

Erin yawns. "Hold on, Sophie's asleep. Let me put her down."

As I'm waiting for her to get back, I go online and look up the address of the college library here in town and jot it down. I also have an epiphany that maybe the woman who raised Mom can help me. Sadie did give her that picture, and she was in their house shortly after Kora passed. Maybe she stumbled on clues—things that belonged to my grandmother, paperwork, or mail lying around.

Erin is yawning again when she returns. "Anyway . . . so if Bernadette says anything to you or if you hear any rumors, promise me you'll let me know."

"Definitely. But like I said, I don't think you have anything to worry about . . . so cheer up, okay?"

"Mmm hmm." She sighs audibly. "So enough about me. How's everything going with you?"

I fall back into my pillow. "Decent, I guess. I was able to write my article yesterday, so now I'm free to do some research on my grandmother. It's going to be harder than I thought, though. Turns out, if I want Kora's medical records, I can't do it. Mom has to."

"Have you already talked to her about it?"

"Yeah, you know how she is. She doesn't want to be bothered with all this, and she's not going to do it just because I want her to."

"Well, maybe she will. Sometimes people you love catch you off guard and do things you'd never expect them to." She sniffles and it sounds like she might be crying.

"Erin, take care of yourself, okay?"

"Yeah, I will." Her tone doesn't sound very convincing.

"When I get back, we'll have dinner at Swain's. We'll order all our favorites. A good bottle of merlot, fried green tomatoes, chicken marsala, mashed potatoes. It'll do you good to have a little bit of fun for a change."

"That would be nice," Erin says, sounding a little perkier. "I'm so lucky to have you for a friend. Thank you for always being there for me even when I'm miserable to be around."

"No problem. You'll get through this. I'll see you soon, okay?"

"Okay, bye," she mutters.

I hang up and realize that maybe Erin's life isn't as perfect as I think.

chapter twenty-seven

PAM

I turn the satellite radio in my Lexus to classical piano and let the chords soothe me as I press my lower back into the leather seat roasting underneath me. I grip my stainless-steel coffee cup, take a sip, then punch the gas to merge south onto the interstate toward the city.

Even though the first few hours of daybreak typically bring me peace, today they don't. After that dream last night, I couldn't get comfortable and struggled to get back to sleep. Then, first thing this morning, I sent John a message telling him I'd have to pass on his invitation to the mountains. He immediately responded back with a thumbs up, which concerned me a bit since he's not an emoji kind of guy.

Because it's a Friday, traffic is light, and two hours later I pull into Dad's driveway. I feel sick to my stomach when I see his house. The white siding is stained with black mildew, the gutters are filled with leaves, and the hedges are blocking the windows. The hostas, which always fanned out so pretty in April, now lie dormant against the pine straw. The front porch light is on, but all the yellowed blinds are closed.

I take a few moments to ground myself, then sling my overnight bag over my shoulder and grab a handful of moving boxes and trash bags.

I let myself in the front door and immediately see that nothing inside the house has changed. The closed floor plan, with walls that block natural light and plenty of corners to bump into if you're up in the middle of the night, feels stifling. The cream walls haven't been painted in decades, and the tan shag carpet is beyond dingy. Even though Dad's been gone for months, the air is still saturated with cigarette smoke.

My sister is sitting at the kitchen table, chair turned around, facing outside, with a cup of coffee and a half-eaten glazed doughnut on a paper towel in front of her.

"Good God, Ivy, my housecleaner could spend weeks in this nasty place. I can't believe you've been able to tolerate staying here all week." I close the door behind me, go straight to the table, and dump the moving supplies in front of her.

"Why, hello to you too, Pam." She dips her doughnut into her coffee and takes a soggy bite.

"Sorry. Good morning," I mumble as I open the blinds behind the beige tweed couch.

Ivy gestures toward the kitchen counter. "Help yourself to coffee and doughnuts. I got a dozen since you were coming."

"Thanks, but I've already eaten breakfast . . . and I got Starbucks on the way." I peer at the stack of boxes by the door and nod in approval. "Wow, you've got a lot done."

"Yes ma'am. The closets and bathrooms have been sorted through, and I've got a charity coming at three to move all the furniture out."

"Good for you, Ivy. Way to be proactive. The sooner I can get out of here the better."

Ivy wads up her paper towel and pushes herself up. "Here, give me a hug. I've missed my baby sister."

I attempt to soften my body against hers, but hugging her feels too awkward and I let go, take a few steps back. She looks offended. But then she clears her throat and takes on the big-sister tone she's mastered over the years.

"Are these all the boxes you have? I think we're going to need more than this."

"I think it'll be okay. I have plenty of trash bags." I hand her a flat box and a roll of tape. "Why don't I go through the kitchen, and you can clear out whatever's left in the bedrooms." I glance at my watch. "Let's try to be done by 11:30. That gives us a little over two hours."

Once we're finished prepping the boxes, Ivy shuffles down the hallway, and I thumb through the music Dad would play when he got a good buzz on. Four records deep, my breath catches in my throat when I see the Sonny and Cher album. It was always Sadie's favorite—the one that was often playing when I'd get home from school.

I slip the vinyl out of the cover, slide it onto the turntable, and place the needle carefully against the edge. I wait until Sonny's raspy voice starts the second verse of "I Got You Babe" before I shake open a trash bag and chuck in Dad's other mint-condition records—the only things presumably worth anything in this house, items we could easily sell to a collector.

Ha, how tragic. My father's true loves are the first to go.

When I was a kid, I'd search for remnants of my mother, for things she might have left behind. Surely there had to be something my dad couldn't bear to part with. But as time passed, I couldn't distinguish what was Mother's or what Sadie bought new. The family of porcelain doves perched on the kitchen window sill, the embroidered pillows on the sofa, the cherub cookie jar, the crocheted afghan I nestled my cheek against every night as I went to sleep. I didn't even know who had chosen the color pink for the bathroom the three of us girls shared.

In the kitchen, I can see Sadie like it was yesterday: at the sink washing dishes, hands chafing from the hot, soapy water, dish towel hanging out of her apron pocket, humming along while she worked. Memories rush back as I inspect the garden outside that's now covered in weeds, with rusted tomato cages holding nothing but tangled brown stems.

Dad tended to that quarter acre of our yard and plowed it each year, but Sadie and I were always assigned the task of planting the tomatoes, cucumbers, and squash—something we couldn't mess up. Dad prepped the holes, and we dropped the seedlings into the dirt. I loved watching those plants transform each year from a tiny, lifeless seed into vibrant green stems, then into actual food that ended up on our dinner table each night. In fact, planting those vegetables each year was a lot like my own life at the time. Dad was a good provider and gave us what we needed to survive, but it was Sadie who loved on us, who gave us sunlight and water so that we could grow into something more than a bunch of struggling sprouts.

On one of our planting days, I asked Sadie where I came from.

"You were just like that seed, honey," she explained, pointing to the ground. "Only instead of growing in the red clay, you grew in your mama's belly into a beautiful baby girl."

"What happened to my mama?"

"I don't know." She took her finger and drew a heart in the soil. "But what I do know is that God needed her to be your guardian angel far more than he needed her down here with us. And that makes her, and you, extra special."

I thought about her words for a moment. "So, if she's my angel, do you think she loved me? Because sometimes I think she must've hated me and that's why she left."

Sadie leaned down and kissed my forehead, smoothing out my braid with her dirt-stained hands. "Oh, she loved you for sure. Why else would she have given you her middle name? Your mother leaving had nothing to do with not loving you."

At the time, I couldn't really comprehend what Sadie meant. But it sounded like a good enough explanation, so I never asked her again. Besides, just being next to her made me feel loved and safe, so I decided God must've wanted Sadie to be my mama instead of some mother who died in a mental asylum.

There was a time in my life when Sadie was everything to me. Then the divorce happened, and Sadie had the nerve to lecture me about all the things I did wrong in my marriage, and how I needed to put Emily first instead of myself. The last thing I needed was for her to bring my shortcomings to my attention. I needed her to love me unconditionally.

Instead, sitting at a corner table in an Italian restaurant on a cold, rainy day, she said, "Your mother would be so disappointed." Even though it was a random thing to say that didn't even make any logical sense, it shook me to my core and I lashed out.

"Why can't you just support me instead of spouting insults?"

Sadie's mouth fell open and her eyes filled with tears. "Pam, I . . . I'm sorry . . . I shouldn't ha—"

"You're right, Sadie. You shouldn't have. Finally, something in this conversation we can agree upon." Then I left the restaurant and haven't spoken to her since.

Shaken back to the present, I slide open the drawer by the sink and drop handfuls of frayed dish towels and dried-up sponges into the trash, then do the same with everything else in my path—not thinking twice about the fragments of my life I'll never see again.

chapter twenty-eight

✤

KORA

When my fingers land on the slick keys of the IBM, the last few stitches of my soul come together like the final squares of the quilt I finished right before Fern was born. Arranging words into sentences dotted with commas and periods makes me feel alive, in control of something. My focus becomes not on the trials of my past, but on going to work each day, keeping my emotions stable, and meeting my deadlines. In this way, writing takes me away from my problems and frees my mind, and I love how filled with pride I feel when I see the finished product.

I've been at *The Flare* for a little over a month now. After a couple of days in the press room, I brought my girls' picture in and put it on my desk underneath a mason jar with a daisy in it —a gift from Rose to congratulate me on getting the job. I love how fearless Ivy looks in this particular photo—one hand propped on her waist, hip jutted out, pouty lips, doe eyes that say she can handle anything that comes her way. Strands of hair are falling out of her ponytail like they always do, sweaty from playing outside for too long. Fern is next to her, blonde curls spiraling out of control, arm draped around her sister, giggling, nose crinkled up, worries floating off her like tufts of a dandelion on a windy day.

Despite the chaos that surrounds me, I've gotten spoiled being alone with my thoughts and not having a child interrupt me every few minutes. *Mama, can I have another glass of milk? Mama, can you help me change my baby doll's diaper? Mama, I miss Daddy. When will he be home from work? Mama, I'm hot, I need a drink of water. Please let me play in front of the fan. Mama, mama, mama.*

But there are certainly plenty of things I miss about my munchkins and would give anything to have again. I used to love snuggling with them under the covers at daybreak, and my heart would always melt when they'd say their prayers at night—sincere, thoughtful utterings with their eyes squeezed shut. Or the peace I felt when we were the only ones at home and I'd watch them playing outside as I smoked a cigarette. I do long for those everyday things I took for granted: the afghan thrown over the couch, the side table by the door where I'd conveniently lay my pocketbook, being able to listen to the radio whenever I pleased, the smell of biscuits baking in the oven.

But this job has been good for me. It's a nice change of pace to have black-and-white facts smother the unpredictable grayness that surrounds me. It's also taught me a lot about the institution. I completed my first assignment about the patients who tried to escape and have written a few more articles since then—about the basketball games in the auditorium, the hospital's chapel, the calls the fire department responded to this month, and the Easter cantata performed and led by our musically gifted patients.

I hold a fresh copy of today's bulletin in both hands and breathe in the elixir of ink and paper. My one-thousand-word article about the new music appreciation classes being offered to patients glistens on the front page. I toss *The Flare* on my desk and pick up today's *Daily Chronicle*. Ever since that first article,

Leo Larson has been detonating scandalous stories like fireworks on the Fourth of July. He reported that because Hamilton Meadow only has forty doctors on staff, a majority of the ten thousand patients never receive a formal diagnosis. Therefore, getting better and being discharged becomes nearly impossible. Also, without diagnoses, patients cannot be segregated by the severity of their illness, so management becomes difficult. To make matters worse, over a hundred disabled children were found scattered in beds around the adult wards. Patients are living in filthy, unsafe conditions, and one patient recently broke a window and attacked another patient, killing her. And last, fifty-five percent of the attendants—the people who spend the most time with the patients—do not have high school diplomas.

As I'm skimming over the front-page news, I hear a sigh behind me.

"Kora, dear, is there any way you can watch Bonnie for me this afternoon? They've called another meeting regarding all this mess with the *Chronicle*, and I'd hate for her to be in my office all by herself."

I pivot toward Hazel Valentine. "Sure. I'd be happy to."

Hazel's niece has taken a liking to me. She spends afternoons at the hospital, where she either plays with her babies in the corner of Hazel's office, or hangs out in the press room to color, draw, or practice her letters.

"And one more thing," Hazel says. "I guess you saw in *The Flare* that there's a dance this weekend at the auditorium. I'd love it if you'd go and write a story on it."

I pause for a moment. I'd seen the full-page invitation from Superintendent Goodwin about the dance, and even giggled when I saw Suzette's cartoon about a doctor asking a patient to dance. "Pretty please with sugar on top?" it said, with the patient planting a pie in the doctor's face instead. But I don't go to dances anymore. I made a promise to the Great and Holy One years ago when he was depriving me of my freedom to walk, and so far, I've managed to keep it.

"Kora?" Darcy butts in. "Is something wrong?" She props herself against the cinderblock wall with a look on her face that says she doesn't understand why Hazel asked me and not her, the queen bee, to cover such an important event.

"No, no. I'm fine," I stammer, then turn to Hazel. "I'd be happy to go to the dance for at least a few minutes. I'll make sure to have my article ready for Darcy to edit on Monday."

Darcy rolls her eyes and Hazel smiles. "Well, good. Perhaps you can go with Rose, that nurse friend of yours. Besides, you never know, this might be your last opportunity to go to a dance here. I bet you'll be discharged any day now."

I'M CAUGHT UP on my work, so once Hazel leaves, I go to the library. I love it here: peaceful, quiet, the musty smell of books, the reading room in the corner, tables where people can spread out, magazine racks, the rows of *Reader's Digest.* A sparkling refuge tucked inside the walls of Hamilton Meadow.

The librarian must have stepped out for a minute, so I take my time perusing the shelves, stopping every few minutes to flip through the fiction books that seem interesting. After about fifteen minutes or so, I decide on *Gone with the Wind.*

Just as I'm pulling the book off the shelf, the door opens.

I glance up and see a man wearing a suit and carrying a briefcase, with his dark hair trimmed in a neat crew cut.

His gaze pierces right through me when he smiles. "Good morning, I'm Leo Larson with the *Daily Chronicle*."

My face warms. "Hi, Kora Mitchell. Nice to meet you."

"I'm trying to find the hospital's annual reports. Do you happen to know where they're kept?"

"Um . . . yes, I just saw them. They're right over there," I say, pointing toward the back of the room.

He nods and says thanks as his dress shoes tap across the floor.

I sit down at a table with my book, and a few moments later, Leo Larson settles in across from me. He flips through the pages of the thick annual report . . . *swish, swish, swish*. Trying not to let the rustling distract me, I leisurely trace the words of the first chapter with my finger.

After a few minutes, he nudges my arm and points to my book. "Everyone says *Gone with the Wind* is the best piece of literature they've ever read. I haven't had a chance to read it yet, but would you agree or disagree with that sentiment?"

I peek at him over the book. "So far it seems pretty good. I'm just on the first chapter, though. I'm a reporter for the news bulletin here at the hospital. Today I had a few extra minutes, so I thought I'd start a new book to pass the time."

He grins. "Ah . . . *The Flare*. I've read some of your issues. It's a good publication. Oh, to be a fly on the wall where you work."

"I'm pretty sure I could say the same about you. You've been causing quite a ruckus around here lately."

"Just doing my job. I'm sure you understand how that is."

I shrug. "I don't care about this place. I'm grateful for my job at *The Flare*, but I still don't get to think for myself. The hospital tells me what to write and I do it."

I read a few more sentences, but I can't concentrate, so I lay the book down in front of me. When our eyes meet, Leo Larson is smiling as if he finds me intriguing. "Just so you know," I say, "I appreciate what you've been doing—reporting on what goes on behind closed doors here. We need someone to expose the truth for us. The patients don't have a voice and you're giving them that. Anyway, I'm sure it hasn't been easy, so thank you."

"Thank *you*." He nods. "You're right, I never get to hear from the patients. But that's not to say I haven't been curious about what their perspective is. From day one, this has been more for me than just chasing a good story. My hope is that once I'm done here, the government will make some serious reforms to Hamilton Meadow."

I nod, then add, "I wrote for a few months at the *Daily Chronicle*."

"Oh, did you now? Why'd you leave?"

"I became a mother."

"Well, if you ever come across a good story, find a way to get a hold of me. I know your mail is censored, but if you ask the right people, they can reach me." He drums his fingers on the table. "You know anything about a Dr. Eugene Hunter who works here?"

"Yeah, that's my doctor. A friend of mine who's a nurse is dating him. I don't particularly care for him, but she seems to think he's a nice guy. Why?"

"Oh, no particular reason. A few things have come up about him, that's all."

We spend the next few minutes reading in silence until he finally speaks again. "Interesting," he says.

"Find what you're looking for?"

"Yes, I wanted to see how many people died here over the past couple of years. In 1957, there were 980 deaths." He scribbles some quick division on his notepad. "So, that means two to three people die each day . . . about a dozen and a half each week. I thought it'd be more than that, but I guess that's still enough to keep those folks down at the mortuary pretty busy."

"I suppose I've been lucky then. No one in my ward has died yet. Or at least none that I know of." I put my hands in my lap and begin twiddling my thumbs. "But you know, there's so many people, even if someone did go missing, I'd probably never even know about it."

MY CHANCE ENCOUNTER with Leo Larson left me feeling a little queasy, and I decide to take Bonnie outside to clear my thoughts. It's a perfect spring day with a bit of a breeze, and the dogwoods and azaleas are in full bloom.

Bonnie lies on her stomach in the grass with her coloring book sprawled out in front of her. Her eyebrows arch as she swipes the green across the sides of the page for the trees, then her lips pucker in concentration when she moves on to the flowers, careful to stay inside the lines. She colors the way I wish Ivy would, holding her crayon just so, carefully selecting each hue, flattening out her little hand on the opposite page to keep the book from moving.

She's working on a picture of Snow White and the Seven Dwarfs. The beautiful girl with black hair and brown eyes peeps out the window, appearing complacent even though she's been snatched away from her home and now lives with little men who work in the diamond mines.

Bonnie squints up at me. "Do you like living here?"

"It's not too bad. I do miss my daughters, though. One day I'd like to have a career like your mama and aunt, and live in a pretty house with my girls."

"But what about a daddy? Doesn't every house need a daddy?"

"Snow White didn't have a daddy in her cottage in the woods, and she was still happy, right?"

"I guess so. But she had the dwarfs." She giggles. "And they sing silly songs all day. You don't need a daddy when you got dwarfs."

Her picture is only half done, but she pushes it aside and rolls over onto her back. Her bangs need a trim, and I brush them out of her eyes, then lie down next to her. We gaze up at the sky, the clouds billowing in fluffy clumps of cotton in all different shapes and patterns.

"So, tell me, what do you see up there in those clouds?"

She takes a minute or two to consider my question as she scans the sky.

"I see a puppy." She points. "See, there's his ears, there's his eyes, and his tongue is hanging out of his mouth. He must be hot up there so close to the sun."

"Do you have a dog? Or some other pet at home?"

"Yes, ma'am. My daddy brought a puppy home for me. He said he found a whole litter in a box sitting right outside his office downtown." She grins. "I'm so lucky. I love my dog more than anything. Her name's Lucy, and she's so cute and sweet, I can't believe someone wouldn't want her. And my daddy also says we're lucky because she coulda jumped out of that box and got ran over in a second. But she decided to just stay there and wait for my daddy."

Bonnie sure does talk a lot. I doubt my girls would be as amused by her as I am. I bet she's the type who would insist on being the mama every time they played house, or be granted the first jump in hopscotch.

"Well, Lucy was probably too scared to jump out. I bet she'd never been to the city before. Can you imagine how terrifying all those sounds and people would be to a dog?"

"Yeah, you're probably right." She nestles her head against my shoulder. "We're still lucky, though."

"Of course you are, sweet girl. You rescued that dog. Gave Lucy love, food, and a nice place to live. Not all pets, or even people for that matter, are given such a special gift."

❧

chapter twenty-nine

EMILY

Sadie Johnson's medical clinic is actually a pregnancy resource center—a brick building sandwiched in the middle of the downtown historic district of Sparrow. Orange mums are planted in flower boxes on the window sills, and the doormat outside is teal with a yellow sun in the middle that says HELLO SUNSHINE. A woman with a weathered face and streaked-gray hair digs through a trash can that's attached to a tree. "Food for my cat," she explains as she stuffs a half-eaten biscuit into the pocket of her baggy flannel shirt.

When I walk in, every seat in the waiting room is taken. All of the girls are younger than me, either teenagers or in their early twenties. One is reading on a Kindle; two have backpacks opened beside them doing schoolwork; a few are on their phones; others just sit and stare, palms resting on their tight bellies.

I go straight to the front desk and a girl wearing a volunteer name tag greets me. "Do you have an appointment?" she asks.

"No, I'm not a patient. I'm a personal friend—well, actually my mom is—of Sadie Johnson's. I was just in the area and thought I'd stop in to say hi. My name is Emily Sharp."

She gestures toward the girls in the waiting room. "Well,

we've got a full house today, but maybe she can spare five minutes or so. Wait a second and I'll check."

I step aside, pick up a magazine, and catch up on the latest celebrity gossip. A few minutes later, a petite lady with shoulder-length white hair dressed in violet scrubs comes out. She pushes her glasses up the slope of her nose and smiles.

"Emily?" she asks. "Is that you?"

I nod and smile. "Yes, ma'am."

"No reason to be so formal. Just call me Sadie, like all the other girls here do." She looks me up and down. "Well, Emily . . . you're all grown up now. I haven't seen you since you were a little bitty thing."

A girl carrying a crying baby comes in, and Sadie waves and says hello.

She turns back to me and claps her hands. "Why don't you come back to my office for a few minutes. I've got a million things going on, but I'm due for a short break. Besides, it's not every day the girl who's practically my granddaughter shows up on my doorstep, now is it?"

"Sure, if it's not too much trouble, I'd like that."

She holds open the door to the hallway. "It's the third door on the right. I have to finish up with a patient, so just go on in and make yourself comfortable."

Her office has a perky feel to it, and I take a seat in one of the retro-style avocado green chairs in front of her desk. The walls are a light yellow, and the sun streams in through the blinds onto manila folders stacked in the corner. A vase of flowers sits on the edge of her desk, and this month's page on the calendar says, *Anyone can find the dirt in someone. Be the one to find the gold.*

The wall to my left is covered with photographs of babies. One picture, in particular, jumps out at me: a baby with dark, almond-shaped eyes and a headful of brown curls. She reminds me of Erin's baby. I smile and reach out to touch the photo, wishing I could massage the little girl's soft, pudgy arms, kiss her cheek, tickle her feet.

"That's one of my favorites too," Sadie says from behind me. "Her name is Stella. She's a miracle baby, born six weeks premature to a scared-to-death, sixteen-year-old girl who wasn't even supposed to be able to conceive because of her endometriosis."

"She's so cute. How old is she now?"

She counts back on her fingers. "Well, I've been doing this for twenty years so that should make her ten by now." She sits down across from me and pats her hands on the desk. "So, what brings you to Sparrow? You're a little far away from home. Your aunt Ivy told me you were living in Baxter now, writing for *Southern Speaks*."

"Yes. I'm here on business, writing an article on the old mental hospital. Mom mentioned you lived in Sparrow now, so I thought I'd stop in and introduce myself."

"Well, I'm so glad you did. And I'm also happy to hear you're writing because it makes our souls light up to do things we love. I know the benefit of that better than anyone." She smiles genuinely. "What about a boyfriend? Anyone special in your life?"

I touch my sapphire necklace. "No, I did, but we broke up a few months ago. Who knows, maybe I'm like Mom—cursed to fail at relationships." I roll my eyes. "I think I'd like to eventually have kids one day, though."

"Well, don't fret. I personally didn't choose the traditional route, and it all worked out just fine for me." She smiles and admires her wall of pictures. "But I consider all these babies my family, and their mamas too. I've been blessed to love and be loved by each and every one of them."

"I can imagine. So, why did you decide to open up this clinic? It seems like a phenomenal place."

She pauses for a moment, then points to a bulletin board behind her that's cluttered with quotes. "E.E. Cummings once said, 'It takes courage to grow up and become who you really are.' I've always tried to follow the path God naturally laid out for me, but sometimes I still fought it . . . or shall I say, didn't appreciate the journey like I should have. It's human nature, I suppose. But when I opened up this clinic, I finally surrendered and started fulfilling what I think is my life's purpose. That's why I'm so passionate about coming to work each day and why I can't see myself retiring anytime soon. I'm so proud of how far it's come and how many girls we've been able to help."

A nurse holding what appears to be a patient file knocks on her office door. "I hate to bother you, but can I ask you a quick question?"

Sadie lifts her index finger. "Hold on a minute," then she turns back to me. "Emily, how long are you in town for, honey? It's ironic that you would show up like this out of the blue because I just can't seem to get your mother off my mind these days. Would y'all happen to be free for dinner tonight?"

"Um . . . I don't know. I'm supposed to be leaving today, and I'm not sure what Mom's got going on."

Her face lights up, and she snaps her fingers. "I know, what about brunch tomorrow? Maybe around ten? And you could spend the night with me tonight. I'd love the company. I have a spacious guest room with its own bathroom and plenty of privacy." She plants her palms on her desk and pushes herself up.

I grin at her enthusiasm. "That might work. I suppose there's no real reason I need to rush back home. I'll call Mom and see what she says, okay?"

"Sounds perfect." She scribbles on a sticky note and hands it to me. "Here's my cell phone number. Just send me a text and let me know what y'all decide."

She's about to walk out the door when I work up the courage to ask her about Kora. "I know you have to run . . . but could I just ask you . . . I'm attempting to do research on Mom's mother while I'm here. I don't suppose you knew anything about her?"

She stops and turns to me with a surprised look on her face. "Oh, honey. That's a big question . . . when I first stepped foot in Daniel Mitchell's home, I was instructed to forget that his wife existed. He wanted his family's life to move forward as if nothing ever happened." She looks down then back at me, her shoulders dropping. "You can't really do that with a person, though, can you? No one is a pencil mark on a piece of paper you can just erase. If you try, they just keep coming back to haunt you. And I think your grandfather knew that better than anyone."

chapter thirty

PAM

I'm in the kitchen bubble-wrapping the last bowl at Dad's house when a text from Emily chimes in: *I stopped by to see Sadie Johnson. She invited us to brunch tomorrow morning at 10:00 at her house. Would you like to meet me there?*

Seriously, Emily? the script in my mind says. *No, I wouldn't like to go.* But instead of declining the invitation, I lay my phone on the counter and seal up the final box with tape and survey the kitchen. Every inch is now ready for a fresh start. And with Dad gone, the house is actually peaceful. The Sonny and Cher album stopped playing an hour ago, and Ivy is singing one of those contemporary Christian songs in the next room. I stack all the boxes next to the front door and take the bags outside to the dumpster.

When I return, Ivy shuffles into the living room and holds up a dainty crystal angel that glistens as the sunlight hits it.

"Wasn't this yours when we were kids?" she says.

I slide my glasses on and am immediately transported. It was the one from my dream last night—the angel on that handsome man's dashboard. "Oh yeah," I say, acting nonchalant. "I used to keep this in my nightstand."

"I thought so, but I wasn't sure if this was the same one."

"How about that." I take the angel and cradle it gently as Ivy tears off a paper towel and dabs the sweat from her forehead.

"Goodness, gracious, Pam," she says, eyeing the kitchen. "You already done in there? You're a machine."

"Yep, we can check the kitchen off our list. I need some fresh air, though. I'm going to take a quick walk."

Ivy sinks onto the sofa and massages her temples. "Whew, I'm lightheaded. I need to get something in my belly. I think I'm gonna go to the gas station and get me some of those good fried chicken fingers. You want some? Maybe it still comes with those tasty little potato logs and corn on the cob."

"No, I brought a salad from home. Thanks anyway, though."

Her face falls as if I've insulted her. "All right. Well, hurry back. There's still plenty more that's gotta be done before those folks get here at three for the furniture."

"Ivy, I'm just going around the block. I'll probably be back before you are."

I slide the angel into my jacket pocket and slip out the door. As I walk down the street I grew up on, I caress the angel, thinking about the day I found it. It was the only thing I ever had that belonged to my mother.

It was dusk on a summer night, and my sisters and I were playing Red Rover with the neighborhood kids. As usual, I was the first one to be called. "Red Rover, Red Rover! Send Pam right over!" I dropped Tommy's sticky hand and made a run for it, but it was no use. I didn't possess enough strength in my frail, ten-year-old body to break through their fingers that seemed to be super-glued together. I hated losing, and I hated that game, so I took off running back home.

I was almost out of the neighbor's yard when the spoiled girl with frizzy hair yelled, "Not only is she little, but she's weak-minded! Just like her mama!"

Her words caught me off guard, and I wasn't sure what to do. So I sprinted to Dad's storage shed, which was always off limits to us girls. "Don't go rummaging through there or else you'll get your butt whooped," he'd always say. But that day I didn't care if Dad caught me, and I didn't care if I got a spanking. At least then he would pay me some attention.

The shed was dank and smelled like sawdust, but it was the perfect refuge. After I caught my breath, I began poking through the items on the shelves: strands of Christmas lights, wrenches, screwdrivers, nuts and bolts, nails, a few empty liquor bottles tucked away. Then I crept to the back wall and discovered a cardboard box in the corner sealed up with shiny, silver duct tape. I ran my fingers along the outside of it, then scooted it out. I thought better of peeling the tape off, but I couldn't help myself.

When I lifted the flaps, a sensation fluttered through my body. Inside were a woman's things. *Her* things. Silky, floral-print shirts, skirts made to be worn with a crinoline, pastel dresses, slips, high heels, bras, books, a rhinestone brooch, gaudy necklaces. But one item stood out from the others: green jeweled clip-on earrings in the shape of leaves. Green was my favorite color, and at the time, I told myself my mother must have known this and would have wanted me to have her most beloved jewels. So, I stuffed them into my pocket.

Digging deeper into the box, I found the crystal angel. It was just about the size of my hand, and I flew her around in the air pretending that she was my mother soaring in heaven, watching over me. There was no way I could bear to part with that angel, so it went into my other pocket.

I stroked the rest of the clothes in the box, picking up handfuls of them and bringing them to my face. But all I could smell was musty old dust, not a mother's scent at all. One dress was exceptionally beautiful—a pink dress with lace etched around the bodice.

As I held it up to admire it, a boy in the distance yelled, "Ready or not, here I come!" I realized the kids were now playing hide and seek and could find me any second, so I gently draped the dress over a piece of lawn equipment, secured the tape on the box, and pushed it back where I found it. Then I grabbed the dress, ran out of the shed, and dashed through our back door.

Sadie was in the kitchen humming "Blessed Assurance" as she washed the dishes. I skirted past her and ran into the bathroom, jerking off my clothes and sliding the dress over my head. It puddled around me, and the arms hung off my shoulders and swallowed my hands. I clipped on the earrings, but they slipped off my tiny lobes and onto the floor. But instead of picking them up, I turned to admire myself in the full-length mirror on the back of the door. I smiled at my reflection as my heart fluttered inside my chest; it was the closest I'd ever been to my mother.

Someone knocked and I gasped. "Pam, you okay in there?" Sadie asked.

"Yeah, I . . . I just got an upset belly." I started wiggling out of the dress, but after a few shimmies, the door sprung open.

"Pam, what in the world are you doing?"

"I found this dress in the shed. I think it's my mother's. I just wanted to try it on. Please don't be mad at me."

Sadie wrapped her arms around me and rubbed my back. "Oh honey, I know you want your ma—"

The front door slammed. All the color drained from Sadie's

face. Dad was home from work. "Sadie!" he called as he stomped down the hallway to use the bathroom before he demanded his dinner.

Suddenly, there he was—hands on his hips, scruffy red face, shirt stained with mud and dried sweat. "What's going on here?"

The blood vessels in Sadie's neck pulsed. "Pam found a dress of Kora's. She was just playing dress-up. That's what little girls do, you know."

"No, I don't know what little girls do," he mocked, "and now I got a whole house of them. Raising little girls was supposed to be my wife's job." He pointed a soiled finger at me. "And anyway, if it weren't for you, your mama would still be here and you wouldn't have to sneak to try on her clothes."

Tears began streaming down my face as shame coursed through me.

He glared at Sadie. "I thought I told you to get rid of everything that belonged to Kora. You better make sure this doesn't happen again. I don't want any part of that bitch in this house." With that, he headed to the kitchen. Seconds later, a beer can popped open.

Sadie kneeled down and took my hand in hers. "Don't listen to him. Here now, you get your clothes back on. Leave your mother's things in here, and I'll take care of them for you."

After I got dressed, I patted the outside of my pocket to make sure the angel hadn't fallen out. Then I hurried to the room I shared with my sisters and tucked it away in my nightstand drawer.

I'm jolted out of my thoughts when I stop to cross the street at the corner of Briarcliff and Cherry. *What did Sadie end up doing with Mother's things that day? Did she throw them away?*

Did she ever go looking in the shed to make sure there was no trace of my mother left behind?

"That's silly," I say out loud. Even if Sadie never disposed of that box, the storage shed collapsed when that tornado ripped through here in the nineties. I remember Dad saying everything was destroyed and that he took what was left to the landfill. If he stumbled on anything of my mother's, I'm sure he would've thrown it away.

I check the time on my cell phone and see Emily's message again. Without thinking, my thumb flies across the letters: *Sure, maybe it would be good to catch up with Sadie. Please text me her address.*

I don't wait for a reply or offer any explanation. Instead, I tuck my phone into my jeans and jog back to Dad's.

✄

chapter thirty-one

KORA

The last time I went to a dance was fifteen years ago. It's been difficult to keep my promise to the Great and Holy One for so many years. I always had to politely decline my husband's invitations to take me for a whirl in the early days of our marriage when he still kissed me goodnight and couldn't get enough of me. Instead, I always listened to the grand stories my girlfriends came back with after a night out on the town. Their infatuation with the Bunny Hop, the Stroll, and the Boogie Woogie. Their gossip about whose husband danced with whose wife. How many petticoats they wore under their dresses, and how perfectly lovely their cardigan, neck scarf, belt, and bag co-ordinated.

Rose and I sit in front of the window with our feet propped up on the sill. Hamilton Meadow is hosting two dances today. One from five to seven o'clock for the patients, which Rose is chaperoning, and another from eight to midnight for the employees.

"If I could get out of going tonight, I would. I'm just not in the mood," I say. "I got lucky last time because almost my entire ward went. And you know me, I relish whatever ounce of quiet time I can get around here."

"Oh, it'll do you good to get out and have a little fun. Besides, maybe there's a patient out there who's on the fence about going to the dance, and your article will brighten their spirits and give them the courage to go to the next one."

"I suppose. Anyway, since I told Hazel I'd go, it's not like I can back out now." I shrug. "How about you? I guess you and Dr. Hunter are going to the employee dance together?"

"Yeah, he's supposed to meet me there. We haven't got to spend a lot of time together lately, so I wanted tonight to be extra special. I even bought a new dress a few days ago." She winks.

"Good, you deserve it. You've been working yourself to death lately." I run my fingers along my hospital dress that wrinkles when I've been sitting too long, wishing now I had the suitcase Mother packed for me.

"Are you still writing in that journal I gave you?"

"Yes, but not as much as I was. I'm usually so tired when I get off work, I just go to the dayroom and crash."

"Well, it's good for you to continue writing out your feelings, so try and keep it up. The brain is peculiar . . . what it chooses to remember, what it chooses to set free. I want you to always remember this part of your life—every detail—how you were able to regain your strength and not only survive, but flourish in the process." She opens up the box of candy Dr. Hunter gave her and offers me one.

I smile and pop a chocolate-covered cherry into my mouth. "Thank you, Rose . . . for everything. And I promise I'll do my best to keep writing."

"Good. And hey . . . speaking of brains, don't you just love how a man thinks? Eugene has been ignoring me for days because I said I'd help out with the patient dance, and then today he thinks he can just show up with a box of chocolates and make everything better. Go figure. Like chocolate's going to make me forget he's been acting like a jackass lately."

I giggle. "Why doesn't he want you to go to the patient dance?"

"Because he wanted to take me into the city before the staff dance to see *Hercules*."

"I think it's sweet that he wants to spend time with you. Daniel and I haven't been out together in ages."

"Well, I invited him to the patient dance, so we'll see if he shows or not. He says there's only so much of this place he can handle before he starts going batty himself."

"I bet." I swallow hard. "So, what does Dr. Hunter think about the newspaper's investigation on the hospital?"

"It depends. If you ask him when he's been drinking, he'll tell you it's going to blow over." She imitates his gruff voice and pushes an imaginary pair of glasses up the slope of her nose. "I'm the best doctor there is . . . I got my degree from Emory . . . I work harder and am more on the straight and narrow than any other employee here."

I laugh.

"But if you ask him in the morning when he's sipping his coffee and going through piles of patient files, he doesn't want to talk about it, or he has something smart aleck to say."

"Has he mentioned getting married yet?"

"No, but he hasn't really been himself lately. His schedule's tighter and he's drinking more. It's all made him more on edge. How about you? When's the last time you had an appointment with him?"

"It's been a while." I tap my foot on the window sill. "Right before I got on at *The Flare*, actually."

"Well, this will all blow over soon enough. It always does, right?" She pats my knee, and her face lights up. "I have a surprise for you."

She reaches into her bag and pulls out a folded royal blue dress. "I brought you something of mine to wear tonight. Nothing fancy, I didn't want to call attention to you . . . but I thought it'd do your soul good to love on yourself a little bit. Every woman needs to do that for herself every now and then, don't you think?"

I jump from my chair and gently take the dress from her. "Oh Rose, I love it! You are so sweet for thinking of me like this."

"Well, go ahead and try it on. We haven't got much time before we have to leave, and I still have to doll myself up."

If childbirth stripped me of my modesty, being trapped at this hospital has surely finished off the job. I slide off my smock right there in front of everyone and wiggle into Rose's dress. It's a little snug in the waist, probably because Rose is younger and has never been pregnant.

"Does it fit?" I ask her. "It's not too tight, is it?" I turn to the left and right, squinting to make out my reflection in the window.

"No, it's just right. But, hold your horses, we're not done yet." She reaches into her pocketbook and pulls out a makeup bag.

I clap my hands. "Really? Am I allowed to do this?"

"Of course. Here, I'll help you." She pops open the compact and hands me the mirror.

When I see the weary face staring back at me, my lungs collapse as if I'm drowning. I *am* like the other women here—sallow complexion, sunken cheeks, a deep rivet between my eyes, frizzy hair I do my best to style without a mirror, sticking up all over the place.

"I look like an old hag. No wonder Daniel doesn't love me anymore."

"Don't talk like that, Kora. First off, you don't look old, you just haven't been able to take care of yourself lately. It doesn't help that the stupid bathrooms don't have mirrors." She holds out the chair for me to sit down. "And second, after I get done with you, you'll be as good as new."

She starts with my hair, taming it with a brush and then teasing my curls, pulling a few pieces out to frame my face. She sweeps ivory powder across my nose, cheeks, and forehead, and blots extra underneath my eyes to lighten the dark circles. Then she smoothes rouge along my cheeks and finishes with two coats of mascara and several swipes of lipstick.

She hands the mirror back to me. "Now what do you think?"

The compact is small but I maneuver it to check myself from all different angles, feeling like a young girl playing dress-up. The mascara makes my green eyes pop, and the plum-colored lipstick is the perfect complement to my brownish-auburn hair. "Well, how about that. It's the old Kora. I didn't think I'd ever see her again."

"I told you she was in there. And you are an absolute knock-out."

I blush. "Rose, I don't know what I'd do without you."

She gives me a hug and the bell rings, sending half the women in the room scurrying to the door just as Mean Jean is opening it.

Rose freshens up her own powder and lipstick then tosses her makeup bag back into her pocketbook. "Well, honey, I've got to go change. See you soon."

❧

I LOCK ARMS with Bernice and Sally as we strut through the double doors of the brick auditorium, just as the first notes of "Jailhouse Rock" begin thumping through the speakers of the jukebox. The energy explodes from the room and makes my belly flutter.

I let go of the girls and take it all in, attempting to relax.

There are hundreds, maybe even thousands of people in here—young, old, men, women—laughing, sobbing, hugging, dancing. Some sit in the bleachers watching the others swing and sway to the beat of the music. Pretty nurses still on duty in their white uniforms dance with elderly men wearing proud smiles. Girls casually pair up with one another, spinning around however they please. Couples swing to popular dances while another group does the Stroll around the room.

I spot Dr. Hunter setting up chairs in the back near the grand piano and electric organ. He's spiffed up in a loud plaid sports coat, one that arrogantly shouts his superiority over us. Not long after, Rose arrives and runs up to him like a cat in heat. I roll my eyes. *I guess that box of chocolates did make her forget what a jackass he is.*

"Come on, Kora. Let's go dance!" Bernice threads her fingers through mine and pulls me toward a group of girls who are jumping up and down with their arms in the air.

I take a couple steps forward, then my fear takes over. My heart drums out of my chest, blending with the melody of the music. I project as loud as I can, "I don't think I can do this!"

Bernice frowns and Sally scans the crowd.

"Yes, you can!" Bernice says. "Come on!"

When I don't move, she leans closer. "What's got you so scared? You're braver than all of us put together."

I shrug. My legs feel heavy like they did when the polio was first setting in, and memories flash through my mind. Sam is holding out his arms in front of me, telling me I can walk, that I just have to believe in myself. I can feel the love and determination that spilled from my heart as I forced my legs forward that day. But then I remember sweating in bed the night I first got sick . . . *Lord, I promise I'll never go to another dance again.*

Promise, promise, promise.

Bernice grabs my face and turns it toward her. "Kora, just do it."

With all the courage I possess, I begin moving from side to side. Bernice holds one of my hands and squeezes it tight. Sally takes the other.

"Kora, you can do this. I know you can," Bernice says.

Another Elvis song comes on, and the three of us hold hands and dance together in a circle. Our arms get looser with each beat, and I think of Rose and all the love she's shown me, how sure she is that everything is going to work out. I think about my girls, too, how one day I want them to be independent and confident, not afraid of anything or anyone.

Bernice smiles and twists one of her legs in the air.

The pounding of my heart fades away, and I drop their hands and start swirling my hips, letting the music soak into my body then flow back out through my legs and arms. I squeal with delight, feeling as if I'm a marionette being magically maneuvered by a puppeteer. Sally follows my lead.

We continue dancing, song after song, until sweat runs down my back and I head to the refreshment table. The girls shuffle off to join another group as I pop the cap off a Coca-Cola. I sip on it while I search the crowd for Rose and Dr. Hunter, but I don't see them. I glance at the clock, tired all of a sudden. *Maybe if I get back before everyone else, I could write my article and then spend tomorrow reading the second half of my book.* Besides, I'm one of the few patients who can come and go as I please because of my job at *The Flare*, so I might as well take advantage of it.

After I finally get Bernice's attention, I point to the door and mouth that I'm leaving. Then I turn around, toss my empty bottle into the trash can, and walk out the double doors of the auditorium as a woman who has just conquered her fears.

❦

chapter thirty-two

EMILY

I glide into the open, airy library of Sparrow Community College and see twenty-somethings camped out everywhere. Students recline in slick, black chairs, catching a few extra minutes of sleep. Others scroll on their phones or appear hyper-focused as they type on their laptops. Artwork covers the walls, and one side has windows that extend all the way from the floor to the ceiling. I spot the Research Department sign, take the stairs, and ask the ponytailed girl behind the computer screen if they have any historical documents on Hamilton Meadow, specifically from the late fifties or early sixties.

She laughs. "Everyone's always intrigued with the institution. Unfortunately, we don't have much, but let me see what I can find for you, okay?"

A few minutes later, she comes back carrying a stack of books. "Sorry, nothing from the sixties, but I did find a few annual reports from the fifties and a couple of other miscellaneous things that might be of interest to you." She hands the stack to me. "Check online in a couple of months, though. I think the state is in the process of scanning in all the old annual reports."

"Okay, thanks for your help."

I find an empty room with a table and plop down. On top of

the pile is the hospital's phone book from 1956. I flip through the fifty or so yellowing pages filled with phone numbers and addresses of doctors, dentists, a beauty shop, police and fire stations, a post office, a dairy, and just about anything else a city would need. There are also three thin psychiatric journals that I skim through then set aside. The only other documents are four annual reports—thick books with worn covers—from 1956 through 1958.

I begin thumbing through the one from 1958. The words make me feel sick to my stomach:

```
The institution is overcrowded and we lack
proper square footage, supplies, and beds to
efficiently care for the patients.

We are deficient in experienced, educated
doctors and lack the funds to pay them proper
salaries.

We feel that a better solution needs to be in
place for alcoholics, mentally disabled
children, and the elderly.

We are having success with electric shock
therapy. This year, 3,178 patients were
treated, 25,150 treatments were given. The
results were as follows: 255 restored, 2,398
improved, 457 unimproved.

Tranquilizers have become an effective
treatment option, which has reduced our need
to rely so heavily on electric shock therapy.
```

There are also pages of statistical information laid out in table form in columns titled *WHITE MALE, WHITE FEMALE, COLORED MALE, COLORED FEMALE*. The meticulous details astound me. Everything you could possibly think of has been documented: the average daily population; patient diag-

197

noses, such as paranoia, schizophrenia, and drug addiction; the two thousand people who were discharged or sent home temporarily on furlough; the number of deaths and what those patients died from; surgeries and treatments received.

In addition, there are pages upon pages of what today feels trivial to document, much less to preserve:

> 835 eyebrow waxes, 975 facials, and 15,101 haircuts were administered in the Beauty Parlor this year.
>
> 2,200 azaleas, 175 rose bushes, and 21 acres of fruit were planted.
>
> The hospital continues to grow their own food in order to feed the patients.
>
> This year, 3,165 hogs were slaughtered, 12,353 bushels of sweet potatoes were picked, and 294,000 gallons of milk were produced in the dairy.

I don't understand. Not only do many of the expenses seem frivolous for an institution that was having financial problems, but I also can't fathom why a hospital that clearly knew how to organize themselves and keep track of every minuscule detail paid so little attention to the details about the patients themselves. *Why wasn't more attention given to the preservation of the patient's medical records? Or the specifics about where they were buried?*

I've seen all I want to see. But just as I'm closing up the book, I spot a map of the hospital with a directory beside it. I run my finger down the list until I stop on the Culpepper Building, which is listed as housing white females. I cross reference the directory with the map: Culpepper is right across the street from the administrative building, which is where I was yesterday.

My breath catches in my throat. *Oh my God, could the women's building still be here?* I stack up the books and slide out of my chair. There's only one way to find out.

chapter thirty-three

PAM

I reluctantly enter Dad's musty bedroom and glance around to see what I'm up against: dirty clothes and underwear still in the hamper, queen bed unmade with blood-spattered white sheets, prescription bottles scattered across the dusty dresser. I open the blinds and pry open the window to let in some fresh air, wondering why he chose light green for the color of his room when such a tranquil color is the complete opposite of his personality.

Even though Daniel Mitchell was my father, he always felt more like a stranger. It feels awkward to be in his personal space, about to go through his most intimate belongings.

For the past few years, I've been thinking more about God, the afterlife, and why we're here. I've never admitted it to anyone, but I still question why my mother died so young. According to my sisters' early memories of her, she was kind, so why was she taken from us when someone like my father was permitted to stay?

I know I'm not the first person to question these things—why bad things happen to good people. But still, it is one of life's great mysteries that's never left me, one I continue to struggle with every day in my profession.

Once Dad died, more questions surfaced. *What was my fa-*

ther's purpose here? He seemed to just go through the motions of life, leaving this planet no better than he found it. Did he never mature into the person he was meant to be? Would his soul get another chance to come back in a new body and make it right? When he died and went to heaven, did God turn him away and give him a life sentence in hell to be tortured for eternity?

Ivy interrupts my thoughts by clearing the phlegm in her throat. The sound is disgusting but it jars me into action. There are still a lot of things that need to be done, and if I'm going to make it to Sadie's house in the morning, I need to get busy.

I open up Dad's closet and get accosted by the pent-up stench of his cigarette-infused clothes. Covering my nose, I thumb through his simple wardrobe of plaid, button-up shirts, three pairs of khaki pants, and jeans wadded up on the floor with a pair of loafers and boots lying on top.

I open up a fresh trash bag and stuff the clothes and shoes in, wire hangers and all. I take another deep breath and hold it as I throw away the rest of Dad's things. In a few minutes, the closet is empty, and I keep the same pace as I move on to the bed where I strip the sheets, pillowcases, and cotton comforter and stack them in the corner.

After I box up the lamp and alarm clock, I go through his nightstand. In the top drawer is a maroon Bible, unused like the kind in hotels. There are also shirt buttons, ink pens, sunglasses, an empty pack of cigarettes, and a checkbook. When I open the bottom drawer, there's much of the same, but also a red and blue striped tie, a few used tissues, and a calendar from 2001. I hurl the junk into a bag when something catches my eye. Resting flat against the bottom of the drawer is a buff-colored piece of paper folded into thirds. I grab my glasses from my pocket and when I unfold the paper, I'm shocked to see my mother's death certificate—a solitary piece of paper that I assume was stashed here years ago and never touched again.

FULL NAME: Kora Pamela Mitchell

AGE: 28

OCCUPATION: Homemaker

CAUSE OF DEATH: Hemorrhage

PLACE OF BURIAL: Hamilton Meadow Hospital

DATE OF DEATH: February 6, 1961

The paper quakes in my fingertips and slips out of my hand. I stumble and collapse onto the bed.

How in the world is it possible that my mother died on the day I was born?

chapter thirty-four

KORA

Sometimes in the spring, when there's a clash of warm and cold air, the sky bursts. But before the storm ambushes the earth, the Great and Holy One gives fair warning of what is to come. Black, white, and gray clouds churn together and blow in fresh air. Two vultures coast, scavenging for dinner, while other birds fly lower, vigorously flapping their wings and delighting in the breeze.

It feels good to be alone without anyone analyzing my every move, granting me absurd privileges that I shouldn't need permission for in the first place. I slide off my patent leathers and step into the grass; the blades are cool and refreshing as they poke through my toes. Dangling my shoes by my side, I take one step and then another and another until I'm halfway across the lawn.

I stop and turn around but don't see anyone. I only hear the leaves rustling, the hum of laughter, the reverberations of the jukebox, and the whoosh of water flowing in the distance. The stillness of the night lures me to play with her, and I have no choice but to oblige.

I put my shoes back on and scurry past the grassy field and into the woods. The crickets have already started strumming their evening chords, and birds watch over me as they rest in the branches. From here the trees block the sky, but surely I've got a few minutes before the rain sets in.

The broad river is up ahead and the rapids cascade over the rocks. It reminds me of the river behind my parents' house that Sam and I would visit to throw stones. We would lie in the sun, read books, and talk about what we were going to be when we grew up.

Jogging down to the river's edge, I find a big rock and plop down on it. It's beautiful here. All the Lord's creatures getting along fine without the interference of man. I lean back and close my eyes, soaking in the moment.

Suddenly, faint footsteps begin crunching through the woods and my eyes bolt open. I sit up straighter but don't turn around because I'm too afraid to see who or what it is.

I catch a whiff of cigarette smoke.

"Why, hello, Kora," Dr. Hunter's voice says. "What are you doing down here?"

I feel like a grizzly bear just squeezed the life out of me. "Um . . . I don't know. The crowd and the noise were starting to get to me."

I stand up and dust off my bottom, imagining he must have followed me.

He moves in front of me with a smirk. A pint of liquor is in his left hand, a cigarette smoked down to the nub dangles in the other. "Huh, you and me both. I wouldn't have even been at this damn patient dance if it wasn't for you. Nope, I'd be sitting downtown in the theater right now with my girl having a nice, quiet evening."

"I'm sorry." I stare at the ground, my heart racing. I take a few steps away from him. The lights of the auditorium peep through the trees. "Well, have a good evening. I promised Bernice and Sally I'd walk back with them, so I better get going."

He lunges after me and catches my arm. Then he leans over my shoulder. His breath in my ear makes vomit rise in my throat.

"You looked hot tonight, Kora. I noticed you from all the way across the room. I saw you dancing. You sure know how to move those hips."

I spin around, my mouth agape. "How can you say that? Where's Rose? Shouldn't the employee dance be starting soon?"

He throws his cigarette down and snuffs it out with the toe of his dress shoe. His tie hangs loosely around his neck with the top buttons of his shirt unfastened, and his sleeves are rolled up to his elbows.

"Well, you know how she's always so uptight . . . I put a little rum in her punch. Just trying to loosen her up a little bit. And what do you know, she can't handle her liquor. She got so sick I had to tote her back to her apartment."

I turn around and start to run away, but he snatches my arm and yanks me toward him. "Do you realize I've always wanted to be with a patient, I've just never had the guts to go through with it? I get *so* tired of always having to watch my back around here. I mean, you're the one locked up, and yet I don't have the freedom to do what I want. There's all these weak women parading around who need a man to take care of them, and I can't do anything about it."

I pull away, but he latches onto me again and pushes me to the ground.

"I bet you patients just lie around in your beds dreaming of making love to a doctor, don't you?"

I prop myself up with my elbows and glare at him. "I may not be happily married, but I *am* still married. And I'm sure my husband wouldn't appreciate you speaking to me like this. Besides, even if I did want a man right now, it sure as hell wouldn't be you."

He slaps me across the face and my head slams to the ground. "How dare you speak to me like that!"

"Leave me alone!" I assert, then scream as loud as I can, praying someone hears me.

He clamps his hand over my mouth. "You better shut the hell up. I see how you flirt with me in therapy sessions. You've been asking for this since the day you got here, and you know it."

He unbuckles his pants and jerks them down. Then he straddles my waist and pushes my dress up, pinning my arms behind my head. "You better not say anything about this. Not to your husband, or Rose, or anybody else. Because if you do, I'll take you down to that goddamn river and hold your head under the water until you stop breathing. And no one will think twice about it. You'll just be another sad Hamilton Meadow suicide statistic. Another inmate who couldn't hack it out in the real world."

Breath sputters from my mouth as I break free from his grip. "Please, please . . . don't hurt me," I say, clawing the ground, trying to find a rock or stick to hit him with. I squeeze my eyes shut and beg him to stop as tears stream down my face.

He pushes his mouth onto mine and I taste the alcohol, smell the stench of his spicy aftershave. I jerk my head away. "Stop!" I keep repeating.

But he doesn't stop. Instead, he forces himself into me.

Finally he stumbles away and leaves me on the ground, believing I'll never have the nerve to tell a soul.

chapter thirty-five

❦

EMILY

The Culpepper Building is three stories and stretches long and lean across the wisps of knee-high grass and weeds. I slide my camera strap off my shoulder and begin snapping pictures. Tangled vines snake up the brick walls and make their way inside through the broken, narrow windows. Overgrown branches jab at the rusted gutters, and a cluster of pine trees pokes out from one section of the roof, which must have blown off in a storm at some point over the past century.

The sound of silence fills my ears. I take a deep breath and squint down the deserted road past the NO TRESPASSING signs and into the distance. My skin tingles as I try to imagine what it must have been like for my grandmother to be dropped off here. Was she scared? Nervous? Indifferent? Or was something so terribly wrong with her that she was oblivious to what was happening?

The wind blows and the building invites me to come closer. My heart rationalizes with my mind: *You can sneak in and out in under ten minutes. No one will ever know you were here.* I look around again, and still there is no one, no cars, no sounds.

I crunch through the leaves and acorns, dodging the mud puddles, beer bottles, and cigarette wrappers, until I'm so close I can feel the energy of the building pulsing through my veins. All the doors are rusted, but they have shiny new padlocks dangling from them, and the majority of the windows are screened with thick wire mesh. Disappointment washes over me. I move toward the back of the building to see if my chances are better there.

Behind a clump of overgrown bushes, I spot a shattered window. I tiptoe as if I don't want to wake whatever is waiting for me inside, then gently wedge my body into the foliage. The bare branches stab my arms through my sweatshirt, and I exhale with relief once I'm on the other side.

In the still space between the bushes and the brick wall, I press my eyes shut and start to second-guess myself. But the voice inside my head chants again. *Go. What are you waiting for? Just a quick peek, then you can go back to Baxter and put all this behind you.* Before I can change my mind, I stick my head through the window and breathe in the cool, damp, musty air. A group of crows screech and fly out of a wide opening where the sun is shining through.

My left leg steps into the window frame before my brain can tell it to stop. I turn sideways and suck in my stomach so I don't cut myself on the shards of glass. I plant my feet on a pile of boards that appears to be fairly safe as my eyes dart in all directions.

The ceilings are caving in and trees have sprouted up in the debris that covers the floor. Ferns thrive in the corners, and moss, algae, and mildew blanket the walls. Over in the corner, there's a row of toilets, dirt-filled sinks, and bedpans hanging on the walls. To the left of me are beds scattered all over the place, covered with stained sheets. My breath catches in my throat and goosebumps spread down my arms.

I zoom in for a few pictures and then hear a deep voice outside. I stop mid-stride as my heart beats through my ears. "Damn college kids. What *is* their obsession with this place? I personally can't wait until they plow this whole place down. It'll sure make our job a whole lot easier."

Water drips and echoes against the walls as the footsteps get closer.

"Yeah, you're telling me," another voice says. "They talked about dynamiting it next month, but who knows if that'll happen with all these liberals protesting it."

I stare at the broken window, considering whether I should try and hide, when a police officer sticks his head in.

We make eye contact and I bite my bottom lip.

"Ma'am, you need to get out of there right now," he says, raising his voice.

"I'm sorry," I offer, walking toward him.

A few seconds later, I'm standing next to a city police officer and a Hamilton Meadow security guard.

"What in the hell were you doing in there?" the policeman asks. "Do you realize this place could cave in at any second? And you're lucky you didn't get attacked by a fox or a coyote. They're always roaming around here in the daytime now."

"I'm sorry. I don't know what I was thinking. I'm a journalist, and I just wanted to get a couple of pictures to go with the article I'm writing."

The security guard plants one of his hands on his hip. "Did you see the NO TRESPASSING signs?"

"Um . . . yes?" I answer truthfully, hoping they'll have sympathy for me.

"What magazine do you work for?"

"*Southern Speaks.*"

"Never heard of it," he spouts in a condescending tone.

"I'm sorry. Really, I am. I was only in there for a few minutes and I'm leaving right now to go back home."

The policeman smirks. "It's actually not that easy. It doesn't matter who you work for or why you were in there. You were trespassing, and that's against the law, in case you didn't know."

Staring at the ground, I slowly nod.

"Look, we've been given instructions from the hospital to arrest trespassers. And if we're not strict about it, people won't take the rules seriously. And when people ramble through here and get injured, they become the liability of the state."

"So, really it's not my safety you're concerned about," I say, probably a little more sarcastically than I should. "You're more worried I'll sue the state if I get hurt."

He presses his lips together and points to his car that's parked next to mine. "Right this way, young lady."

We walk silently back toward the road. As he's typing in the information from my driver's license, Graham pulls up next to us. Smiling, he rolls down his window. "Hey Riley, you're not about to arrest Emily, are you?"

"Why, you know her?"

Graham gets out of his truck. "Yeah, she's a friend of mine. I guess this might actually be my fault. I told her I'd show her around if she wanted, but I've been so busy with work, I haven't been able to get around to it."

Graham turns to me and winks. "I'm sorry, I guess you got tired of waiting."

I dust off my clothes with my hands. "Yeah, I guess."

The security guard returns to his truck, mumbling something I can't understand.

The policeman rolls his eyes. "Oh, good God. All right

then . . . you're free to go. But you better not let me catch you out here again. Your boyfriend won't always be able to bail you out, you know."

I feel lightheaded as he tromps back to his car.

Graham turns to face me. "Emily, what in the world are you doing here? I thought you'd be gone by now."

Staring at the ground, I start to explain.

chapter thirty-six

PAM

I pick up my mother's death certificate and read through it again. There's a lump in my throat and my hands are shaking as I try to make sense of what this means.

First, there's the obvious: if I was born on the same day my mother died, there's no way I had anything to do with her commitment. That creates a whole slew of other questions:

Was she committed while she was pregnant?
Were conjugal visits at the hospital allowed?
Is it possible she was the victim of foul play?
What was the real reason behind her commitment?
Why did Dad lie to me?
Why did he lead me to believe it was all my fault?
Who was he trying to protect?

Years ago, I buried the pain of my mother's death and the trauma that resulted from my father's emotional abuse. My therapist professed this was a defense mechanism—an attempt to survive and to forget that my mother abandoned me, and that I was the reason she was gone.

Once Emily was born, I closed myself off even more. I never talked to her about her grandparents, but that didn't stop the curious, innocent nature of a child. She still probed into a life I was desperately trying to forget.

Why don't we ever visit Papa?

Does he ever invite us to his house?

Is my grandma in heaven the way my friend's nana is?

Did your mama let you sleep in her bed when you had a bad dream?

Did your mama teach you how to braid hair?

I was an expert at dodging her questions or crafting an eloquent, but vague response that made her hush up in a hurry.

But now, this death certificate changes everything.

It not only resurrects my mother from the grave, but it's evidence that some sort of secret was buried with her.

I run my finger along the word "hemorrhage," and for the first time in my life, I feel empathy for what my poor mother must have gone through. Adrenaline pumps through my veins like it does right before I stride into the courtroom for a new trial.

I grab my phone off the nightstand and find that the nearest Kinko's is five miles away, in the old Winn-Dixie shopping center. Then I open Emily's email and read through the court order. Even if my mother's medical records aren't available, I have to at least try to obtain them. I'll never be able to forgive myself if I don't.

The movers will be here in an hour, but Ivy is in the next room snoring, so I step over the bags scattered on Dad's bedroom floor and tiptoe past her open door. Hopefully, I can make it to Kinko's, fax the documents to Sparrow Probate Court, and make it back before she wakes up and starts asking questions.

I don't call or text Emily to let her know I've decided to cooperate. I contemplate calling John, but since it's a sunny Friday afternoon, he's most likely playing golf.

Besides, I don't have to answer to anyone. No one, that is, except for myself.

chapter thirty-seven

KORA

I somehow manage to drag myself out of the woods and onto the lawn. Despite the pain I feel, the smells and sounds of the earth comfort me: damp grass, night air, crickets chirping, bats flapping, frogs croaking.

I warm my hands between the tender flesh of my inner thighs and arch my back to soothe the pang above my tailbone. I'm not sure how much time has passed, but the music is still blaring from the auditorium. I can't see much in the dark, and my right eye is swelled shut. But in the distance, I see flashes of lightning crack open the black sky. I close my eyes and count the seconds out loud to make sure I still have a voice, that I'm still alive. *One Mississippi, two Mississippi, three Mississippi.*

After only a minute, I hear footsteps. I seal my lips and hold my breath. *What is it? A stray dog, a coyote, a raccoon? Dr. Hunter again, coming to finish me off?* I try to push myself up, but my arms give out from underneath me and I fall back to the ground. Finally, the steps come to a halt.

"Kora?" Hazel Valentine's gentle voice whispers. "Kora, is that you?" She touches my shoulder and rolls me over. "What happened? Are you okay?"

My dress is still bunched up around my waist, and she eases it down over my thighs.

"I'm okay," I mumble.

"Oh, Kora . . . please don't tell me you were raped."

I nod and start to cry.

"Do you know who it was?"

I don't answer.

She wraps her arms around me and helps me sit up. "Well, don't worry. I'm here now." She wipes the grass and dirt from my face. "Do you think you can walk?"

"No, I just want to stay here."

"You can't. The employee dance ended fifteen minutes ago. You've got to get back to your ward or else the hospital's going to think you tried to escape. If you go back now, I can tell them you were late because of me."

"But . . . I'm afraid. I'm afraid he'll come back for me."

She massages my back. "Dear, he can't get to you in your ward. But you can't tell anyone about this. If they think you're being promiscuous or causing trouble, they'll take away your privileges. That means no more writing, no job, and no more time outside by yourself. And if you accuse someone of raping you, it's your word against his. I assume it was an employee who did this?"

I nod again as my bottom lip quivers.

"Around here, it's the sane against the insane. And who do you think they're going to believe?"

Tears pour down my cheeks and Hazel hugs me, letting me soak the shoulder of her dress.

"Kora, you can't let this break you. Just think about your girls and how much they need you. You've got to pick yourself up, move forward, and pretend like this never happened."

She smooths out my hair and pats my face dry with her

sleeve. Then she stands and pulls me up by my hands. Pain shoots through my stomach and down my legs. I grit my teeth to keep from collapsing.

"Oh, Kora . . . are you sure you're going to be okay? Tell me the truth because I'll take you to the hospital right now if you need me to. I don't care what they say."

"No, I'm fine." I wipe my nose on the sleeve of my dress.

"All right then, let's get out of here. The storm will be here any second."

DANCE NIGHTS AT the sleeping ward are always loud because the women have a hard time settling down. But Mean Jean has no problem reeling them in by sending someone off to be shocked. By the time Hazel brings me in, Jean's already got the girls scurrying into their beds. She doesn't even care that I'm late or that something terrible has happened to me. She just points with a scowl on her face and commands me to get in bed.

After Hazel tucks me in, I curl up with my flimsy pillow, trembling uncontrollably. I can't stop the tears, but I breathe slow and steady to try to calm myself. With each breath, though, I can smell Dr. Hunter. I desperately wish I could take a shower but Mean Jean would never allow it. I can only imagine how glorious a shower would be in the confines of my own home, with the luscious lather of Ivory soap and hot water instead of the institution's unscented soap, lukewarm water, and a crowd of gawking women. Yes, back home I was trapped in my life with Daniel Mitchell, but at least if I needed time to myself, I had the freedom to lock the bathroom door or go for a walk.

I roll onto my stomach and push my aching face into my

pillow until my lungs beg for air. Currents of shame, grief, and disappointment pulse through me. *I've been intimate with a man in a way God never intended. My body no longer solely belongs to my husband. Was Dr. Hunter right when he said I asked for what happened? That I deserved what I got? Probably. After all, over the years I've turned into a weak, wretched, waste of a woman. I couldn't even hack the asinine tasks of motherhood, homemaking, and taking care of my husband.*

I want to erase this night from my memory just like Hazel said, but instead I begin agonizing about what is going to happen.

Will Dr. Hunter let me go home?

If I turn him in, would anyone believe me?

Would he actually try to kill me if I told the hospital what he did?

Can I lose my job over this?

What am I going to say to Rose tomorrow when she sees me? The truth would kill her. Would she even believe me, or would she think I came on to Dr. Hunter first?

I try to divert my thoughts by pretending I am somewhere, anywhere, but here.

I picture my girls and me at the beach on a hot summer day. I'm wearing my favorite pair of shorts—the pink ones that fall just past my knees—and a floral button-up shirt tied at the waist. The girls are in their bathing suits, hair plaited, with blistered noses. They build sandcastles, splash in the waves, hunt for shells, and tuck their dolls under a towel to protect them from the sun.

Suddenly, the sea air smells like urine. I'm jolted back to reality when Sally jumps up, strips the sheets off her mattress, and slides her nightgown over her head. Wearing nothing but her bra and panties, she wads the soiled laundry into a tight ball and crams it underneath her bed. Then she sits on the naked mattress and drapes a blanket over her shoulders, rocking back and forth singing the first few words of "I'll Fly Away" like she always does this time of night.

I imagine the butterfly I saw the other morning coasting over both of us, swooping between the spindles of our bed. Perhaps the Great and Holy One delivering grace and protection. I reach under my mattress and lay my hand on the cover of the Bible I've yet to begin reading again. *Dear Lord, please take this pain from me. I need you to help me. Please, please, please.* I start to hum, then sing "I'll Fly Away" with Sally, the tune I've belted out dozens of times on Sunday mornings. She glances over, gives me a little smile, pats her heart.

The night sky weeps, and the wind whips through so abruptly and fiercely, I expect the windows to shatter any minute. Lightning illuminates the room like a strobe and a low rumble of thunder follows. I reach over and hold Sally's hand. Our singing slowly fades into bits and pieces of the melody until Sally drifts off, snoring lightly.

I slip my hand out from hers and pull the blanket up to my chin. Even though I've always been afraid of thunderstorms, I somehow manage to fall asleep.

WHEN THE SUN finally comes up, Rose nudges me. "Come on, Kora, get yourself up," she says.

My back is to her, and I keep my eyes shut, not budging.

"All right, then, I'm giving you five more minutes, but that's it." She moves on to wake the other girls, and I massage the throbbing that's spreading into my eye sockets. For once I'm glad there are no mirrors here because I have no desire to know what I look like.

I drag myself out of bed and keep my eyes toward the floor as I slip on my dress and slide into my shoes. There are no off days at the institution, no veering off schedule, no chance of sleeping in and skipping breakfast.

I catch a glimpse of Rose from across the room. She is pale today and her hair's a mess. She's not even wearing lipstick or mascara like she usually does. I sidle up to the end of the bathroom line and keep my head down as Rose makes her way past each girl.

"Josalyn, fix your dress, it's on backwards."

"Sally, I know your bra itches you, but when you have boobs that big, you have to wear one."

"Bernice, I know you're about to pee on yourself, but press those legs together."

"Why Loretta, certainly you can have a hug. We all need one every now and then."

When Rose reaches me, her mouth drops open.

"Kora, what in the world happened to you?" I try to keep my head down but she tilts my chin up. "Who hurt you?"

Before I have a chance to change my mind, I blurt out, "It was one of those interns from the university. I'd never seen him before. He raped me on the way back from the dance last night."

Lying to my best friend, I reason, means no one gets mad, no feelings are hurt, and nothing has to change. I can attempt to forget this ever happened.

Unless, of course, I'm pregnant.

✂

chapter thirty-eight

EMILY

Graham and I sit on the tailgate of his truck and watch the police and security guard speed out of sight. "So, I guess I should explain to you what I was doing here," I say.

"I have to admit, you've sparked my curiosity. You don't exactly strike me as the law-breaking type." He laughs.

"I know, I just got caught up in the moment. Clearly, I wasn't thinking. I do kind of have a reason, though." I pause and take a deep breath. "My grandmother was a patient at the hospital back in the early sixties, and she died here. And no one in my family knows why. I think this might've been where she lived."

"Ah, the inquisitive spirit of the journalist. Makes perfect sense now."

"And it's been a lot more difficult than I thought it would be to dig up information on her. I'm really frustrated . . . I feel this overwhelming need to have something solid to hold on to with all this. And I guess I felt like going into that building would give me that."

"What are you trying to find on her?"

"I'd like to have her medical records, but my mom has to request them, and I'm not sure at this point if she's going to do that. And I'd also like to know where she's buried."

Graham gives me a confused look. "It surprises me that your

mom's not all over this. I've heard this place was pretty sketchy back then. She knows that, right?"

I roll my eyes. "Yeah, but for whatever reason, she chooses to block it all out and pretend like it never happened."

In the distance, bells echo slow and steady through the desolate campus. I glance around, trying to figure out where the sounds are coming from.

"The chapel," Graham explains. "Even though the hospital doesn't hold services there anymore, the chimes still play at the top of every hour. That particular song, 'What a Friend We Have in Jesus,' plays every day at noon."

The melody sends a shiver up my spine, and I wait until the last note plays before I continue. "So, how did you even know I was at the Culpepper Building to begin with? You stick a GPS on me the other night at dinner?"

He smirks. "I was out grabbing a late lunch when I saw your car. The cops are right, you know. It's not safe out here."

"Well, I appreciate it. I'm glad my record will remain squeaky clean thanks to you." I laugh.

His face relaxes into a smile. "You know you can make it up to me by having dinner with me tonight."

I take a few seconds to answer, genuinely considering it. Once Mom agreed to have brunch tomorrow at Sadie's, I agreed to meet Sadie at her house at six o'clock tonight for dinner. Though I'm sure she'd understand if I decided to do something else, I don't feel right about canceling.

"Um . . . I can't. I mean, I could and I'd like to, but I decided to stay in town for another night and I've already made other plans." I hate the way my words come out, as if I'm just making an excuse to not go out with him.

"Okay, well, I guess this is goodbye." He jumps off the bed of the truck, then helps me down.

I tilt my head and look deep into his eyes. "Thanks again, for everything. It's been really nice getting to know you."

He gives me a crooked smile, one that seems to convey disappointment, then hops into his truck and drives away.

chapter thirty-nine

PAM

When I return from faxing the court order, Ivy is peering out the window. She's pale and her eyes are puffy as if she's been crying.

"Ivy, what's wrong?" I ask.

She points to the backyard, where the pond is. The grassy shores around it are now thick with weeds and fallen tree limbs. A thin film of scum covers the water and ripples with the breeze.

"While you were gone," Ivy says, "I remembered why they sent Mama away. Or at least I think I do unless my mind is playing tricks on me."

"Really?"

"Yeah, it just came from outta nowhere. When I woke up from my nap, all these scenes started piecing themselves together. And it's crazy because the memory was so vivid. Like I was a kid, and it was happening all over again." Her eyes well and she takes a tissue out of her pocket.

I haven't sincerely hugged my sister in a long time, but I wrap my arms around her and let her weep, not even caring that her cheap, caked-on makeup is likely ruining my Michael Kors sweatshirt.

"Shh, it's okay, Ivy. Here, let's sit down." I keep one arm over her shoulder as I help her to the couch. "Tell me what you remember."

She takes a deep breath.

"I'm not sure how old I was, but it was winter because I remember it being cold in the house. Daddy wasn't here. He must've been at work or off doing whatever it was he did back then. Mama was a mess and had been crying all morning. She shouldn't have even been at home alone with us that day, she was so bad off. And there was a baby, Pam. I don't remember the details, but I remember Mama being pregnant and then for some reason, the baby didn't make it. And it broke her . . . she wasn't the same after that." Her leg bounces nervously and she tries to steady it with her hand.

"Anyway, she dressed Fern and me up in our lace socks and best dresses. We went outside, and she loaded us up in that old blue Chevy and drove us through the backyard to the pond. Right when she got to the water's edge, she stomped on the brake and I fell to the floorboard, hitting my head on the glove box. That's when I knew something was really wrong with Mama because she started laughing so hard, she peed all over herself and didn't care. It didn't make sense . . . Mama was always so sweet and kind. If she was in her right mind, she would've scooped me up right then and there, wrapped her arms around me, and comforted me. But she didn't."

Ivy whimpers and I squeeze her to me. "It's okay, Ivy. Just take your time."

She takes in a breath and continues. "Instead, she yanked Fern and me out of the car and told us we were going swimming. Right there in the middle of that freezing cold day with our church clothes on. Fern was too young to know any better, but I knew something wasn't right, so I took off running toward the house. But she caught me and dragged me back. She made us all hold hands and then she guided us into the water. When we were up to our waist, she told us we were going to heaven to help Jesus take care of our baby sister. And that we didn't need to be afraid once the water was over our heads. We just needed to look for the bright light and stretch as far as we could to reach out for Jesus."

My hands shake and I pull my arm from around Ivy.

"Anyway, I was scared to death. Practically convulsing because that water was so cold. I was truly terrified I was going to die. And Mama's glassy eyes and that smile on her face . . . well, it's no wonder I've suppressed that awful day all these years."

"So, what happened?" I whisper.

"I remember the water was up to my chest and up to Fern's neck . . . and then Grandma came running toward us from out of nowhere. She was screaming at Mama, 'What in the hell are you thinking?' Grandma didn't wait for her to answer, though. She seemed so old . . . she was always complaining about how bad her arthritis was. I thought we were in trouble if she was going to try and save us. But she ran into that water and grabbed Fern and me. She carried us back to the grass, then wrapped us up in her sweater.

"Mama just stood there, banging her fists into the water. She was sobbing, hollering, cussing out Jesus for taking her baby away. Once Grandma got to her, though, she just fell into her arms. Mama was at least a foot taller than Grandma and still had a belly from being pregnant. For a second, I thought the sheer weight of Mama was going to drag Grandma down, but she didn't waver. The next thing I remember was them walking back toward the house, and Fern and I following after them."

I shake my head, trying to process it all.

"So that was it," Ivy says. "I think Mama went to bed and didn't get up until Daddy hauled her off to Sparrow." A stoic expression spreads across her face. "But it's the most bizarre thing, Pam. You weren't there. I guess you could've been taking a nap or maybe even with Daddy. But if the reason Mama lost her mind was because she had a baby who died, that would mean you had nothing to do with it."

I put my hand on Ivy's leg. "Well, I have something to tell you too . . . maybe we've finally reached our moment of serendipity. We've certainly waited long enough for it." I take in a breath. "I found Mother's death certificate today when I was cleaning out Dad's room."

Ivy's mouth falls open. "Are you serious? What did it say?"

"It said Mother died from a hemorrhage. But I'm confused because it says she died the same month, day, and year that I was born."

An odd look crosses Ivy's face. "Your birth certificate doesn't say you were born at Hamilton Meadow, does it?"

"No, it says I was born at St. Joseph's. But I plan on getting to the bottom of this."

"How?"

"While you were asleep, I sent over a court order request to Sparrow. I'm hoping Hamilton Meadow still has Mother's medical records so we can figure out what the hell all this means. Emily's actually the one who suggested we do it. She's in Sparrow right now working on an article. The institution is finally selling all that land and plowing those old buildings down."

Ivy's eyes widen. "Oh, Pam. What if after all these years we finally find out what happened to Mother? Why, I thought I'd go to my grave never knowing."

"I guess anything's possible," I say. Then I put my arms back around my sister, clutching onto her like never before.

chapter forty

KORA

A few weeks ago, when Rose was talking to me about how the mind forgets certain things while others remain imprinted in our memory, I knew exactly what she was talking about. Because I remember every detail about the day I buried my baby girl, Violet, and lost my mind in the process.

She was born prematurely on a cold, overcast Saturday in December—fourteen days before Christmas—the day we were supposed to go hunting for a tree in the woods. The girls and I already had the orange slices dried, the paper snowflakes cut, and the popcorn strung.

Violet was only three days old when she passed. She had a headful of auburn hair and a sweet smile, favoring me, not her daddy. We buried her in town, at the cemetery across the street from the Baptist church, in the same white lace gown her two sisters wore when they were babies. Lying in that two-foot pine coffin on the yellow-and-green checkered quilt Mother sewed for her, she looked like she was simply taking a long afternoon nap.

We had just gotten home from the funeral when Daniel started his usual demands. "What's for dinner?" he barked from the kitchen table, arms stretched out on the starched placements.

I laid my clutch on the spic-and-span countertop and slid the glass casserole dish—the one my Sunday School class brought—out of the way. I closed my eyes and breathed in slowly. The proper and disciplined response was on the tip of my tongue, ready as always, to spill dutifully from my red, lip-glossed mouth that I touched up on the way home. But instead of the answer Daniel expected, the one that never faltered or sounded selfish, I said, "I'm going to lie down. I don't feel well."

"But I'm hungry." His biceps bulged as he pushed himself up and planted his hands on his hips.

I was exhausted, weak, emotionally depleted. I hadn't slept for more than two hours at a time since the baby was born, and I'd only been able to choke down a piece or two of toast each day. The thought of cooking dinner, or even the menial task of rolling out biscuit dough, made me feel like draping myself over the train tracks downtown and letting a locomotive plow over me. Besides, even if I could've mustered up the strength to cook something for supper, there was no way I could have blessed our food and poured out gratitude to a Lord whose motives I questioned.

"Eat what the church brought over," I said, starting toward the bedroom.

"I don't want that. I want *you* to cook me something for dinner."

My anger boiled like the pot of grits I forgot on the stove that morning. I spun around and sank my eyes into his. "No!"

He moved toward me, leering at me like he wanted to put his fist through my face. "Are you going to let me down twice this week? First, by not taking proper care of our baby, and now giving me attitude about dinner?"

I tapped my foot against the hardwoods that I polished the day before I went into labor. From Daniel's perspective, it was all my fault that the baby came four weeks early. Something I did wrong: ate too many biscuits piled high with apple butter, didn't drink enough milk, smoked too many cigarettes, didn't get enough rest.

"I said I'm going to bed," I repeated. I was surprised how venomous my voice sounded, how strong, even though I felt like my knees could buckle out from under me at any moment.

He stepped closer to me, his face just inches from mine. Violet had only been in the ground for an hour, and Daniel already reeked of tobacco and Southern Comfort.

"Cook me dinner!" He pounded his fist on the wall.

My belly tightened into a cramp and I brought my hand to it, squeezing my legs tightly together as blood gushed into the sanitary napkin clipped onto my panties. I stumbled backward just as the girls ran in through the back door.

Ivy stopped when she saw me. "Mama? Are you okay? Please don't be sad, Mama."

Her voice jerked me out of my head for a moment. I tried to put a response together for her, but my thoughts were scrambled.

"Ma—ma!" The two syllables came at me in slow motion.

"Shut up!" Daniel yelled. As usual, I flinched, afraid that he was going to hit one of my babies—or me in front of them.

Logically, I knew what I should do. My girls needed me to tell them their sister was an angel in heaven and not to worry, that Daddy wasn't going to hurt them. My husband needed me to cook his damn dinner with a smile on my face and keep on being a stellar wife and mother. But instead, my legs gave out from under me and I sank to the floor. My grief erupted in sobs. The words *Why me, Lord? Why, why, why!* felt as though they were going to burst from my eyes, mouth, nose, ears.

Daniel stood over me and said something I couldn't make out. I cupped my hands over my engorged breasts, and my body convulsed. In that moment, I could no longer feel the scars of childbirth between my legs, the tumultuous eight-month journey that dead-ended into a thicket of briars.

Oblivious to Daniel and the girls, I sank into a dark abyss, consumed with thoughts of how the doctor never should have taken baby Violet early, even if I was having contractions . . . of all the things that went wrong in labor . . . how she wasn't kicking or crying when she came out . . . how I wished I had someone's hand to hold when I was pushing. Thoughts of how it only took two pallbearers—Daniel and his brother—to carry that tiny coffin. Thoughts of the way my heart felt ripped from my chest when they plopped the first shovel of dirt onto her and then another and another. Thoughts of when Joanne brought me a pan of biscuits and a jar of pear preserves the morning after my baby girl was born. "She's just beautiful, Kora," she had said. "She's just little. Don't you worry, she'll pull through. She's strong like her mama."

But that was a lie.

That baby girl wasn't strong. And back then, neither was I.

chapter forty-one

EMILY

Sadie lives a few minutes from the city down a side street with well-established trees and quaint, older homes. A thick layer of leaves covers the lawn in front of her white brick ranch with black shutters. She and I pull into her driveway at the same time, and she gets out of her beige SUV holding our dinner.

I get my suitcase out of the backseat and meet her on the front sidewalk. "Thanks again for letting me stay with you." I look up. "I love your home."

"Thank you, honey. I'm happy to let you stay with me. We are practically family, after all."

She unlocks the front door and shows me to my room. Her house is homey but not cluttered, with clean, crisp white walls and dark hardwood floors. I drop off my things, go to the bathroom, then head back to the dining room.

Sadie's sitting at a circular table with generous portions of fried chicken, mashed potatoes, and green beans piled on our plates. She's poured both of us glasses of iced tea.

"This looks delicious," I say, taking my seat.

"It's the next best thing to home cooking. I love being in the kitchen, but sometimes I just don't have the time for it."

"I get it." I pick up my fork.

"Before we get started," she says, "let's pray." She bows her head and closes her eyes. "Dear Heavenly Father, Thank you for the splendid beauty of this day. Thank you for our blessings and for bringing sweet Emily here tonight with all the grace that you possess. Thank you for this food that we are about to receive. Please allow it to nourish our bodies and spirits. We ask all this in your strong and holy name, Amen."

I slowly open my eyes and wait for Sadie to pick up her fork.

"Now, honey, I want you to make yourself at home." She slides a big bite of mashed potatoes into her mouth. "So, how's your mother doing these days?"

I start picking at the chicken with my fingers. "Pretty good. She's been dating the same guy for a few years and still working hard as ever."

"And your father? Do you still talk to him?"

"Kind of . . . we chatted about a month ago. He's still in New York, so we don't see each other that much. Every year he says I should visit for Thanksgiving or Christmas, but I always decline. I mean, I've always been so worried about how Mom would feel about it. For some reason, when they divorced, I felt like I had to choose sides . . . like it was impossible to have a relationship with both of them without making the other one mad." I shrug. "I may end up going if I can get off work, but I wanted to see what Mom had going on first."

"I always liked your dad . . . I thought he was a good fit for Pam. She apparently didn't think so, though." She laughs. "By the way, I'm sorry I didn't go to your papa's funeral. I thought it'd be a little hypocritical of me if I showed up, considering I refused to speak to him when he was alive and well."

"If you two didn't get along, why did you work for him for so long?"

"Well, for one thing, I was young . . . and a little afraid to stand up to him, I guess. But I mainly stayed for the girls. They stole my heart the moment I met them. They were like my own children. It was hard when I had to leave them."

"Did you ever want children of your own?"

"I suppose I felt I could take it or leave it—motherhood, that is. It was never a burning desire for me because I was always fulfilled in whatever I was doing at the time. I wanted children, but my soul didn't need them to be happy. You may know what that feels like."

"Yes, ma'am. Writing makes me happy, but I think I want kids too." I take a sip of my tea. "Why did you decide to become a nurse?"

"After I finished taking care of Pam and her sisters, I knew I felt most fulfilled when I was helping people. Especially children. So, I went to college and became a nurse."

"How did you end up helping young, pregnant girls?"

"Well, when I first became a nurse, I worked in labor and delivery, and out of all the other positions I held over the years, that was always my favorite. So, I'd like to think that's when the seed got planted." She butters a roll and takes a bite. "And then, a few years later, there was a fifteen-year-old girl I taught in Sunday School who got pregnant. She saw me in the grocery store one day and spilled her soul to me in the parking lot. She wanted to keep the baby but believed it was impossible. She said everyone was giving her a hard time and no one understood what she was going through. That day, she and I sent up great big prayers in the front seat of my car. That was the moment I knew there was a real need to help girls like her. But at the time, it was just an idea. I didn't know if I'd ever really do it."

I nod as she takes another bite of roll and chases it with tea.

"And then . . . I don't know if your mother ever told you this . . . but I was in the delivery room with her when you were born. I'll never forget the look on your mother's face right after she delivered you. She had these crocodile tears flowing down her face. And love. Oh, sweet Jesus, she had big love. I didn't think she was capable of loving like that. You saved her, Emily. Just by coming into this world, you did what I'd been trying to do for decades."

My eyes widen. "You really think so?"

"I know so."

"Do you mind if I ask what happened between you guys? You seem like you were so close. I can't believe you haven't spoken in what . . . over twenty years?"

"Well, it's complicated. It was really just a misunderstanding. I never should have allowed the distance between us to go on for as long as it has."

"What about my grandfather? Why do you think Mom's relationship with him was so strained?"

"Well, I can tell you it wasn't her fault. Her father made her life hell, so she never wanted anything to do with him. She always wanted to get away from him. 'Crazy free,' that's what she said she'd be if that ever happened." She shakes her head and laughs. "There was one time when she was about twelve that she literally packed up and ran away. She of course didn't go far—I spotted her at the back of our property, past the pond, where the pasture met the woods. I'd get out my binoculars every thirty minutes or so and check on her, just to make sure she was still there. I tell you, that mother of yours . . . she was just fine. Playing cards by herself, reading books, taking naps on the ground.

But then I started cooking dinner and lost track of time, and before I knew it, that sun made its way across the pond and sank beneath the trees. When Daniel came home, she wasn't back yet. Ooh . . . he went ballistic, calling her names, slamming things around . . . even knocked a hole in the drywall. Once he simmered down, dozing off with a beer bottle between his legs, she finally snuck back in. But when he heard that screen door creak, he woke up."

"Oh no," I say, anticipating the worst.

"Oh no, is right. He went outside and clipped the biggest switch he could find and wore her butt out." Sadie leans back in her chair. "Pam never ran away from home again. But that whipping didn't stop her. She learned how to run away in her head. And that's what her problem is . . . she's still doing that. All these years later, that girl's still trying to be crazy free."

chapter forty-two

✤

PAM

The charity came a couple hours ago and took all the furniture and boxes of things we thought were salvageable, leaving only mine and Ivy's twin beds so we have somewhere to sleep tonight. I sit cross-legged on my old yellow comforter with chains of daisies strung around it as Ivy and I both savor bites of the pepperoni pizza we ordered.

"So, you're heading out tomorrow, I guess," Ivy says. "We got a lot more done today than I thought we would."

"Yeah, I'll probably leave around eight. I'm actually going to Sadie's house for brunch in the morning. Emily met up with her in Sparrow, and she invited us over."

"And you said yes?" She raises her eyebrows. "I'm impressed. It'll be nice to catch up with her, won't it?"

Ivy seems a little melancholy and I wonder if it's because she wasn't invited. After all, Sadie was also her mother figure for years. For a moment, I wonder if I should extend the invitation to her, but she saves me by not lingering on it. "I don't know how you keep up such a fast pace at your age. You always got something going on. I can't keep up with you. But you and I always have been different like that, I suppose."

I smile, appreciating the closeness we shared earlier. "You know, when I was a kid, I always looked up to you. I would have done anything to be your friend. But you were always going your way, and I was going mine."

Remorse spreads across her face, and she lays her paper plate on the bed. "I'm sorry I wasn't there for you the way I should've been. And I also hate things with you and Daddy were always so strained. I guess I was just selfish. Back then, I never thought of anyone but myself."

"It's not your fault. I guess we were all just doing the best we could with the cards we'd been dealt. It wasn't your responsibility to take care of me, or make me happy, or protect me from Dad. But yeah . . . growing up in this house was definitely a struggle for me."

"Well, you would've never known it. You were always stronger and smarter than me and Fern. And everyone could see it. I never helped you because I didn't think you needed it. You seemed to do just fine on your own."

I sigh. "Ha, now you tell me. And here I thought you ignored me for all those years because you hated me. Just like Dad did."

She tips her head in a sad, sentimental way and places her hand on my leg. "Dad didn't hate you, Pam. And I've always wanted nothing but the best for you. I'll admit, there was a time when I was envious of your success. I was stuck at home cooking, cleaning, and raising kids. I probably was a little more standoffish than I should have been, but now I understand we just had different lives. One journey wasn't better than the other." She shrugs lightly. "All us girls have struggled with our pasts, but I think Daddy's death gave me and Fern closure. I don't think you're quite there yet . . . but I hope you figure it out because you deserve to be happy."

"Thanks, Ivy. I appreciate you saying that." I lean back on

my elbows. "You know, you're right. I always thought once Dad passed, I would be free. Free from the guilt, the hurt, the disappointment, the hate. But those feelings are still there, and I don't know how to make them go away."

A sound hums from my pocket. I pull out my cell and see John's photo—the one he let me snap one night when I was acting silly after a third glass of chardonnay. I ignore his call and slip my phone back into my jacket.

Ivy tilts her head. "Pam, when are you going to give that man a chance to love you?"

I sigh. "I don't know if I can."

"Don't be silly. Everyone's capable of love. Even Daddy was capable of it. In fact, I think he was a little like you, the way he built a wall around himself and wouldn't let anyone in."

"I'll call him back later, I promise."

"You don't have to promise me a thing, dear. You're old enough to make your own decisions now without your big sister bossing you around." She stands up and yawns. "Well, I'm gonna call it a night and turn in early. I'm exhausted."

"Me too, I guess." I toss my paper plate into the trash bag and Ivy holds her arms out.

"Thank you, Ivy. For everything," I say, relaxing into her hug. "I'll keep you posted with what I find out about Mother, okay?"

"Everything's going to work out fine, Pam. I just know it." She kisses me on my forehead and walks out of the room.

chapter forty-three

KORA

The morning I lied to Rose about who raped me, she let me take a long shower, doctored my face, and allowed me to spend the day alone in the sleeping ward. She agreed with Hazel and said I should keep quiet and do everything in my power to forget about what happened. But like a vase that shatters and is glued back together, I might have looked fine on the outside, but upon closer inspection, it was obvious I'd never be the same again.

By the time I figured out I was pregnant, it was summer. Rose had recently broken up with her debonair boyfriend, so I finally told her the truth. She promised she wouldn't tell Dr. Hunter, but she was so angry if one of the help-patients in the kitchen snuck her a butcher knife, she probably would've made sure he never had the privilege of conceiving again.

After I told Dr. Hunter I was pregnant, I asked to go home.

"You've got to be kidding me," he said. "You're going to stay right here where I can keep an eye on you. What if I send you home and you tell someone what happened? I don't know about you, but I don't think that makes much sense for me to allow you so much freedom. Besides, Kora, don't you know I care about you? Now that you're pregnant, I must monitor your condition to make sure you don't become emotionally imbalanced again."

Being the intelligent and arrogant man he thinks he is, he's got it all figured out. His plan is for me to stay here at the hospital until the baby is born, then put my child up for adoption. At that point, if I've been a good girl, he says he'll permit me to go home.

Blah, blah, blah. How kind of him.

But what Dr. Hunter doesn't know is that I've already lost one baby, and I'm sure as hell not going to lose another. The love I feel for this child, despite the brutality under which it was created, fuels me to keep hammering out articles at *The Flare* and escape the confines of this hell hole. I have to. I'm determined to get my second chance as a mother.

Had all this happened last year, I strongly suspect that Dr. Hunter would have sent me on my way and gladly put this whole ordeal behind him. But since the *Daily Chronicle* has ambushed Hamilton Meadow, he doesn't want anyone asking questions. No, it's easier for him to play dumb and pretend he has my best interest at heart. Anyway, everyone is so distracted by the media attention right now and consumed with fear, no one will likely even notice or care that my belly is getting bigger every day.

After the first few articles Leo Larson wrote, the cannons have continued to fire here at the hospital. Doctors and nurses have quit or gotten fired, and because of the publicity, the governor even paid us a visit and started his own investigation.

Through all of this, I can't help but wonder, *What would Leo Larson think about what happened to me?*

The day after Dr. Hunter explained to me how the details of my pregnancy would be handled, Rose brought me an old copy of a *Wonder Woman* comic book she found in the dayroom. As I pored through the pages, I had an epiphany: my words can be used as weapons. My truth-laden golden lasso could be comprised of vivid adjectives, powerful verbs, and clear, concise sentences. And the bracelet I use to deflect Dr. Hunter's bullets? Why, it's genius really . . . the article I'll turn in to the *Daily Chronicle* with the following headline: HAMILTON MEADOW DOCTOR ON CHOPPING BLOCK FOR RAPING PATIENT. I know if I can get the newspaper behind me in this battle, I can win the war.

But writing an exposé about my rape and pregnancy is only one piece of the puzzle.

Rose called Mother and told her everything. I don't know if Mother feels sympathy for me, but I do know she and Daddy now have a taste of what it's like to share a life with my husband. Not only did Mother admit that Daniel was demanding and unreasonable much of the time, but she was also pretty perturbed that he'd been gone for three days and no one had seen or heard from him. "Tell Kora she can live with us until she finds a job and a place of her own," Mother said to Rose.

I smiled when I heard that. Daniel Mitchell was finally no longer a peach in my family's eyes—and that helped me set up the next piece of my plan.

Lucky for me, Rose's friend who works in labor and delivery—a girl who hasn't been able to conceive—is going to help me. Her job is to stall, professing she wants to adopt my baby, until I'm discharged and can get my article published with the *Daily Chronicle*. Then, I'll march up to the hospital and take my baby home. My parents are a little uneasy with my master plan, but since I am now the property of the state and therefore have to be respectful of Dr. Hunter's wishes, they understand I have little choice but to be cooperative and outsmart him at his own game.

❧

MOTHER AND DADDY brought the girls to see me today. I need to sew Ivy some new dresses because she's shot up like a weed, and baby Fern is speaking in full sentences now. We sat on the lawn in front of the administrative building, reading a chapter of *Charlotte's Web* and gobbling up the peach cobbler Mother baked. It was the best day I've had in a long time.

Now that they've left, I enjoy the shade of my favorite oak. I scrunch the loose curls that are to my shoulders now and tilt my head back. The sun warms my face through the branches, and I blot the perspiration beads from my forehead with the handkerchief Mother gave me. As I do, I notice a monstrous anthill a few feet away, and it makes me think about the house I shared with my husband—a place that shielded us from the weather, where everyone had their own job to do, and our children obediently followed along behind us. A lovely place that surely would last forever as long as everyone continued to follow the rules.

Hmm . . . not that I would do it, but I wonder how long it would take for those ants to reconstruct their life if I were to stomp on their red dirt mansion the way Daniel tried to destroy my life. I imagine some ants would perish, but others would scurry off to safety, eventually working hard enough to rebuild their home, and possibly even make their life better than it was before.

I gaze into the distance at the lanky, parched pine trees, the patches of dead grass, and the craters of cracked clay. It hasn't rained in weeks, yet the dry weeds and pink-throated snapdragons seem to rejoice as they sway gently in the breeze.

It seems like it's been ages since I've set my problems on fire and today the conditions are just right for it. I strike a match in my mind and picture all the things that would make the flames grow when a good gust of wind comes along: limbs that fell in the storm the night Eugene Hunter raped me, Daniel Mitchell's 150-proof moonshine, the medical books lining Dr. Hunter's office. I imagine the inferno roaring as the flames climb higher and expand farther, close enough to feel my skin bubble and my lungs burn.

I blink once, twice, three times as the fiery blaze comforts me. I push my chair back where the fire can't blister or smother me, yet is still hot enough for me to pretend like I'm being sterilized from everything that's gone wrong in my life. Smiling, I feel at peace for the first time since my baby was conceived. All I need now to complete this sweet scene of justice is a sloe gin fizz, a couple of cigarettes, and some Elvis playing in the background. And of course, the companionship of my notebook and a pen.

✤

chapter forty-four

EMILY

Sadie strikes a match and lights a set of white pillar candles. The scent of vanilla wafts toward me as classical piano music plays from a radio on the kitchen counter. On the table, lace placemats, china plates, coffee cups, and crystal glasses join a pitcher of orange juice, a carafe of coffee, cream and sugar, a quiche, and a platter of generously iced cinnamon rolls.

"Do you need any help?" I ask, pouring myself a glass of orange juice. "Mom should be here any minute."

"No, honey. I'm almost done," she says. "Besides, I enjoy having someone to take care of. Sometimes it gets lonely living here all by myself."

I smile. "I'm enjoying being here with you too. It's a nice change of pace for me." I walk into the living room and sink into Sadie's recliner. A half-finished puzzle sits on the coffee table: a yellow house on a lake surrounded by autumn trees, a rowboat in the water, and kids playing in the yard. I sip on my juice as I watch Sadie flutter around the kitchen. It's nice to see her wearing something other than scrubs.

"The cinnamon rolls smell amazing," I say.

"Why, thank you," she says. "It's my mother's recipe. I used to make these all the time for Pam and her sisters when they were little."

I laugh. "Maybe that's why Mom was such a fan of canned cinnamon rolls when I was a kid."

"Well, that Pam never liked to cook. She was always too busy for that sort of thing. But the Lord gave us all unique talents. It'd be kind of boring if we were all walking around here doing the same thing, now wouldn't it?"

I nod. "How'd you become such a good cook?"

"When you get to be my age, you're the sum of your life experiences." She slings a dish towel over the oven handle and surveys the tidy kitchen. "It's pretty simple, actually. I always liked to eat good food, so I learned how to cook good food. A 'foodie' is what I think they'd call me nowadays."

I'm about to comment when the doorbell rings.

"I guess that's your mother. You know what Pam's always saying, 'If you're not early, you're late.'"

"Yes, ma'am. You know my mother well." I push out of the recliner as Sadie smoothes her apron before opening the door.

Mom stands on the porch looking pale, absent the abundant makeup she typically wears.

"Pam, it's so good to see you!" Sadie engulfs her in an embrace. "Gosh, it's been much too long."

Mom eyes me over Sadie's shoulder. "It has."

I expect them to share a more sentimental reunion after all these years, but Mom appears to feel awkward and Sadie seems to instinctively know better than to push it. So, she simply holds Mom out at arm's length and says, "Thank you, honey, for making the drive all the way out here."

Mom smiles as she steps inside. "Smells like home," she says. Looking at me, she adds, "Every Saturday morning Sadie would make us those cinnamon rolls. Sometimes I think that's how I made it through my childhood—knowing there was always that reward waiting for me at the end of the week."

Sadie takes in a breath. "It's nice to know you have some good memories."

Mom hesitates, then shrugs her shoulders as if to say, *Yeah, some.*

"Well," Sadie says, clasping her hands together, "I've got everything ready if y'all would like to go ahead and have a seat."

It still feels odd to me that twenty years of silence between Mom and Sadie hasn't warranted a more emotional moment of reconciliation, but Mom matter-of-factly says, "This is lovely. I didn't have anything for breakfast, so I'm famished." We both sit down at the same time. "I actually drove from the city this morning. I was at Dad's helping Ivy get his house ready to sell."

Her words surprise me. I had no idea she was out of town.

"Well, that explains why you were so quick to accept my offer," Sadie says. "I'm sure you were looking for an excuse to get out of *that*."

Surprisingly, Mom laughs. "Ivy found a buyer for Dad's house, and since I had the time, I decided to meet her there. It was a last-minute kind of thing." Reading my look, she adds, "Emily, I would've told you, but I figured I wouldn't bother you with my drama."

I narrow my eyes and swirl my juice as Sadie invites us to say the blessing. I follow their lead and bow my head as Sadie prays. Right after she says "Amen," she passes the quiche to Mom, keeping their conversation light. "So, Pam, how's Ivy doing these days?"

"She's pretty good. A little wound up about selling Dad's

house, but she'll get through it. I actually enjoyed my visit with her."

"Well good, I'm glad to see you girls are getting along these days," Sadie declares as she pours the coffee. "Were you able to get a lot done?"

"Thankfully, yes. This time next month, that old house should be history. Then I can finally put all this behind me."

Sadie and I elect not to comment as we scoop quiche onto our plates and pass around the cinnamon rolls.

After about ten minutes of small talk and awkward silence while we eat, Mom turns to me. "So, Emily . . . have you found out anything about your grandmother?"

I start to reply when Sadie clears her throat. "Before Emily answers that," she says, sitting up straighter in her chair, "if it's okay, there's something I'd like to say first."

Mom shrugs. "Sure."

Sadie starts tapping her fingers together. "This is hard for me, so I'm just going to say it . . . before I lose my courage like I've done so many times. Pam, I actually know more about your mother than I've let on for all these years . . . and Emily, I wasn't completely honest with you yesterday either."

Mom moves her napkin from her lap to the table. "Does this have anything to do with how my mother died? Because I found her death certificate yesterday when I was cleaning out Dad's bedroom. That's actually one of the reasons I came here today . . . to ask you about it."

Sadie's wrinkled face relaxes into a smile. "I guess I've lived this life long enough to not let God's timing surprise me anymore." She looks down, shaking her head. "Actually . . . yes. It does have something to do with that. Before I came to work for your family, I was a nurse at Hamilton Meadow . . . from 1958 to '61. I . . . was your mother's nurse . . . and her friend. She knew me as Rose, which is my middle name."

Chill bumps spring up on my arms and Mom looks perplexed as she calmly sets her coffee mug down. "You *knew* my mother?"

"Yes, I did. And that's why I invited both of you over this morning. It's time I finally explain everything that happened back then." Sadie walks over to her desk, where she pulls a spiral-ringed book from the top drawer. When she returns, she lays it in front of Mom. "This is the journal your mother kept when she was at the hospital. She enjoyed writing, so I bought it for her as a therapy tool, to get her feelings out on paper. She always hated talking to the doctors, plus she was shy. But she surprised me and ended up writing quite the story in this little book."

Mom's hands are shaking as she picks up the journal and flips through the pages.

"How did you get this?" Mom finally asks.

"Kora kept it under her mattress. Once she passed, I took it. Then I quit that hell hole and never looked back."

Mom blinks slowly. "Why are you just now showing this to me?"

"Your father wouldn't let me tell you anything about her. Back then, no one talked about mental illness. People didn't go around announcing if a family member wound up at Hamilton Meadow."

"So, all those times when I was a little girl . . . when I came to you begging to know what happened to my mother, you knew . . . and you never told me? How could you lie to me for all these years?"

249

Sadie's face softens with sympathy. "It was never easy. But I couldn't have told you back then. You were just a child. You wouldn't have understood."

"Yeah, but I'm almost sixty now."

Sadie takes another deep breath and puts her hand on Mom's. "You're right, I should have told you sooner . . . I'm sorry for that . . . truly I am. Being estranged all these years hasn't helped. But I think by the time you leave today, everything will make more sense."

Mom's eyes fill with tears again as she places her palm on the smooth brown cover of the journal.

Unsure of what I should do, I ask Mom if she wants me to read it out loud.

Mom pauses then slides the journal gently toward me. "Okay."

I open the book to the first delicate, yellowing page and run my fingers along the swirls of Kora's exquisite handwriting, my heart pounding in a nervous yet excited cadence as I begin to read.

chapter forty-five

PAM

By the time Emily reads the last page of my mother's journal, I know about the days leading up to her commitment, her stay at the hospital, and the triumphs and tragedies that transpired during her months there. And then it abruptly stops. The room is quiet as my mother's story settles into the pit of my soul. I can't imagine the despair she must have felt. I wish I could hug her, hold her hand, tell her how very sorry I am.

It has all become clear to me. "I was that baby, wasn't I?" I whisper.

Sadie nods gently. "Yes."

A myriad of emotions and questions catapult through me. I can't believe what I've just heard, but it makes sense now. Why Dad played favorites with my sisters. Why he refused to love me. Why he made me feel guilty all those years. I sniffle and bite my bottom lip, then leave the table and go into the living room where I can briefly be alone with my thoughts.

Sadie and Emily let me pace for a few minutes, then I feel their loving arms across my back.

"Why don't we sit down," Sadie says.

Sadie guides me to her recliner and she and Emily sit across from me on the couch.

"How did she end up dying?" I finally ask. "It sounded like

she was doing better, like she had a plan to get out of there."

"Oh, yes," Sadie affirms, "your mother had a plan, and nothing was going to get in her way. To be honest, I was never convinced she had clinical depression because she bounced back so quickly. I really think she was just mourning the death of her baby and was broken from being Daniel's wife for so long."

"That makes sense," Emily says.

"Yes . . . but . . ." Sadie hesitates. "Things at the institution kept getting worse and worse, and when Kora was almost full-term, Dr. Hunter came in drunk one morning and told the nurses to give her electric shock therapy."

I dig my fingers into the arm of the recliner.

"What exactly is that?" Emily asks.

"Electrodes are secured around the head like a headband. Then, electrical currents are sent through the brain, which causes a seizure. Back then it was used for pretty much any nervous condition. It was horrible. The hospital did it on Mondays, Wednesdays, and Fridays . . . seventy-five to eighty procedures a day."

"Oh my God," Emily says. "That *is* horrible."

I'm deeply disturbed hearing this, but also confused. "Why do you think Dr. Hunter told the nurses to do that to her? Was he trying to kill the baby . . . to kill *me*?"

Sadie shakes her head. "No, no, I don't think so. I think he was worried the hospital was going to find out what he did. I think it was his way of trying to destroy the evidence."

"What do you mean?" Emily asks.

"Well, electroshock causes a chemical reaction in the brain, and one of the main side effects is memory loss. It was the perfect solution for Dr. Hunter because he wanted Kora to forget about what happened that night down by the river."

Emily's mouth drops open. "He was allowed to do that on a pregnant woman? And he could do it without her permission?"

Sadie shrugs. "Yes . . . and I know it sounds barbaric because it *is*. But they say electroshock on pregnant women is safe. They still do it on some females today if the benefit outweighs the risk."

All I can do is shake my head.

"And once Daniel had her committed," Sadie continues, "she became the property of the state and essentially lost all her rights."

I lace my arms over my chest. "Well, wasn't that a convenient way to shut her up. I guess that's what killed her?"

"No, not technically. But it did make her go into labor . . . and then during childbirth, the blood vessels that run to the placenta that are supposed to contract and pinch off on their own . . . they didn't. And your poor mother hemorrhaged, Pam . . . that's how she died."

I feel a tear fall down my face and swipe it away.

Sadie leans forward. "But sweetheart, you managed to come into this world completely unharmed. And when I saw you, I gave you Kora's middle name because I knew while you were in her womb, her fortitude was woven into every fiber of your being."

I manage a slight smile of gratitude for my name, but the internal conflict I feel is overwhelming. "All those years I thought *I* was the one who drove her crazy . . . that *I* was the one who emotionally broke her. And now I find out it was literally *because* of me that she died."

Sadie's face contorts with compassion. "I know this is all so hard to hear, Pam."

I shake my head. "Why does my birth certificate say St. Joseph's, then?"

"Dr. Hunter changed it. He didn't want anything tying you to him. And things were so chaotic then, no one noticed or cared about a little detail like that. Honestly, you were gone before anyone had a chance to think twice about it."

Questions line up in my brain, and I fire off the first one. "So, how did you end up being our nanny?"

"Kora made me promise if anything ever happened to her that I would take care of y'all. She didn't want Daniel raising you girls by himself. So, once you were born, I went and paid him a little visit. I told him his other daughters deserved to know their sister, and if word got out that Kora was pregnant and he didn't take the baby, everyone would assume he wasn't the father." Sadie shrugs. "As far as everyone was concerned, he technically could have been your dad. He visited Kora that one time and no one really knew what went on up there. I'm sure Kora's friends gossiped amongst themselves in the beginning, but no one ever had the gall to confront Daniel or you girls about it."

"Wow," Emily mutters.

"But I also guilt-tripped him," Sadie adds. "I told him Kora would still be alive if he'd given her more time to recuperate after their baby passed. And then I put the icing on the cake and gave him a deal he couldn't refuse. I told him I'd be his live-in help free of charge, that I'd handle the child rearing and also do the cooking and cleaning if he'd agree to take you."

"And he agreed," I say, knowing he would have been a fool to turn down such a sweet deal.

"Of course that selfish man agreed. As long as I promised to never tell you the truth."

I look away, my understanding of my childhood becoming clearer. But bitterness creeps in. "So why, after he died, didn't you come to his funeral and tell me then. That would've been the right thing to do, regardless of what was going on between me and you."

"Oh, Pam," Sadie says sympathetically, "that's easier said than done. I really didn't think it was the time or place, especially not having seen you since that silly fight we had. I did try to talk myself into going, but I just couldn't make myself do it. Please understand . . . I despised Daniel. He tossed your mother to the curb like a bag of trash . . . and then he made me lie to you. I hated him for being an unfit father . . . that without me there to keep your family afloat, God only knows what would've happened to you girls. Don't get me wrong . . . I see God's plan clearly now, but back then, I certainly had doubts, times when I felt angry and jealous of my friends who had families of their own to take care of."

But I *don't* understand. "You make it sound like you were the innocent victim. Like you didn't have a choice. But you had choices, Sadie. Many of them."

Sadie sighs. "Again, for what it's worth, I'm sorry, Pam. Yes, there were hundreds of times over the years that I could have told you, but I'd always back out at the last minute. Like the day of our fight. My purpose in coming to see you that day was to share your mother's story with you—I thought it would comfort you to know the struggles your mother went through with Daniel. I thought it would give you strength if you knew how strong, independent, and confident she was. And deep down, I blamed myself for your divorce. Maybe if I would've explained why Daniel was resentful toward you, and maybe if you knew how fiercely your mother loved you, you would have allowed yourself to be happy."

I look away as Sadie keeps talking.

"That day, I actually had Kora's journal in my pocketbook, but once we started talking and you opened up to me about the divorce, my emotions took over and I found myself getting angry with you. You had the perfect life—the life I yearned for—and yet, you chose to throw it away. I shouldn't have said the things I did, but you left before I had a chance to explain myself. So, at that point, I decided maybe Daniel was right . . . that I should leave well enough alone. And so, from that point forward, I pushed you and your family out of my mind and kept my days filled with work, or school, or volunteering."

Sadie's words are too much for me to absorb right now. I stare out the window until my eyes start to burn. "What ended up happening to Dr. Hunter?" I finally ask.

"The last I heard, he was living about thirty minutes from here, out in Whitley County. He got married and had children, I believe. After Kora died, he quit his job at the hospital, and I heard through the grapevine that he opened his own practice and stopped drinking . . . I guess he tried to turn his life around."

I roll my eyes. *Don't they all.* "Did you ever think about turning him in to the police? Didn't you worry he might abuse other patients?"

"Yes, but it was a different time back then. If Hamilton Meadow would have known, they probably wouldn't have done anything about it. It would've been Hunter's word against Kora's. And whose side do you think they would've taken?"

I lean my head into the recliner. "Well then, I guess he thinks he got away with raping my mother."

Sadie nods. "Probably."

I pause briefly then rise from the chair. "Then I think it's time he knows his secret's been exposed. Maybe I'll even press charges. As far as I'm concerned, it's never too late for justice to be served."

Emily and Sadie look like they feel sorry for me.

I grab my purse. "I'm serious," I throw at them.

Talking accomplishes nothing. I should know because I've spent a lifetime hiding behind words, behind arguments. The only thing that gets results is taking action.

When I get to the door, I toss a glance at Emily. "By the way, I sent that court order to the county. So, I guess we'll request Mother's medical records once the judge signs off on it."

Emily looks at me sideways. "Okay."

Then I turn to Sadie. "I'm sorry you're on the receiving end of my anger. I know you did a lot for me when I was young and I'm grateful. It's just that I really can't wrap my head around the fact that you kept this secret from me all these years. A secret that would have completely changed my life."

I turn abruptly away as the tears start flowing, and then walk out the door, slamming it behind me.

chapter forty-six

EMILY

Sadie and I stare at each other, not knowing what to say. I, too, am overwhelmed by all this news, but it isn't as close to me as it is to Mom, and I'm able to sort through the facts with a more rational frame of mind than she can right now.

Sadie finally rises and I follow her into the dining room to help clear the dishes from the table.

"I wish that would've gone better," she says, scraping the plates.

I pat her gently on the back. "It was a lot to take in."

"I know, but . . ."

"Don't be too hard on yourself. I can't help but think if I'd minded my own business, Mom would still be in her safe haven of denial and could've been spared a lot of pain."

Sadie turns on the faucet. "I was going to tell her anyway and I mean that. None of this is your fault, honey, so you just go ahead and forget you ever said that. Plus, I'm hoping it's like any other wound . . . once the air hits it, the healing process will begin. I know Pam's got to sort through all this in her own way in her own time."

She shuts off the water and turns to me.

"For what it's worth," I say, "I understand why you never told

Mom the truth. And I can only imagine how hard it must've been for you to sacrifice getting married and having kids of your own. And you did all that for a friend and for children who weren't even yours."

Sadie wrings the dishcloth and her eyes dart away for a moment. "Thank you for saying that . . . but I also had my own selfish agenda. I had to take care of my family at the time . . . and I know I should've been doing that with a generous heart . . . but most of the time it felt like a burden I couldn't escape from. To be honest, the Mitchell family was my ticket out of Sparrow."

"Really?"

She nods. "And even more than that, I wanted to get as far away as possible from that hospital and Eugene Hunter."

"Why did you go to work there in the first place?"

"Well, I guess because helping people and coming to their aid when they were in distress was instinctual for me. I've been that way for as long as I can remember."

"How old were you?"

"I went to work in July, a week after my eighteenth birthday. Back then, you could earn your associates degree in nursing through on-the-job training. Besides, Hamilton Meadow was always desperate for help and had more patients than they knew what to do with. The pay wasn't that great, but the benefits were. We got free rent, healthcare, meals. It was exhausting . . . we pretty much had to work 24/7, and there were ninety patients in my ward. But it was a good gig for an eighteen-year-old girl with no prospective husbands in sight."

I laugh. "If you say so."

Sadie flashes me a smirk. "But I also genuinely wanted to help those poor people. I really hoped I could make a difference in their lives. But once I got there and realized how limited the hospital's resources were, all I could really do was love on them . . . and that didn't cost the state a dime."

I smile at Sadie's generosity. I realize she felt trapped caring for her parents, but she could have worked somewhere that wasn't so depressing. Instead, she chose to bring some light into people's lives who probably had very little, if any, light left.

"How about we retire to the living room," Sadie offers. "The dishes can soak and get cleaned up later."

I settle next to her on the couch, kick off my shoes, and hug my knees to my chest.

"So," I venture, "I know my grandfather was a real piece of work. How did you manage to live with him all those years?"

"Well, that's true about Daniel . . . he was a pistol most of the time. But I loved taking care of your mom and her sisters. I was never one to mind changing a dirty diaper, or waking up in the middle of the night to feed a baby, or keeping little ones entertained. It was easier than working at the institution, even when Daniel was bellyaching about something." She laughs then becomes serious. "The hardest part for me was being there, in my best friend's house . . . as if I'd just jumped into her life and taken over where she left off."

"I'm sure that did feel strange." I look away for a moment, considering what it would be like to step into Erin's life right now. "What ever happened to the article my grandmother wrote about the hospital?"

"I don't know. She told me it was in her journal, folded up in the back. But when I took it that day, it wasn't in there."

"Did you tell Dr. Hunter she wrote it? Maybe he took it . . . or maybe that's why he had extra incentive to shut her up."

She pulls back slightly. "Oh, honey . . . do you really think I would've done that? I never would have intentionally hurt Kora or put her in jeopardy in any way whatsoever."

I start to apologize, but Sadie jumps right back in. "My boyfriend raped my best friend. Can you even imagine how furious I was at him? How betrayed I felt? It took me years before I could release my anger and forgive him."

"I can only imagine. I'm sure that wasn't easy for you. It's just odd that the article disappeared like that."

"I agree. I was always curious who found it and what they did with it. I know it probably ended up getting thrown away, but still, it would've been nice to have put it away for safe-keeping."

"Or maybe you could've had it published."

Sadie raises a brow. "Maybe . . . especially since Hamilton Meadow was such a hot topic back then. But even though the newspaper loved to report on a good scandal, I don't know if they would've published Kora's article. It was a man's world back then. Women, whether victimized or not, dead or alive, typically weren't allowed to voice their opinion." She studies her puzzle, then bends over the coffee table and picks up a piece that she pops into place. "Eventually, though," she continues, "people started listening. There were plenty of accusations over the years questioning the safety and abuse at Hamilton Meadow."

"Did you witness a lot of that?"

"Some . . . but, in my opinion, it wasn't as terrible as the media always made it out to be. A lot of patients did get better and return home, and for every bad employee, there were a hundred good ones. You know how it is. Plenty of positive things happen in this world, but unfortunately, they're not as newsworthy."

I nod. "Well, my grandmother sure was lucky to have you as her nurse. Thank you for everything you did for her."

Sadie smiles. "You remind me of her. You know Kora was about your age when she was committed. That's why I was a little dumbfounded this week when you showed up at my clinic. I felt like I was seeing a ghost. And I admit, I certainly wouldn't turn away from her soul if she did happen to pay me a visit."

I laugh. "I do see the resemblance . . . but now that I've read her story, I know we have a lot more in common than just looking like each other."

Sadie puts her hand on my knee. "Emily, I know your grandmother would be so proud of you. I think she would feel that because of you and your mother, all her struggles were worth it."

I put my hand over hers. "That's a nice thought. I just don't understand how you've been able to keep your faith all these years. After all you've been through, you still seem so strong and sure of yourself."

Sadie sighs. "I am where I am today *because* of faith. Your grandmother taught me the value of that. It's ironic, isn't it? The people who come into our lives at just the right moment and give us little morsels of wisdom?" A sentimental look crosses Sadie's face. "Say, would you be interested in seeing where your grandmother is buried?"

"Really? I thought most of the graves were unmarked."

"A lot of them are. But I know exactly where your grandmother's buried. I go there every year on Pam's birthday. I sit down by the creek, next to the metal post that marks her gravesite, and have me a good long chat with Kora about everything that's going on down here."

"That's really sweet. I'd definitely love for you to take me there."

"I'd be happy to." She gently pulls her hand away and stretches. "But we'll have to go tomorrow. I don't think I'm up for it today."

"Tomorrow's fine. Would you mind if I spent the night here again?"

"Of course not. And invite your mom to go with us if you think she'd be open to it."

I make a face. "I think I need to give her a couple hours to cool down. But maybe I could talk her into it. I assumed we'd never know where Kora was buried. So regardless of what Mom decides to do, I'm in."

"Good." Sadie spots another puzzle piece's home and I mosey over to the window.

The wind picks up, and the trees sway. If I'd brought my running shoes, I would head out for one of those long runs where I blast my music and don't come back until my hair's soaking wet and my thighs are numb. Instead, I ask Sadie if she minds if I check my email.

"You go right ahead. To be honest, unearthing this secret has taken a lot out of me. I think a nap would feel pretty good right about now."

"I bet. Don't let me stop you." I pull my phone from my purse, but instead of tapping the email icon, I scroll through my contacts instead. When I reach Graham's name, I suddenly have a flash of the kind boy in Kora's journal who helped her when she had polio. *Too bad she didn't end up with him instead of my grandfather*, I think.

I reach up and touch the necklace I've worn every day since

Colin and I broke up. I haven't been able to bear the thought of throwing away the last memory of our life together—the love we shared, the dream I had for our future, the hope I hung on to that he would change into the man I so desperately needed him to be.

But knowing my grandmother's story has given me the courage to do what I should have done a long time ago. I slide my hands behind my neck and unclasp the necklace. Then I stride into the kitchen, wrap it in a paper towel, and drop it into the trash can.

"Sadie? Would you mind if I stepped out for a little bit?"

"Not at all."

"Okay, thanks. I met someone here this week . . . a really nice guy . . . and if he's up to it, I think I'd like to see him again."

"Well, that sounds like a wonderful idea. Stay gone for as long as you want. If I happen to not be here when you get back or if I've already gone to bed, just look under the mat for the key." She sits up and faces me. "And thank you, honey, for understanding and not holding all this against me. Don't you worry, everything's going to work itself out."

chapter forty-seven

🦋

PAM

The second I got in my car, I pulled out my phone and looked up Eugene Hunter's address in Whitley. Then, I reversed out of Sadie's driveway and wound through the streets of the neighborhood and onto the highway as questions pummeled my mind.

Is shock therapy painful?

Was Mother conscious when she gave birth to me?

Did she hold me before she died?

The statute of limitations for rape is fifteen years, but what if the perpetrator confesses?

Since Mother is deceased, can I still press charges?

Could the hospital or the doctor be sued for malpractice?

Because I only take cases dealing with sexual harassment or gender bias in the workplace, I don't get involved much in rape. But John sometimes does. Thinking maybe he can help me, and hopeful he isn't upset with me for being distant lately, I pull off the road and call him.

"Hey, stranger," he says over chatter and country music pulsing in the background.

"Hi. It sounds like you're out. Is now not a good time to talk?"

"No, it's fine. The kids were actually free this weekend, so we went to the mountains. We're at a fall festival up here."

"Oh, okay then, since you're busy . . ."

"No, no, I can talk. I'm just passing the time at an art exhibit while the kids listen to a band and eat funnel cakes. Just give me a second to get out of this crowd so I can hear you better." He breathes into the receiver as the noise fades away. "I was beginning to wonder when I was going to hear from you again. Did you get everything at your dad's house squared away?"

"Yeah, I left this morning. I'm not home, though."

"Oh? Where are you?"

"Remember how Emily was going to Sparrow for the magazine and she wanted to do some research on my mother while she was there?"

"Yeah?"

"Well, she ended up contacting Sadie to see if she knew anything. And . . . I'm in Sparrow—just left Sadie's house . . . you won't believe what she told me."

I then proceed to tell him everything about my mother, her journal, and the rape.

"Dear God, Pam," he says softly. "That's terrible. What are you going to do?"

"I think I have the right address for Hunter, so I'd like to go see him. I know he's old, but I want to confront him about what he did to my mother. Do you think that's completely crazy?"

John's quiet for a moment. "Well, if that's what you really want to do . . . you shouldn't go by yourself. Call Emily and have her go with you."

I sigh. "I don't know if she will."

"I bet she would. But if not, if you can wait till tonight, I'll go with you."

My heart swells. John's still willing to be by my side, even after all I've put him through these past few weeks. "I appreciate it, but you don't need to do that. You'll be exhausted once you get home. But let me ask you . . . what would you think if I wanted to press charges against him? Do you think I'd have a case?"

"Hmm . . . I don't know if that's the best idea. But maybe. It would obviously depend on what kind of solid evidence you could get against him."

"Well, I have the journal. But the article Mother wrote conveniently disappeared." I think for a moment. "I keep my tape recorder on me. What if I could get him to confess? I could record our conversation when I go over there. If he does confess and our DNA matches, would that nullify the statute of limitations on rape?"

"I'm not sure on the specifics. I'd need to read up on it a little bit. But just because DNA could prove he's your father, it wouldn't prove he raped your mother."

"But there's also Sadie's testimony. I could have her subpoenaed."

"Are you sure you'd want to do that? How old do you think this guy is now?"

"I don't know. Early nineties?"

"Oh wow. Well, why don't you go see him first and get some of your questions answered. Then, call me when you leave his house and let me know how it goes."

"Okay, I'll keep you posted."

"And Pam . . ." he says, his voice becoming serious. "Be careful, all right?"

I want to tell him how much I love him, how good it feels to have him worry about me, how much I appreciate him always being there, even when sometimes I don't deserve it. But I don't. Instead, we say our goodbyes.

I rest my head on the steering wheel. *Daniel Mitchell never worried about me.* When I was five and I'd climb to the top branch of the weeping willow beside our house, he was never concerned I might fall. When I was in the third grade and I'd walk by myself to the store to buy candy, he never told me to look both ways before I crossed the street. When I brought home an F in eighth-grade math, there were no consequences, no lecture about how he expected more from me or how disappointed he was. And when I was sixteen and came home at three in the morning with liquor on my breath and a black lace bra hanging out of my purse, he was drunk and snoring on the couch.

I guess that's something my mother and I have in common.

Daniel Mitchell obviously never cared about either one of us.

chapter forty-eight

EMILY

Graham and I are meeting in downtown Sparrow in the courtyard in front of the college. I get there a few minutes early and see him on the other side of the lawn. He's playing football with a little boy in baggy jeans and glasses strapped around a headful of curly brown hair.

The boy sprints across the lawn and Graham jogs backward, throws his arm behind his shoulder, then spirals the ball. When the boy catches it, Graham pumps his fist in the air. "That a boy! Good job, Jacob!"

The boy's face lights up, and a smile spreads across it.

Graham sees me and waves. "Hey, I'll be there in a few!"

I give him a thumbs up and find a seat on a metal bench in front of a quaint church. The courtyard is teeming with people enjoying the pretty day. College boys are taking turns balancing on a low tightrope; a couple is lying on a quilt in the grass with their arms draped around each other; a little girl learning how to ride a bike wobbles down the sidewalk as her parents follow behind her.

I tip my head toward the sky just as the sun illuminates the kaleidoscope of colors on one of the stained-glass windows of the church. I close my eyes and relish the warmth on my face.

When I open them, Graham is striding up. "Thanks for waiting on me."

"No problem." I look behind him. "Where's your friend?"

"His mom just picked him up."

"He seems like a good kid."

"Yeah, he's great." He pulls his hoody off and smoothes his black T-shirt against his muscular chest. "He's the nephew of one of my buddies at work. He doesn't see his dad that often and I come out here to play with him for an hour or two on the weekends."

I smile. "I'm sure his mom appreciates that."

Graham nods. "I think so." He slides onto the bench next to me. "So, what's going on? I thought you would've left by now."

"Yeah . . . me too. But . . . something's happened."

"Uh oh, you didn't end up going back to that building, did you? I took a risk talking that cop into letting you off the hook." He laughs.

"Ha, ha, very funny. No, I think I've learned my lesson on the subject of trespassing." I playfully punch his arm. "Everything that's happened in the past twenty-four hours has been legal, although still insanely intense."

He swivels toward me and leans back on one hand. "Tell me about it."

"Okay, but first . . . I want to apologize for kind of giving you the cold shoulder yesterday. I'm not usually like that. I just have a lot on my mind."

"No worries."

I take a deep breath and bite my lip, then I spill everything I've just learned about my grandmother.

"Whoa," Graham says, sitting up and putting his arm

around me. "I don't even know what to say. I'm so sorry. Have you talked to your mom since she left?"

"No, I thought I'd give her a little space."

He shifts to face me. "She'll come around. Sometimes the truth hurts, but it still feels better than not knowing."

"Yeah, I know. I just wish Mom got that."

"Deep down she probably does. It's just going to take her a while to sort through everything."

"I guess." I look out into the courtyard and let the crowd distract me for a moment.

I feel Graham's hand on my knee. "I'm curious what *you* think about all this."

I turn to him. "To be honest, I've got so many things swirling through my head right now, I don't know what to think. All I know for sure is, Kora was a good wife, a good mother, and a good person. She didn't deserve any of this."

Graham nods. "What do you think your mom's going to do?"

"Well, she acted like she wanted to go to the police, but I don't know if she has a case since it happened so long ago. She's requesting Kora's medical records, though, so maybe she can use that as evidence."

Graham smirks. "Yeah, if the hospital still has them."

I mirror his cynicism. "Exactly."

"I suppose I can see where your mom's coming from."

"I can too. But if she's going to pursue something legal, I want it to be for the right reason . . . to punish that doctor for a crime he committed. Not because of her own personal vendetta. I mean, it's not like putting him away is going to make her feel any better. The guy's probably close to a hundred years old by now."

"I hear you. But it's hard to say what you'd do if you were in her position. It sounds like she's got a lot of things to figure out before she makes any decisions."

"Yeah."

"Do you have any interest in meeting your biological grandfather?"

I open my mouth to answer, then hesitate. "I guess I'm not opposed to meeting him, but I definitely don't see myself having a relationship with him. Because of what he did, our family's roots were planted in poison."

"Well, let me ask you this: as Kora's granddaughter, do you think he should be held accountable for a crime he committed sixty years ago?"

I stare at the college boys still goofing around with the tightrope.

"I'm not sure if he should go to jail. I think we all make mistakes, especially when we're young and immature. And realistically speaking, I don't know what good comes out of putting him in prison at this point. He's too old to learn a lesson or to live his life differently, and he'd just be a financial burden to the state. And who knows? What if Sadie's right and he genuinely regretted that decision he made as a young man? Maybe he *has* spent the rest of his life trying to right a wrong. If that's true, I don't know if I could support Mom's decision to press charges."

Graham sits up straighter. "Well, I kind of see it like your mom does. If you break the law, there should be consequences. Unless of course, you're trespassing." He winks. "Then I give those criminals a little more leeway."

I shake my head and toss him a playful leer. "You're not going to let me live that down, are you?"

"Nope."

We both laugh, and then I become contemplative again.

"You know, I think what's eating at my conscience the most is that I started all this because my boss was pressuring me to come up with a good feature story to boost our sales."

"Well, you clearly got what you wanted. The question is, are you going to write about it?"

"I don't even know if Kora's story is mine to tell. And I wouldn't want anyone to think I was taking advantage of a bad situation or using her tragedy to further my own career. Somehow it just doesn't feel right. Or at least right now while it's all so raw, it doesn't." I let my eyes run up Graham's chiseled forearm. "Anyway, thanks for suggesting we meet here."

"Sure. I love this place. Sometimes I like to come here and pray, work through whatever's going on in my head. There's just something about it here that makes me feel like I can handle anything that comes my way."

"Such the wise man, you are."

"Not really. I just try to pay attention a little bit as I go along. I've still got plenty to learn."

"Don't we all."

Graham chuckles but I can see his mind has switched gears. "So, tell me . . . are you over that guy you mentioned the other night at dinner?"

I look away. I do still think about Colin sometimes. I miss going to bars and dinners and movies with him. But now I wonder if what we had was really love . . . or if I was so determined to be with someone, I tried to turn our relationship into something it never had the strength to be.

"I think I'm over him," I finally say. "Why do you ask?"

"Because you're a great girl, and I'd like to get to know you better." He jiggles his leg nervously. "Would you maybe want to chill at my place later? Maybe grill out or something?"

Before I have a chance to think about it, I say, "Yeah, that would be nice."

I've never met a guy like Graham before. When I was sixteen, there was Drew, who was always forgetting his wallet when we'd go out. Then came Ben, a sensitive soul who always brought both Mom and me flowers, even though she'd always throw hers away the moment he strolled out the door. College boys were much the same. Travis, who went to school fifteen hours a week and lived off his parents' credit card. Sam, who could just smile and get anything he wanted. Scott, a pre-med student with a weakness in grammar, who was always talking me into writing research papers for him. And then Colin—the combination of every bad boy I'd ever dated rolled into one.

My phone rings and I grab it from my bag. I tilt the screen to show Graham who it is.

He scoots to the other side of the bench and raises his eyebrows. "Well, I guess she's ready to work through it."

My heart is racing when I answer.

"Emily, I got it," Mom says, breathless. "I got Eugene Hunter's address. Sadie was right. Apparently, he's still alive." She pauses for a few seconds and I reach for Graham's hand. "I was hoping . . . well, I was hoping you'd consider meeting me at his house right now."

chapter forty-nine

✤

PAM

Eugene Hunter lives in an older, upscale neighborhood with lots of pines and hardwoods. I arrive before Emily and park out on the street in front of his house. Although there's a black Volvo in the driveway, the blinds are closed, and it looks like the lights are off.

I study his brick ranch with green shutters and matching front door and try to decide whether or not he's the type of person who appreciates the things he's been given or if he takes them for granted. His grass has already gone dormant for the winter, and overgrown azaleas crowd the pine islands. The red-leafed bushes in front have a few sprigs out of place but are still in good shape, not leggy like his neighbor's. The water hose is tightly wound against the house, and the rusting door of his black mailbox is hanging open.

I recheck my watch and sigh. Emily should've been here five minutes ago. My lower back is aching so I step out to stretch, then grab the tape recorder from my purse and tuck it into my pocket just as Emily pulls up.

I zip up my jacket as a gust blows through and clutch my arms against my chest.

Emily strides up, giving the house a once-over, then turns to me. "So . . . what's your plan?"

I pause, knowing this whole thing is spontaneous and possibly a mistake. "I just need answers. After I left Sadie's, I called John and he says we've got a potential case."

"Wow, okay. So I guess we knock?"

"I guess so." We approach the door and I rap on it. The house remains silent as I tap my foot on the faded monogrammed doormat. I peek through the sidelight on the left. "I see a light on in there." I knock again, but still nothing. My chest feels tight, and I take a deep breath as I reach for the knob. It turns with a whiny creak.

Emily steps back and shakes her head. "No, Mom, we are *not* going in. I've already trespassed once this week, and it didn't turn out well."

I give her a confused, but stern look. "Don't be silly. I'm sure he's here. Why else would a car be in the driveway?"

"Fine. But for the record, I don't think this is a good idea."

I reach into my pocket and press the record button on my tape recorder. As I push the door open and step inside, I'm accosted by a horrid scent. It reminds me of that nursing home where John's mother is locked away—a peculiar combination of elderly funk mixed with urine, dust, and filth.

"Oh my God," Emily whispers loudly, covering her nose and mouth.

I urge her down the silver carpet through the entryway.

"Hello?" Emily calls out. We both survey the formal living room decorated with floral curtains and rose-colored velour furniture and exchange appalled glances. "Eugene, are you home?"

We pause for a moment and listen, but still nothing.

We continue walking into the kitchen. On the counter, speckled-brown bananas lie next to green-tinted potatoes that have started sprouting roots, and a bowl of soggy cornflakes with curdled milk sours the air. We follow the sound of a TV on low volume and discover it in the den off the kitchen. A couch draped with a quilt and pillow sit across from it, but no one is there.

Emily walks over to the bay window at the edge of the kitchen that looks out into the yard. "That must be him," she says, pointing.

Standing in the distance holding a rake is a small man, maybe 5'7" or so, with thinning white hair. His short-sleeve plaid button-up shirt is tucked into his baggy khaki pants. Heaps of leaves surround him, and he seems dismayed as the wind scatters them all over the yard.

"What do you think he's doing out there?" Emily asks. "He doesn't seem quite right."

I take a deep breath. "I don't know, but I'm ready to have a little chat with him."

I open the door, and he glances up. Squinting, he adjusts his glasses and waves the rake in the air. "Whatcha doing in my house? You better get out of here before I call the police!"

I step down off the deck as he takes a few steps closer. The rake slips out of his fingers and falls to the ground. His eyes are on Emily as we approach him.

"How'd you get here?" he asks her, confused. "I didn't do it, and you know it. Can't prove anything."

I study his deep wrinkles and notice white, wiry chest hair poking out of his shirt. A cut on his arm seeps blood. I also notice his golden brown eyes that are the same shade as mine.

"Are you Eugene Hunter?" I ask.

His mouth falls open, and the crease between his eyebrows

deepens. He takes a few steps back, mumbles something under his breath, then picks up his rake again.

I remain cool, calm, collected. "My name is Pam Sharp."

He squints again. "Who?"

I stand up straight. "I'm your daughter."

His eyes widen and splotches suddenly run up his neck. He undoes the top button of his shirt and begins clawing at the skin on his arms. "Daughter? I don't have a daughter. I . . . I . . . don't have any children. You don't know what you're talking about."

He turns back to Emily and studies her.

"She looks like her, doesn't she?" I say. "The woman you raped in 1960? Maybe you remember my mother's name—Kora Mitchell?" I point a crimson nail at Emily. "But she's not Kora. She's your granddaughter."

He starts mindlessly running the rake through the grass. "I didn't do it. Didn't do it. Didn't do it."

I march over to him and yank the rake out of his hands, tossing it to the ground.

"Get off my property, or I'll have you arrested!" He's angry but trembling as he stares me down.

"No, Eugene Hunter. *You* are the one who should be arrested. And don't you tell me what you're going to do! I'm not some woman locked away in an insane asylum with no rights. I'm the one calling the shots now, not you! Do you understand?"

His bottom lip quivers as he stares at me. Finally, barely over a whisper, he says, "So, you're the baby."

"Yes. All grown up now. Raised by a man who hated me for the crime that *you* committed. A man who spent every waking moment making sure I paid for the death of my mother."

Emily steps between Hunter and me. "Mom, none of this was ever your fault. When are you going to realize that? It wasn't then, and it's not now. Nothing you say or do to this man is ever going to change what happened."

Eugene looks back and forth at us, unsure of what to do.

"I knew I shouldn't have asked you to come," I snarl at Emily. "I knew it was a mistake."

Emily looks as if I've just slapped her. "I just wish you would've given us both a little time to process everything that's happened . . . some time to weigh our options and decide the best way to handle all this."

"Well, guess what? I'm out of time." I point to Eugene. "And he's sure as hell out of time. He's kept this secret for years, and he's finally going to pay for it. I don't care if it's the last thing I do, everyone will know what he did."

Eugene begins mumbling again. "Didn't do it. Didn't do it." Then he shuffles behind me and heads toward the house.

I start after him but Emily grabs my arm. "Let him go, Mom."

"And what? Give him a chance to call the police?"

"I doubt he'd do that when you've threatened to have him arrested. Just let him go."

I shake my arm from Emily's grip and shake my head.

"You know, Mom," Emily says with an edge in her voice, "it kills me how hypocritical you are about telling the truth."

My mouth drops open. "How dare you."

"What? You've spent a lifetime lying to me. You never told me anything about your childhood. You've refused to tell me what happened between you and Dad. And those are just the big things you've kept from me. I'm your daughter and I barely know anything about you."

"This is hardly the time or place to have this discussion, Emily. My biological father is in that house right now, and it's not your decision if I want to bring justice on him." I start to walk toward the deck then pivot back toward Emily, who's looking at me as if I've lost my mind.

"Fine. If it's so important to you to know what happened between your dad and me, I'll tell you. I cheated on him. And that's kind of a difficult thing to explain to your daughter. But yes, that's why he left. Big freaking deal. People cheat all the time."

Emily looks gobsmacked.

"Don't play dumb. If you think back to that day he left and read between the lines, I'm pretty sure you could have figured it out on your own. And as far as my mother, I told you—there was nothing to say about her. If Sadie would have been honest with me sooner, yes, I probably would have told you more."

Emily's face flushes. "All I know is you've been fighting this your whole life, and it hasn't gotten you anywhere. If Eugene goes to jail, what do you gain from that besides a lot of stress? I hate that all this happened just as much as you do. I hate that Hunter raped my grandmother. I hate that Kora was institutionalized for something that today would be easily treatable. But most of all, I hate you had to grow up without your mother and that I missed out on the opportunity to know an amazing woman." She motions toward the house. "But nothing we do today will change any of this. I think it's time you accept your past and leave it behind you. If you won't do it for yourself, then do it for me."

I see tears well up in Emily's eyes as she sweeps past me, clearly bent on leaving. When she reaches the side of the house, she abruptly turns around. "I'm spending the night with Sadie again tonight. In the morning, we're going to see where Kora's buried if you'd like to join us."

My shoulders fall. I want to tell her I'm sorry, to come back and let me give her a hug. I want to promise that I'll do better in being the mother she deserves. But the words stay trapped.

"Or don't come," Emily retorts. "At this point, I don't really care what you do."

chapter fifty

❦

EMILY

I make my way to the front of Eugene's house and sprint to my car. I can't help but wonder what he's thinking, or what Mom might do now that I've left her there with him, but Graham is expecting me. I send him a text letting him know I'm on my way over, and he quickly replies that he'll be outside on the back deck waiting for me.

My hands shake as I key Graham's address into my GPS. If Mom comes to her senses, she'll be leaving any minute, and I don't want to face her again right now. I have no idea if she's sorry or if she's mad at me. I just want to get to Graham's as soon as possible.

Graham lives a few blocks from downtown Sparrow on a street with cottage-style houses painted in monochromatic colors. The neighborhood has a calming effect on me: kids ride their bikes on the sidewalk, a boy plays fetch with his lab in the front yard, a husband and wife are having a cocktail on their porch.

I park in Graham's driveway and freshen up a little before I head to his backyard.

He's on the deck with a bottle of red wine, a platter of cheese and crackers, and a fire in the chiminea. A Kenny Chesney song is playing softly through an outdoor speaker mounted on the cedar railing. He glances up, smiling. "So, how did it go?"

I managed not to cry in front of Mom, but when I lock eyes with Graham, I lose it.

"Oh no . . . come here." He wraps his arms around me. "I'm sorry, Emily."

He lets me cry into his chest for a minute before he pulls me back and gently wipes my face. "I guess things didn't go well with your mom."

"No, it was terrible. The doctor's old, Graham. Really, really old . . . and he's senile, I think . . . but Mom's still being adamant about pressing charges."

Graham caresses my shoulder, then pulls me to his chest again.

I sniffle and force a smile, then abruptly change the subject, not wanting him to think I'm a drama queen. "I like your place."

He gives me a compassionate smile, seeming to read my motive. "Thanks. I usually rent an apartment, but it's always so noisy. I decided to go with something a little more private this go around." He pulls me away gently. "Would you like some wine?"

"Yeah, that'd be great."

He pops the cork from the bottle and pours us each a glass.

"Maybe this will help," he says, handing it to me.

Graham throws a couple pieces of wood on the fire and stokes it. I sit, smiling as I think of Kora and how she coped by burning her problems. *Maybe I should try that. I definitely have some I'd like to incinerate at the moment.* I also think of Erin; campfires remind me of her. I always looked forward to her autumn invitations to visit her family in Alabama. I remember watching her parents, fingers threaded together, the ease with which they laughed, the way her dad would play songs on the guitar that her mom knew every word to, and how their eyes would connect every once in a while, as if nothing could tear them apart. Those nights always left me with a yearning to have a normal family with parents who still loved each other.

Graham sits across from me and leans in. "What are you thinking about?"

"How do you know I'm thinking?"

"Because I pay attention. Your eyebrows—they move when you're deep in thought."

"They do? No one's ever told me that before."

He smirks self-assuredly. "Well, it's a fact."

I take a sip of wine. "Just thinking about my friend Erin."

"Oh right . . . the one with the baby."

"Yeah. She's been back at work for a couple months now."

"That's got to be hard. How about you—do you see yourself with kids one day?"

"I think so, but Erin's got me second-guessing myself. Maybe there's a reason I haven't found the right guy yet. Sometimes I think I might be better off by myself." I set my glass down and tap my finger against the stem. "How about you? Do you want children?"

"Oh yeah, for sure." He pops a piece of cheese into his mouth and chases it with wine. "So, why do you think you're better off by yourself? You're a smart, pretty girl. You could have any guy you want."

I eke out a half laugh. "That's very sweet of you to say, but I'm not exactly the best relationship material. Who knows, maybe I get it from Kora and my mom . . . but when it comes to guys, I typically make bad decisions."

"That surprises me. Why do you say that?"

"I don't know. Somehow I always wind up with the guys who'd rather party than get married and settle down."

"But you don't stay with them. That says something."

I look pensively into the fire. "I guess I owe that to my mom. She's insanely independent. She's hated every guy I've dated, but you're right, I do come through for her in the end."

"You mean you break up with the guy?"

I laugh. "Exactly."

Graham swirls the wine in his glass. "I think you just haven't met the right person yet. I've had my fair share of failed relationships too. I'm actually divorced."

"Really?"

"Yeah, we got married our senior year in college, and once we started our careers, we grew into two different people. I learned a lot from that relationship, though. Now I really think I know what kind of girl I want to spend the rest of my life with."

"Sounds like my mom. She's with someone now who's the polar opposite of my dad."

"Interesting." Graham slides a piece of cheese onto a cracker. "How did you leave it with her today?"

I roll my eyes. "We got in this huge fight and all this pent-up frustration came spewing out. I mean, she's condemning everyone for keeping secrets, and yet she has plenty of her own . . . like she finally broke down and admitted that the reason she and my dad got a divorce was because she was having an affair. I think that's really what pushed me over the edge."

"You never knew?"

"No, I knew there was a big fight. I was there for that. There was a lot of screaming, and I remember my dad saying she was crazy and that he hated her. Then he stormed out and slammed the door so hard a picture fell off the wall, and that was it. Everything in my life was fine one day and then completely demolished the next. He must've packed up his things when I was at school because two weeks later, he called and said he had moved to New York."

"Wow, that must've been really hard. Do you ever see him?"

"No, I've only seen him once since I turned eighteen."

"Too bad someone would take being a father for granted like that. I'm guessing you'll probably be more appreciative once you get in a healthy relationship because of how you were raised."

"You think?"

"Well, yeah. Divorce is a lot like death. It's very humbling. It gives you a perspective on relationships that other people don't have."

I pair a cracker with some cheese. "Did you know that fifty percent of marriages end in divorce?"

He squints at me. "Yes . . . a statistic that I think scares a lot of people out of saying 'I do.'"

"I know, right?" I take a bite, cradling the crumbs. "I think deep down I'm a dreamer, though. I may get pessimistic sometimes, but I still want the happily ever after."

"I know what you mean. When I got married, I had this master plan for my life. But nothing worked out the way it was supposed to, and I've learned to be okay with that. Trials can strengthen our faith and make us better people if we let them."

"I've never been to church," I blurt out. "My mom never took me, which is interesting to me because Sadie seems so religious. You'd think if my mom grew up going to church, she would've at least discussed the concept of God with me. But I guess like everything else in our relationship, she never got around to it."

"The only reason I went to church was because of my aunt. Once my dad passed, she stepped in and got me through it. My mom was usually working on Sundays, and my aunt helped silence the what-ifs that were eating me up."

"What do you mean?"

His jaw tightens. "Like what if my dad lost those extra fifty pounds the doctors were always hounding him about. What if he took his blood pressure medicine? What if I minded better when I was a kid and didn't stress him out so much? What if we all did everything we were supposed to and because of that, he was still alive?" He turns to me. "But . . . losing my dad taught me the answers to those questions don't really matter. All we can do is accept that some things in life are out of our control, and there's nothing we can do about it except to pray and show appreciation for what we *do* have."

Graham's words strike a chord with me. Haven't my own what-ifs been wreaking havoc on my life? *What if I met the right guy? What's going to happen if I don't? What if I'm trapped in my dead-end job forever? What if I could change Colin? What if Mom and Dad never got a divorce?* I've spent all this time and energy worrying and expecting certain outcomes, and all it's resulted in is disappointment.

The fire pops, and Graham throws another piece of wood on. The sun's starting to go down, and I tip my glass to get the last swallow before getting up to warm my hands near the flames.

"Our twenties are supposed to be the best time of our life," I finally say. "Sometimes it hardly feels that way, though. There are just so many things to navigate through, so many things to figure out . . . so much pressure to start the rest of your life and make the right choices."

"Yeah, but it's not all bad. Tonight's good, right?"

He puts his arm around me and I rest my head on his chest. I close my eyes and breathe him in—the musky scent of the fire mixed with cologne and red wine. I think about how I've always felt guarded around guys. I could reveal my top layer and maybe even the next one after that, but I've never allowed a man to know my heart before. The problem is, I don't even know how to do this . . . have real love, a healthy relationship, everything else that comes with it.

Graham faces me and strokes my cheek, staring deep into my eyes like he gets what I'm thinking even though I haven't said a word. Then he leans down and kisses me. His lips are moist, warm, hungry for me. My heart races as my breath catches in my chest.

Warmth floods through me and all the screaming thoughts that have been distracting me lately disappear.

All I see, feel, and hear is Graham.

The man quite possibly sent here to save me from myself.

chapter fifty-one

🦋

PAM

After I left Eugene Hunter's house, I checked into the Best Western in downtown Sparrow. I just didn't feel like I was in the right frame of mind for a two-hour drive back to Baxter.

Maybe Emily is right. Perhaps I do need some time to think about all this. Time to think about where I go from here, and time to really accept the fact that the man who raised me is not who I thought he was.

Kicking off my shoes, I plop down on the bed in front of the television set and turn it to a Lifetime movie. It's already midway through, so I have no idea what it's about. It quickly fades to background noise as I think about the drama of my own movie running through my head. Even though I don't regret what I did today, it still feels like I've made a complete mess out of everything. And for the first time, I question if pressing charges against Eugene Hunter *is* the best choice.

My chest feels tight, and I stretch my arms over my head. I switch off the TV and sit in silence, hoping that the answers I so desperately need will present themselves. I've essentially given up on religion over the years, but every now and then, I utter a prayer. I clasp my hands together, but the words don't come. I sigh with annoyance in case God is up there listening.

My mind drifts to my mother, to the events leading to her

commitment, her death. All I know about electroshock are depictions I've seen in movies, which are likely overdramatized. But regardless of the physical pain she endured, I can't imagine what it must have felt like to be forced into having a treatment she didn't want or need—and worse, to have her fate ultimately determined by two psychotic men.

I've read a few cases online about healthcare freedom. A husband who tried to force his wife, the mother of his two children, to have chemo and radiation even though she wanted to seek a natural alternative. Parents who lost custody of their daughter with autism because they refused to give her the treatment the hospital recommended. A group of mothers and fathers who sued the state of California for the freedom not to vaccinate their children due to their personal and religious beliefs. But I never hear about similar cases regarding mental health. Surely they exist, but I'm guessing we rarely hear about them because the victim is too mentally unstable to be trusted, or listened to, or taken seriously. I'm suddenly curious if people with mental illness are still, even today, denied some of their basic, fundamental human rights.

My hands tremble as my crossed leg swings back and forth. My chest still aches, so I stand up to stretch some more. I tilt my head from side to side, extend my arms in front of me, squeeze my shoulders.

John's always teasing me about my nervous habits. If he were here right now, he'd be sitting in bed with the pillows propped behind him and his eyebrows perched in amusement. And insisting that although this is a serious matter, I'm getting myself far too worked up.

I realize now that I miss him.

I grab my cell and call. When he answers on the first ring, I bite my lip, hoping I'm not on speakerphone with his kids in the car.

"Are you back yet?" I ask as cheerfully as possible.

"Yeah, perfect timing, I just dropped the kids off. Did you and Emily go over to that doctor's house today?"

I take a deep breath. "Yeah. He's still alive, although he seems a little out of it. Emily met me there, but we had a terrible argument. I want to press charges, but she thinks it's stupid. I don't know, it's a mess. All of it. And then to top it all off, Sadie wants to show us where my mother is buried tomorrow morning." I start to pace in the cramped hotel room.

"Well, if you go tomorrow, it'd probably give you closure. What's Emily's reasoning for not pressing charges?"

"She thinks Eugene is too old. She says she doesn't see what the point is."

He snickers. "And you don't get that? Pam, I love you, and I don't want you to get mad at me for saying this, but I want to make sure you're really clear about why you want to do this. Is it truthfully because you're seeking justice, or is it because you think punishing this doctor is somehow magically going to solve all your problems?"

I take a minute to genuinely consider what he's just said. "I *do* want to punish him for robbing me of a mother. And call me crazy, but I also think he should pay for raping and essentially killing someone." I stop mid-stride. "Why do you never take my side on anything?"

"I'm not taking *sides*. I see no problem making this man pay for what he did. I just want you to make the right decision. And anyway, Pam, we're in a relationship. It's okay if I disagree with you every once in a while." A siren blares past him, and he pauses for a moment. "Why don't I come there right now. We can have dinner, discuss the pros and cons. I can even go with you in the morning to the cemetery if you'd like."

"No . . . no, John. I think I just need to work this out myself. This is my battle to fight, not yours."

"But don't you see, Pam? You don't have to fight for everything that's wrong in this world. Sometimes shitty things happen to us, and we're free to just accept it and move on."

My frustration builds as I scratch the polish from my thumbnail. "Maybe *you and I* should just move on," I say.

"Wow. That's subtle."

"I'm sorry. I just . . . I just don't know if you can ever be the man I need you to be."

"And who's that? Because I'd really like to know."

"Look, I don't know what I want. I just know I'm tired of pretending like I'm happy with you when I'm not."

The line falls silent.

"Well, okay then," John finally says. "I can agree with you that we're not as happy as we used to be. So maybe it does make sense for us to take a break for a while."

"I couldn't agree with you more."

John is clearly done with the conversation and says a curt goodbye.

I stare at the screen of my cell. I've always feared I would lose John, but I didn't think it would ever really happen. Who could blame him, though, for not wanting to stick around when I'm so difficult sometimes? What do I expect when I reel him in when I need him and push him away when I don't?

The tightness in my chest throbs as I reflect on how many times I've witnessed how stubborn people can be regarding their opinions. When they believe something strongly enough, they can't be talked out of it because they believe wholeheartedly that they are correct. But an opinion is just that—an opinion—choices and beliefs based upon our past experiences, morals, and preferences.

Maybe John and Emily disagree with me, but I'm going to fight for what I believe in, just like I always have. Only now I know it's not only because I'm a lawyer who's made a career out of standing up for what's right, but because I am my mother's daughter.

❦

chapter fifty-two

EMILY

I toss and turn under the quilt of Sadie's guest bed, staring into the darkness. Even though I have plenty of other things on my mind right now, I can't stop thinking about Graham. How I felt when he kissed me, the easy way our conversation flows, the chills that go through my body when our arms touch. But even though things between us are better than any connection I've ever had with a guy, fear still hovers over me and makes me question everything.

Could we really make a long-distance relationship work?

What if he doesn't like me once he gets to know the "real" me?

What if he's tempted to cheat on me if we're not able to see each other that often?

What if my heart gets broken again?

Eventually, my body relaxes and I fall asleep, but I have short, vivid, violent dreams. Colin taking me to a secluded cabin in the woods and holding me against my will. Riding a roller coaster with Mom and getting stuck right before it barrels down a hill that disappears into the clouds. Free-falling, then running through a cemetery, yelling Kora's name into a dense forest.

It is pitch-black, and I can't see where I'm going; if there's a moon out, the canopy of trees above me is blocking the light. Suddenly, I hear panting and growling and turn to find a pack of coyotes with glowing green eyes behind me, exposing their teeth. I twist around and try to run, but a set of claws plunges into my back and I lunge forward and fall—down, down, into a black abyss until I thud against the ground. I immediately panic. *No one's ever going to be able to find me down here. What if I never see Graham, my mom, or Erin again? What if Graham falls in love with someone else?*

The coyotes continue to prowl above me as if they're trying to figure out the best way to get to me. Dirt crumbles down and splatters around me. Then something sharp jabs into my thigh and blood soaks through my jeans. When I look down, I see a numbered metal post wedged into my leg. *A patient's burial marker?* I take a deep breath, steady my hand, and pull it out in one swift motion. Pain sears through my leg and more blood pours out. The coyotes lift their noses into the air and begin howling. I try to stand, but my leg is numb and collapses underneath me.

I scream in desperation. "Help! Kora! Mom! Help me!" My heart races and I swallow hard as I listen carefully for a response.

Instead, a lustrous white light appears above me and I shield my face with my hand. Someone is beside me, and even though I can't make out the details of the woman's face, I know from the silhouette that it's my grandmother.

She reaches out and takes my hand into hers. "Don't worry, I've got you, sweet girl. There's nothing to be afraid of now." I blink slowly, taking in her beauty. The coyotes yelp then run away.

"Do you want it?" she asks.

"What?" I whisper.

"Courage . . . courage to go after anything you want in this life. The confidence to believe in yourself. And faith to over-come the fears that prevent you from being all that you were created to be." She reaches down and places her hand on my heart. "It begins here." I smile and lay my hand over hers as love radiates through me. Even though there is so much I want to say to her, all I'm able to do is nod. Kora extends her hands into the sky. "Oh, Lord, hear her plea for help!" Her voice echoes into the forest, then she disappears into the night.

I wake with a gasp and am confused by the light in the room. *Is she still here?* Then I realize that between the gap of the blind and the window, a full moon is brightening the darkness. I close my eyes and let the beams shine on my face as an over-whelming sense of peace floods through me. Seconds later, I fall into a deep sleep.

chapter fifty-three

✠

PAM

I've decided to visit Mother's grave, not because I want to, but because it's the right thing to do.

When I arrive at the cemetery, it's eerie but beautiful. Rows of numbered posts are perfectly positioned just a few feet apart from one another like dominoes. Scattered around them are more of the same posts, along with traditional headstones that have weathered and turned black with age. The sun shines in streaks through the bare hardwoods and lands on a statue of an angel that guards the cemetery like a poised ballerina. One of her arms is stretched upward, and her body is elongated, graceful as if she could take flight at any moment.

Sadie's SUV is parked in the grass, and she and Emily are standing side by side waiting for me. I park and walk toward them.

"Am I the only one who feels hollow right now?" I say.

Emily gives me a look that says, *Good morning to you, too.*

"Well," Sadie says, "I'm used to coming here. But I can understand why you might feel uncomfortable."

I point to an area close by. "Why are the posts in that spot so close together?"

"No one's actually buried right there. But it makes quite the statement, doesn't it?" Sadie shades her eyes with her hand. "A while back, landscapers found gobs of those posts pulled up and scattered through the woods. And then about ten years ago, a group was formed to restore the cemetery, and they decided to create this memorial with some of them."

"So, why do some have names and dates on them like a regular headstone?"

Sadie shrugs. "I don't know. I guess sometimes the family would pay for an upgrade, or maybe it was replaced later."

"How many people are here?" Emily asks in a soft voice.

"I believe around twenty thousand. But all the bodies aren't here. There are other cemeteries on the property . . . they're just not as easy to get to, and they haven't been maintained." Sadie hesitates for a moment and glances between Emily and me. "You ready to do this?"

We both nod and step aside to let Sadie lead the way. I can tell Emily's not sure how to read my mood after our fight yesterday, so she keeps to herself as Sadie takes us into the woods and down a path that's overgrown with weeds, vines, and saplings.

"It was misting the day we buried Kora," she says, looking over her shoulder toward us. "I kept my head down as I followed behind her parents, the preacher, and the six male patients who were carrying her coffin. There were puddles, mud, and fallen branches everywhere. I was glad we were granted a reprieve from the weather for an hour or so because it had been storming off and on for two days while Kora had been at the hospital mortuary."

Sadie stops for a breather.

"Are you okay?" Emily asks. "We can take a break if you need to."

"No, I just need a minute or so to catch my breath. Don't you girls worry about me. I might be old, but I can still run circles around those young girls at the clinic. Besides, we don't have too much farther to go."

We hike in silence until we finally reach a clearing in the woods. Sadie points to a marker that's off by itself: number 1583. Within acres of pines and bare oaks, the post sits next to a tall, healthy evergreen. "There she is. That's where Kora is buried."

Emily and I trudge ahead of her and stop at the rusted, metal post. A chill sweeps through me. "So, this is how the state chose to dispose of their property. Jesus, most pets nowadays are treated better than this." I cross my arms. "My poor mother."

Sadie sidles up and puts her arm around me. "The patients dug her grave that morning. The dirt was still fresh, not too muddy. It was a simple service. The preacher from the Baptist church in town read the twenty-third Psalm, and then he placed his hand on her coffin and said a short prayer. Then he promised us that she was in a better place and could finally rest in peace."

I feel my hands tremble and ball them into fists.

"I'm sorry, Pam. For everything," Sadie says. "If I could've changed what happened to your mother or prevented it from happening, I would have . . . surely you understand that."

Sadie's words sting, but I allow my heart to fill with compassion. I nod, knowing she's right.

"And even though I've chosen to remain optimistic over the years, that doesn't mean I truly understand why Kora had to suffer like she did . . . why all this turned out like it did. I've had to go through my own evolution of acceptance—not only for what happened to Kora, but also, for the role I played in her death. I've learned how to love myself unconditionally. But I had to get to the root of that trauma, look it straight in the face . . . feel it, accept it, and then heal and move forward."

Emily squats and runs her finger over the engraved numbers. Then she starts pulling up the weeds around Mother's grave and smoothing out the pine needles with her sneaker.

"Were you with her when she passed?" I ask. "She must've been absolutely terrified."

"Yes, I was holding her hand. Right when I got word of what had happened, I rushed to the hospital. But I want you to know, Pam, that despite everything that happened to your mother, you gave her purpose and courage. Once she got pregnant, she knew she needed a career that would allow her to be independent so she could leave Daniel. She could either give up or fight for what she wanted. And once she settled into that warrior mentality, she said she felt more alive than she had in years. She may have lived within the confines of Hamilton Meadow, but inside she was finally free. All of that to say, I think when she passed, you can have peace that she had no regrets."

Emily stands and wraps her arms around Sadie.

"I know Kora sure would be proud of both of you." Sadie squeezes Emily with one arm and reaches out for my hand with the other. "In your own way, you're getting to do everything she ever dreamed of. I believe the brain is hardwired when we're born to guide our heart and soul to fulfill our purpose in life. Sometimes we fight it, or we don't see it because our past traumas have hidden the truth, but the intelligence is there . . . we've just got to get out of the way and let nature do its job."

I think about that for a moment, wishing I knew where I was being guided and hoping for a fresh perspective that would allow me to see things differently.

"You know," Sadie continues, "the three generations of women in your family remind me of the journey monarch butterflies make each year. They travel from Canada to Mexico in the winter—a 2,500-mile trek—and then back again in the spring. The distance alone is impressive, but the real miracle is that except for the generation that hibernates, the monarch's average life span is only three to four weeks. So, as one generation dies, another is born and comes into this world knowing exactly which direction to fly to ensure they ultimately reach safety."

"Wow," Emily says.

Sadie nods. "Amazing, right? And I think it's because they innately know their species is beautiful, talented, and intelligent. And without each one of them doing their part, they would become extinct."

"And they end up in the same places every spring and fall?" I ask.

"Yes. The monarchs are gifted with a keen sense of direction and instinct, but scientists also think they may possess genetic memories of their ancestors. They know which way to travel because maybe in some sense, they've already made the journey." Sadie shrugs. "Like you girls. You've never met Kora, and yet I can see so much of her in both of you. You may feel lost at times, but I know you're right where you're supposed to be."

Sadie's words land on me like a balm, and suddenly, all the anger and frustration that's been brewing inside my body fades away. I reach out for Emily's hand and she tentatively places it in mine.

Sadie takes a few steps back and faces both of us. "I'm glad to see you two making up."

"Truce?" I ask Emily, and she nods gently.

"Good." Sadie's eyes dart between us. "Because I need to tell y'all . . . yesterday I called an old friend I used to work with at the hospital. I wanted to see if she knew anything about Dr. Hunter. She said she didn't know him and his wife very well, but they did go to the same church for a while. Apparently, when his wife died a few years ago, his mind started getting bad. And now he's been diagnosed with Alzheimer's." Sadie turns to me. "His daughter is putting him in an assisted living facility this week."

Emily grimaces. "Daughter? But he said he didn't have any children."

"With Alzheimer's, short-term memories go first. Things like what you ate for breakfast, appointments, recent conversations. Long-term memories—like what he did to Kora—are harder to forget because over time, they've been replayed in the brain over and over again and a strong emotional attachment has been formed. But even still, people can forget their own children. It's heartbreaking."

I gape audibly. "I can't believe this is happening."

"Well, if it's any consolation, if you decide to let this go, Dr. Hunter is already serving a life sentence. Usually, our brain buries the past so we can psychologically survive. But for him, the guilt, pain, and fear from sixty years ago is likely just as vivid today as it was back then. In fact, probably more so. And to be honest, I don't even know if he'd be able to mentally comprehend a prison sentence if he's as bad off as they say he is."

I feel my eyes well with tears, and I can't stop them when they start to fall.

I let go of Emily's hand and Sadie hugs me. "For what it's worth," she whispers into my ear, "I don't think Kora would have wanted you to press charges against Dr. Hunter all these years later. I think she would want you to take all those fragmented pieces of your soul and mend it back together . . . move on with your life and be happy. And I also think before you can forgive him for what he did to your mother, you first have to forgive yourself."

"For what?" I squeak out between sobs. "I didn't do anything wrong."

"You're right, you didn't. You were lied to and manipulated. You were raised with a preconceived notion that your mother was sick, taken away from you, and that it was all your fault. And that misconception doesn't just go away overnight. You need to forgive yourself for a tragedy you never had anything to do with. Forgive yourself for not asking more questions . . . for trusting your father and even for trusting me. You couldn't have known any better. It was *our fault*, not yours." She holds me at arm's length and looks into my eyes. "You've got decades worth of anger you think you can get rid of by prosecuting a ninety-year-old man who made a horrible mistake sixty years ago. I get it, Pam. If anyone knows how deeply he hurt your mother, it's me. But I just don't see where it gets anyone at this point. You've spent your entire life letting this eat you up. And now, you finally have the opportunity to be free."

Sadie pulls a tissue from her pocket and hands it to me. I wipe my face then slide my sunglasses back on. "I know you're right. I just need some time to process all of this."

Sadie nods and pats my shoulder. "I know."

I turn and start back toward my car, hoping they both understand why I feel the need for space. As I make my way through the woods, I feel a glimmer of hope that I can indeed release the guilt, anger, resentment, and hurt I've been harboring all these years. I know it's complicated to be a mother, and I can't imagine how arduous it was for mine. For so long, I was angry at her for deserting me, but she didn't deserve that. I understand now she was just doing the best she could at the time.

And I guess, for that matter, so was Sadie.

❧

chapter fifty-four

EMILY

As I drive to meet Graham, I think about the conversation at the cemetery, and how I, too, have stifling emotions that need to be set free. Resentment toward Mom for always being so caught up in her career; Erin for getting the job I wanted; Colin for his flirtatious, self-centered behavior. But the day Dad walked out on us planted a pretty robust seed. I haven't given it much thought over the years, but now I can see how it impacted my life, the decisions I've made, and maybe even my self-worth.

I'm passing by the old hospital mortuary when Erin's name appears on my phone.

"Hey, what's up? I was going to call today to check on you."

"Well, Sophie's feeling better. She did have an ear infection, but Michael's leery about giving her antibiotics, so he wanted to see if it would clear up on its own. It hasn't been a fun experience, but I think she's on the mend now." She sighs. "But anyway . . . I'm calling to let you know I turned in my two weeks' notice on Friday. I assume Bernadette's going to offer you my job, so I just wanted to give you a heads up."

"Really? Are you sure that's what you want to do?"

"All I know is I need some time to figure out what's important to me and what *truly* makes me happy. Because honestly, I don't have any clue what that is anymore. Nothing is turning out like I thought it would. I hate to admit it, Emily, but I'm miserable. I'm doing good each day if I've showered and have clean clothes on."

"Maybe you have postpartum. Have you talked to Michael about it?"

"No, but I've had friends with postpartum. I don't think it's that. I just think I'm trying to do too much. I feel a lot better now that I've gotten some rest. And you know how on top of things my mom is. She's not going to let anything bad happen to me."

I smile. "I'm sure she's worried about you."

"Yeah, it can get kind of annoying at times, but I know she means well." I hear Sophie babbling in the background. "What about your mom? Did she decide to sign that court order? Were you able to find out anything about your grandmother?"

I sigh. "It's a long story. I'll have to fill you in later when I get back home. But long story short, I'm still in Sparrow and Mom is here too. Right now, I'm driving to say goodbye to the *most* amazing guy I've ever met."

"Oh no . . . does it have to be goodbye?"

"I don't know if I can see a long-distance thing happening. I'll tell you about it later."

"Well, either way, I'm so stinking jealous. You have nothing to tie you down and no one to answer to. You are free, my friend."

"You know what's funny? I've been envious of you for years. But I guess no one's life is perfect."

"Envious of *me*?" She laughs. "I've had enough challenges this year to last me a lifetime."

I pull into the parking space in front of the administrative building. Graham is lying on a blanket in the grass, and the stray dog I saw earlier this week is by the trashcans, nose buried in a metal bowl, inhaling food that someone must have left for him.

"The thing is, Erin . . . it's kind of surreal because in a weird way, I feel like I'm finally getting everything I've ever wanted . . . or that I will when the time is right."

"Well, if you finally stumble on what you're looking for, don't let it go. Just follow your heart. You'll figure it out."

"Thanks, Erin. I don't know what I'd do without you. I hope you follow that same advice."

"Aww, thanks. Call me as soon as you get back, okay? I want to hear every last juicy detail."

After we say our goodbyes, I jump out of the car and jog down to meet Graham.

"Hey you," he says. He puts his book down and stretches out his arm. "I saved a spot for you."

"Thanks." I lie down next to him and inhale the sweet scent of his leather jacket.

"I guess things went well this morning?"

I close my eyes and revel in the warmth of the sun on my face. "Yeah. It was nice to see where Kora was buried, and Mom came too. I think it was good for her. She was pretty quiet, but I think maybe she was feeling better when she left."

He leans his head against mine. "I can't wait to meet this mom of yours."

"Really?"

"Yeah. I said I wanted to get to know you better, and your mom is a part of your life, so of course I want to meet her."

"But what about the fact that I live in Baxter and you live here? Don't you think it would to be hard for us to keep in touch?"

"When I finish up with this job, I could quit working for Cash. I have a business degree plus some experience now, so I can do pretty much anything I want."

"Where would you live?"

"Anywhere." He shrugs then laughs. "I actually like it here." He props himself on one elbow and gazes at me. "Do you? Maybe we could both live in Sparrow."

"And what would I do here?"

"I don't know. Freelance, maybe? Or, I think the city has a local magazine similar to *Southern Speaks.* I know for sure they have a newspaper."

I give him a slight smile. "Right before I got here, Erin called and said she's not going to be working for the magazine anymore. So chances are they're going to offer me her job. It's what I've always wanted."

A serious look spreads across his face. "I guess it would make sense for you to stay in Baxter then."

"Who knows," I groan, "I'm so confused. I never dreamed in a million years she'd quit."

Graham gives me a deep look. "You know what you want. All you have to do is make up your mind and go after it." He swipes a strand of hair from my forehead. "You know, last night after you left, I read some of your work online. You're really talented, Emily. You could get a job doing anything you want. Don't feel like you have to settle at *Southern Speaks.*"

"You make it sound so simple."

"I think it could be." He leans in and brushes his lips against my hair. Then he finds my mouth and we share a passionate kiss.

We lie for a few silent minutes in each other's arms, and I can't help but wonder if we could make things work out.

Finally, I sit up. "This is so hard . . . but I need to get back home. I have a lot to do before tomorrow morning. And definitely a lot to think about."

"I get it." He stands and helps me up. "You all packed and ready to go?"

"Yeah, my bag's in the car." He skims his fingertips along my back as I secretly yearn for him not to let me go.

Tell me to quit my job.

Beg me to stay for another night.

Ask me out to dinner, or watch a movie, or go for a walk around the city.

Do anything, as long as we're together.

"I'd like for us to at least keep in touch," he says as he pulls away from me.

"I'd like that too."

We hold hands as we silently make our way up the hill toward our cars. When we get to the top, I bury my face in his shirt. What I feel inside is clear, I just can't make the words come out of my mouth. Graham seems to be everything I've ever wanted in a man, and I can't bear the thought of getting in my car and never seeing him again.

"I don't want to leave you," I say.

"Then, *don't*." He tilts my chin up and caresses my cheek. "I want to be with you, and I don't care where we live or what we do for jobs. I know we haven't known each other very long, but I definitely think we should give things a try."

"You make it sound so easy."

He smiles. "It *can* be easy. And in case you haven't figured it out yet, I'm falling for you."

"Really?"

"Yes, really." He playfully rolls his eyes. "I love everything about you. The way your eyebrows dance when you're deep in thought. The way you're scared to death to allow yourself to fall in love. Your inquisitive nature. Your ambition. But mostly, I love how I feel when I'm with you. And even though it's early, I believe what we have is worth taking a chance on."

Boys have declared their love to me before, but no one's ever told me why so effortlessly, so thoughtfully, so true. I can't ignore the way Graham makes me believe in love, real love, and the way he makes me feel fearless. I think for a moment about Kora—her strength, her talent, her beauty—and how she rose from a pit of despair and strove to create a better life for herself. I also think of Mom and what a powerhouse she is. How she created a life so dramatically different from the one she had as a child. And Sadie, with her morals, confidence, and independence—the sacrifices she made so that Mom and her sisters could have a better life. I feel so blessed that these women have molded me into the woman I am today.

I rest my forehead against Graham's. "I think I'm falling for you too," I whisper.

"Does this mean we're gonna try and make this work?"

I slowly nod as tears fill my eyes.

Graham wraps his arms around me. As our lips come together, my body melts against his, and I know I'm exactly where I was always meant to be. I just needed Kora to show me the way.

chapter fifty-five

✦

PAM

One Week Later

Motives for the bad decisions people make have always intrigued me. Sure, some people are malicious—as if their heart has been carved out with a sharp knife, and they only feel satisfied when they're torturing another human. But that's almost always because they've been traumatized or deeply hurt themselves. We all tend to judge situations and make decisions based on how we were raised or on past experiences.

When I think of it this way, I can't help but wonder: if we knew what actually drove people's motives, would it be easier to have compassion, forgive, and to move on with our lives? Would we be less likely to jump to conclusions? And furthermore, if we take into consideration the reasoning for our own belief systems and thought patterns, as adults can we reevaluate these habits, determine what our own truth is, and possibly forge a new path?

This epiphany shifts something in me and I realize I'm finally done being a victim of my circumstances. I'll never know why Eugene Hunter raped my mother or why that particular vile act is what sparked me into existence. Maybe Dr. Hunter had his own demons he was fighting. Maybe he was abused as a child, or maybe he grew up seeing his father abuse his mother. Perhaps he allowed the destructive and powerful nature of fear, manipulation, and greed to hijack his soul.

And Sadie . . . even though at first I felt like she betrayed me, I have a better understanding now of why she took the path she did when I take her motive into consideration. She didn't make the decision to keep a secret from me because her heart is flawed; she did it because she felt she was doing the right thing. And do I really have the right to hold that against her? Especially when I, too, have made a lifetime of bad choices? Is it fair to disregard all the nurturing, selfless acts she did for me over the years?

Even Dad had a motive for mistreating me. Regardless of the circumstances surrounding my conception, I'm sure it killed him having a child under the same roof who wasn't a Mitchell—a little girl who was a daily reminder of all the tragedies that followed baby Violet's death. Perhaps he thought by instilling fear in me, I'd be more easily controlled, and therefore I'd never question the story he fed me. Maybe he was grieving in his own way. And if I'm giving him the benefit of the doubt, maybe in the beginning he was genuinely trying to protect Ivy and Fern by shipping Mother to Sparrow.

This week, I've come to accept that our past experiences transform us into the people we become, but ultimately, we have the freedom to make our own choices moving forward. And for me, it starts with putting my past behind me and not filing charges against Dr. Hunter. I might even try to reach out to his daughter—my half-sister—and see if she's willing to get to know each other.

I've also rethought my relationship with John. When I got back from Sparrow last Sunday, I drove straight to his house and professed my love to him. I'm not sure what exactly made me realize it, but in that moment I knew we were meant to be together, and I begged him to forgive me and promised to change my ways. I didn't know if he'd be willing to give me yet another chance, but shockingly enough, he said he still loved me.

John is asleep on my couch right now with the newspaper resting on his chest. My heart swells when I look at him, when I think of how he's stood by me when he could have easily given up and moved on.

My phone rings and I grab it quickly, hopeful it doesn't wake him. "Hey, Mom," Emily says. "Graham and I are about to head over. Are you sure you don't need me to bring anything?"

"Nope, I've got it all taken care of." I cradle the phone with my neck as I grab a potholder and take the spinach dip out of the oven. "I can't wait to see you. I know it's only been a week since we left Sparrow, but it seems like forever, doesn't it?"

"I know. I can't wait for you to meet Graham."

"I'm looking forward to meeting him too. It'll be nice to put a face with a name."

Emily pauses. "You know, Mom . . . I've always had a plan, but right now I'm just kind of going with the flow."

"Well, that's good."

"Really? You think that's a *good* thing?"

"I do. You're like me, you listen to your head far too much, and sometimes that can get in the way. Don't worry, you'll figure it out. What does your gut tell you to do?"

"To find a writing job that's a better fit for me and to give Graham a chance."

"Well, there's your answer. Don't make it more complicated than it is."

Emily is silent and I imagine my words rolling around in her mind. Before she can say anything, though, I feel my heart open to her too.

"I haven't told you yet . . . but I'm so proud of you for doing all of this . . . for pushing me out of my comfort zone and encouraging me to dig deeper for information about my mother. And I'm grateful you didn't give up on me. I know you were pretty upset with me."

"It's okay. I'm just glad you got the answers you needed," Emily says.

"You want to know something else? I understand what Sadie meant when she said I changed my mother. Because from the moment you were born, you have slowly but surely been changing me for the better. And honestly, if it wasn't for you, I'm not sure where I'd be right now. So, thank you."

The line falls silent again and Emily sniffles. "Thanks for saying that, Mom, but I really didn't do anything special."

"Yes, you did. If it wasn't for your courage to do what I never had the guts to, I never would have known what an incredible mother I had. I would have never known I have a half-sister. And the man who raped my mother would've left this earth without anyone ever confronting him about what he did."

"Well, I'm glad it all worked out. But actually, the truth of the matter is, I was just looking for a racy ghost story for the magazine." Emily laughs.

"Well, you are my mother's granddaughter. I guess now we know where you get that feisty journalistic spirit."

"I guess so."

"And Emily . . . I know I don't say it enough . . . but I love you, and I'm so very proud of the woman you've become."

"I love you too, Mom."

"See you soon."

After we hang up, I stare at the box on the table. The judge signed off quickly on the court order and I was able to request Mother's medical records, but yesterday Hamilton Meadow called and said they were unavailable. Over the years they must have either been misplaced, damaged, or thrown away.

But I ended up getting a better surprise.

I open the flaps of the box and am overwhelmed by the sight of my mother's things. This is the same box I found that day in Dad's shed all those years ago. With all the commotion last weekend, I never got around to asking Sadie what happened to it. But after I left Dad's, Ivy discovered it in the crawl space underneath the house. We decided our grandmother—Kora's mother—must have hidden it there at some point. Ivy shipped it to me, and it just came this morning.

As I run my fingertips along Mother's cool polyester blouses and take in the musty scent, tears fill my eyes. I'm touching something my mother touched, something she wore, and a current of energy runs through me, as if Mother herself is reaching out to me.

Underneath her blouses I find her Bible. I flip through the tissue-paper-thin pages with underlined passages and notes scribbled in the margins and discover two pieces of folded-up paper near the back. My hands tremble as I slide them out.

Typed on an old IBM is Mother's article with the headline: HAMILTON MEADOW DOCTOR ON CHOPPING BLOCK FOR RAPING PATIENT.

My legs feel weak and I lower myself slowly into a chair. The article my mother planned to turn in to the *Daily Chronicle*, the one she hoped would expose Dr. Hunter, never saw the light of day. Or did it? Maybe it was never published, but perhaps word got out about it, and that's why she hid it in her Bible—and why Dr. Hunter ordered the electroshock therapy. I can't help but wonder if Eugene's long-term memory is still intact, if he'd tell me what really happened. But I abandon that notion as quickly as it comes to me. No matter what the details may be, I'm certain the story that eventually killed my mother is in front of me—minus the ending she had such high hopes of bringing to fruition.

A tear slides down my cheek and lands on the paper, smudging the print. I momentarily feel bad for marring such a precious document, but then I look up and see that the sun is casting a particular light on Mother's crystal angel, the one that now resides on the sill above the kitchen sink, making it sparkle. I rest my hand on my heart and smile.

Oh, Emily, I think to myself. *You're never going to believe what I just found.*

Thank you so much for reading *Crazy Free*. Although most of my research for this book was garnered from Central State Hospital in Milledgeville, Georgia, by 1955, over 550,000 people resided in state hospitals across the United States. Each institution of course had its own set of challenges, but for the most part, the gist of the stories was the same: lack of money, overcrowding, investigative reports on poor conditions, bodies placed in nameless graves, and patient-run newspapers. In contrast, today those same institutions are facing similar circumstances: abandoned and deteriorating buildings, properties for sale, and the creation of advocacy groups.

Kora was a fictional character, but based on my research, I believe what happened to her was possible, and my heart aches for those who endured suffering as she did. But, just like anything else in life, good things accompanied the bad. In fact, the more I learned about this time in our nation's history, the more I was completely blown away by how involved women were in the care of these patients. The movers and shakers included occupational therapy aides, music therapists, nurses, wives of government officials, and miscellaneous church and women's groups.

Mental health has come a long way since 1960. Medicaid and Medicare were created, federal funding became available, and awareness, empathy, education, medication, and treatments improved. Patients were gradually discharged from the state-run mental asylums and could no longer be committed against their will. They transitioned into regional hospitals, community clinics, and small group homes. Less serious cases became the family's responsibility, or people went home and took care of themselves.

Although the rights of the mentally ill have certainly improved over the years, mental illness continues to be a problem that plagues our nation. With the prevalence of crime, and the staggering amount of homeless, drug addicts, and prisoners in this country, I wish a better solution existed—one that would benefit the health and safety of both patients and society in general. However, funding continues to be a problem and medication isn't a one-size-fits-all cure. Even after all these years, the brain continues to be as big of a mystery as it ever was.

For photographs, discussion questions, and more information on *Crazy Free*, please visit www.crazy-free.com.

acknowledgments

To God, the best storyteller—the master of showing not telling—thank you for lighting up my life with your magnificence. Special thanks to my grandparents who breathed life into this novel when I was a child and young adult. Although this story evolved over the years into one completely different from my grandmother's life, if I'd never found that *All About Me* book she filled out when I was a kid, the dream would never have been born.

I am also deeply blessed to have found Stacey Aaronson through the Women's Publishing Summit. I will be forever grateful that I found the perfect publishing partner, editor, and designer to make my dream a reality. Her encouragement, pure unbridled joy, and confidence was exactly what I needed at the end of this decade-long writing journey.

I extend a special thank you to Sylvia, a nurse at the Georgia state institution for forty years, who took the time to patiently answer all my questions. Also, a big thank you to Mary for giving me and my friend Lisa an excellent tour of the grounds at Central State Hospital.

To my other friends and family who gave me encouragement through this process, thank you so much for your support. Julie and Lisa, thank you for agreeing to read my first few chapters and offer suggestions, and many thanks to Kelly for proofreading the final copy. I am also grateful to Ginny Yttrup for critiquing partial early drafts.

To my parents, thank you for keeping our family history alive and for instilling such a strong work ethic in me. Thanks to my sister for all the gab sessions about ghost stories and all the other things we can't talk about with anyone else.

Last, I am so grateful to my family who spends day in and day out with the craziness that comes with writing and publishing a book. Tim, thank you for your love and support, and for listening to me talk about these characters for years as if they were real people. And to my three sons, who have taught me more about life than I could ever imagine . . . may you always fearlessly chase after your dreams. I am so very proud of the men you are becoming.

about the author

TORI STARLING holds a bachelor of arts in journalism and is the author of the blog *Jake's Journey with Apraxia*. She is married with three sons and two gorgeous fur babies. *Crazy Free* is her first novel.

www.crazy-free.com